THE MARKED STAR

Shadow Watchers

VICKI HINZE

MAGNOLIA LEAF PRESS

The Marked Star

Published by Magnolia Leaf Press
Niceville, Florida, USA

Print Edition Published by Magnolia Leaf Press
2018. ISBN: 978-1-939016-23-2
Electronic Version Published by Magnolia Leaf Press,
2016. ISBN: 978-1-939016-17-1
Cover Design by VK Hinze

Related Books:

Crossroads Crisis Center: Forget Me Not, Deadly Ties, Not This Time

Shadow Watchers: The Marked Bride, The Marked Star

CONTENTS

THE MARKED STAR

PROLOGUE

Silicon Valley
Five Years Ago...

THE ARMED AGENT PARTED THE LIVING ROOM WINDOW BLINDS then peeked out to check the street. *Dark. Still. Calm. Normal street traffic. No kids outside; too late for that.*

Grateful for it, he remained on edge. Hyper-alert. Nerves sizzling. Even in the dead of night, moving her was dangerous. To her, and to him.

He called back over his shoulder. "You need to hurry."

Fear had her eyes stretched wide, her weary face pale, and her hands shaking. "I'm going as fast as I can."

"Go faster." Only a fool would believe word hadn't gotten out that she'd reported the strong-arm attempt. Her enemies likely knew exactly what she'd said and done before she'd left headquarters. They'd probably ordered her contract hit before she'd gotten to the waiting car. "This is the last place in the world you're safe."

He shouldn't have brought her here. His chest tightened even more. He knew better, and he should have refused. It's just that she'd had a life; an everyday, average life and it had been snatched

1

from her. She'd pleaded with him to let her come and get a few things. Seeing how much it meant to her had gotten to him; he was only human.

She had grabbed photos, important papers, an old doll, and a little memorabilia—the kind of things that define a life and can't be replaced. Surely, she was entitled to that much. She'd forfeited everything else: her home, family, and career—even her identity.

He checked the street again. An old man with stooped shoulders and dark hair wearing glasses walked into view, led down the sidewalk by a frisky, leashed dog. The man didn't so much as glance at the house, which allowed the agent to release a staggered hitched breath.

The dog paused to do its business on a patch of grass near the mailbox, leaving the man mostly hidden by her car. It stood parked in the driveway and unmoved, just as it had been for the past two weeks.

Not daring to trust his eyes and ignore his senses, the agent remained alert, half-holding his breath again, straining to see clearly through the cracks between the blind slats. He held his gaze firmly on the man's head and shoulders. Why was he bent over? Likely only hurrying the dog.

Something tingled deep in his gut. He'd been an agent too long to not recognize the feeling, and stilled. Everything seemed normal, calm, yet his nerves strung tighter until they crackled like live-wires. *Why?*

Having no answer, he watched and waited not daring to so much as blink. Finally, the man with the dog walked on, shuffling down the sidewalk as if on a leisurely stroll. In due time, he made the corner, then disappeared from sight.

Slowly, the tension inside began to uncoil and the agent released the finger-parted blinds. They snapped shut. Startled by the silence-splitting sound, the woman gasped. "Sorry." He turned from the window to look at her. "Who owns a chocolate lab?"

"The Parkers. Three doors down."

Good. Good. Legit. "He's out walking the dog."

She stopped in her tracks, a smiley-faced beach bag dangling from her wrist. "*He?* There is no *he.* Linda Parker is a widow. It's just her and her daughter." The gravity of her own words hit the woman hard. She nearly stumbled. "Oh, God. It's them. They took Bruiser. It has to be them—"

Her car in the driveway exploded.

The force of the blast popped his ears, blew out the living room windows. He dove, slamming into her, knocking her off her feet. Sprawled on the floor, he covered her with his body, cupping her head in his hands, shielding her from flying debris.

Glass rained down on them. Slivers and jagged spears stabbed into his back, his legs, his arms and hands. If combustibles were in the garage…

A secondary explosion rocked the house, nearly lifting him off her. She screamed.

"Stop it!" He whispered a swift warning. "They need to think we're dead or they'll be back."

Low and throaty, she mewled and pressed her dusty hand over her mouth to muffle the sound.

When the remains settled to fine dust sparkling in the air, he scrambled to his feet and pulled her up with him. "You okay?"

"Yes—no." She darted her gaze, dazed and confused. "They bombed my house."

"Yes, but you're okay." He checked her over, saw no blood. "You hear me? You're okay." He spoke slowly, distinctly. "We have to go now." Crackling filtered through the wall. Something in the garage had caught fire.

"But—but I dropped my bag—"

He spotted it in the debris. The air still thick with sheetrock dust, insulation, and smoke, he snagged her bag from the rubble and tugged at her arm, urged her down the hall, through the kitchen, and toward the back door. His shoulder clipped the wall. Pain shot through his arm. His sleeve and hand were speckled with blood. "If you want to live, we have to get out of here—now. Do you want to live?"

"Yes." Tears slid down her face, streaking her dusty cheeks. "Yes, I want to live."

CHAPTER ONE

Thursday, June 4th, 11:52 p.m.
London, England

"Congratulations, Elle." Her tour manager, Neil St. James, seated his black-framed glasses on his nose with a delicate forefinger. "You're a hit in London. Twitter is on fire—you're trending."

"That's wonderful news." The applause inside the Royal Albert Hall had been thunderous. The concert had gone off without any major hitches and the audience had responded exactly as she'd hoped it would to *New Dawn*, her latest release. Elle had poured her soul into that song, written it with such hope... Deep satisfaction spread through her chest. Deep, yet not deep enough to assuage the guilt that had her seeking refuge in music in the first place.

She dropped her gaze. Inspiring others was a start, and if she kept at it, maybe one day she could forgive herself.

But that day wasn't today. "I'm going to take a walk."

Neil didn't seem surprised. "Of course."

She paused and sent him a quizzical look.

"The band told me about your post-concert walks."

"It's the adrenaline rush." Performing always pumped her up. After concerts, she had to walk to settle down and get grounded. "Some artists drink. I walk."

"It's nearly midnight." Worry flickered through his eyes. "Shall I come with you?" He looked around, searching. "Where's Charles?"

"I'll be fine, and he'll be close. He's always close." She smiled, then recalled her usual bodyguard was home in the States. Charles, the replacement hired by Neil, stayed more in the shadows but he too hung close by. Seeing no reason to amend her comment, she added, "I won't be long."

Neil persisted. "Where will you walk?"

"To the hotel." She grabbed a light sweater in case of a late night chill and realized she'd forgotten the name of the hotel. "Neil—"

He looked down at her, his eyes huge and distorted by his thick glasses. "The Royal Park. It's a boutique hotel. Everyone's told me at least once that you favor boutique hotels."

She did. As much time as she spent in them these days, having a homey rather than a hotel feel to retreat to went a long way toward keeping her in the right frame of mind. She'd been away from home over two hundred seventy days in the past year. No one like her could stand that much hotel living and stay sane much less balanced.

"It's a block from Hyde Park," Neil said, pointing. "You can't miss it."

"Thanks." Elle eased her arms into the sweater and snagged its sleeve on the amethyst ring her father had given her to celebrate the European tour. Elle loved its stone and ornate gold setting. Her birthstone was diamond, but her father had opted for amethyst, no doubt because it was purple. Purple had always been special to them. As far back as she could remember, the color had carried a special meaning they never shared with anyone else.

She gently unsnagged her sweater then stepped out into the night and onto the sidewalk. Small groups of people milled up and down. Glad the sidewalk wasn't deserted, she walked on, diverting her face when coming close to anyone to avoid being recognized.

A couple came out of a bar, laughing. Another couple joined them and the foursome chatted about a movie they'd all seen. One loved it. One didn't, and neither of them could get the other two to express an opinion either way. *Normal conversation. Ordinary. Real.*

Trying not to envy them that, she kept moving. Half a block down from the Hall's entrance, three men snagged her attention. They had been in front of her but now lagged behind, and they weren't talking, just walking together silently, their expressions intense and serious, their gazes fixed and distant.

Fighting off a shiver of unease, she picked up her pace. At the corner, the men closed the gap, coming nearer to her. The hair on her neck stood on end. A ripple swam through her stomach, firing a warning. She looked for her bodyguard but saw no sign of him. *Didn't it figure?* Recalling his instructions to her, she stopped at the curb. A dark van pulled in and stopped. She turned her back to it and faced the more immediate threat: the three men. She stared at them, letting them know she was aware of them and taking mental notes. Her guard had told her that nine out of ten times that direct look was enough to get people to back off.

The middle man's eyes widened and his mouth opened.

A second later, something slammed into Elle's back. Beefy arms closed around her, and he lifted her off her feet. A rank-smelling cloth doused in some kind of chemical covered her mouth and, jostling her, deflecting her flailing arms, he half carried, half dragged her into the dark van. She stretched to reach the frame of the side door and missed. It slid shut behind her.

Beefy arms tossed her onto the floor. She landed with a thud, her head swimming. Someone rammed a fabric hood over her head. She couldn't see a thing, couldn't remove it; they restrained her arms with some kind of thick strap. Tight, digging into her skin. Her heart raced, her mind whirled. She fought them with her bound hands, her feet, and felt a needle prick her thigh. "No! No!"

"Shut her up!"

"I'm trying."

The injection burned, and soon she couldn't fight anymore. Her limbs felt heavy, leaden. Her head woozy, she stilled, face down on the van's floor. Her body rocked—the van accelerating. It sped off into the night.

"Is she out?" A male alto asked.

"On her way." A second one told him.

She had to get out of here. Survival rates plummeted once an abductor got you in a vehicle. But she couldn't move and her mind was functioning as slow as sludge. How could she run if she couldn't move? Couldn't think? "Who are you?" she mumbled, her voice foggy and thick. "What do you want?"

"Put her out." An irritated third man—a tenor—lifted her hand. Removed her ring. "And keep her out for the duration."

For the duration…? Oh, sweet mercy. They intended to kill her.

Her heart sank. She was going to die. To die, and she couldn't do a thing to stop them…

CHAPTER TWO

Saturday, June 6th, 3:20 p.m.
Seagrove Village, Florida

"You may kiss the bride."

Reverend Brown, the minister at Seagrove Church, smiled at Mark Taylor and his bride, Dr. Lisa Harper.

Seated in a groom's pew, Nick Sloan suffered only a tiny shaft of envy. Mark was a good man. Nick could substantiate that opinion; no problem. Mark had been Nick's former Shadow Watcher teammate and he was the current head of PSC, the now ex-team's private security consultant firm. More than five years of personal observation had given Nick valuable insight. Mark definitely was a good man—and most important to Nick, Mark was trustworthy.

Hard lessons learned early had taught Nick not to trust anyone, but over the years, Mark consistently and repeatedly had earned Nick's trust. As he had gotten to know Lisa, he'd come to respect her, too. She hadn't been dealt an easy hand, but like most of the team, she had endured and survived. She'd become a doctor at Crossroads Crisis Center and she certainly faced her fears head-on, though honestly she hadn't had a lot of choice about that. Some of her challenges would break just about anybody and have them curled in a ball, hiding in a dark corner until they could depart the fix and wing their way to heaven or hell. Not Lisa. No, she coped, and she spent her free time teaching at-risk women self defense.

Lisa was bent on never again being anyone's victim.

Nick's money was on her succeeding.

Of course, the whole team had taken on the additional risks of being in one place simultaneously, making themselves easier targets, and shown up in Seagrove, Florida to watch Mark and Lisa marry. Tim, second-in-command, innately classy and sophisticated, came with his wife, Mandy. Joe, cool from the cradle, a woman magnet, and the undisputed king of contacts came with Beth, the one woman who kept him in knots and seemed immune to his charm. Sooner or later, Nick predicted, they'd also marry. Sam, the Civil War reenactment and NASCAR enthusiast, and the best background expert with the most highly honed intuition Nick had ever seen in a single operative or security consultant, came alone. And Nick, always alone, was the techie who could make computers sing soprano in any known language where a speaker had something to say worth hearing. Together with Mark, they were the entire former Shadow Watchers team and the current security consultant associates at PSC. They were also friends.

At least, as friendly as Nick allowed. He did share more with them than with anyone on Earth. He'd die for any of them, but he also kept his bare-bone secrets tucked in his personal closet where bare-bone secrets belong.

Regardless, the whole group had waited a long time for this ceremony.

"They look happy, don't they, bro?" Joe said from his seat in the pew beside Nick.

At the altar, Mark and Lisa turned to face their guests. Their blinding smiles beamed joy. "They do today," Nick said.

"Come on, Nick." Sam sighed. The absence of his usual ball cap or do-rag had his long hair unfettered. With the shake of his head, his red curls rioted. "Can't you ever just be happy for someone happy?"

Tim and Mandy sat in the pew in front of Nick, Joe, and Sam. Both swiveled their heads to look back and whisper a potent, "Sh." Tim's warning came with a scowl.

What was their problem? Nick shrugged and stood with the other guests then watched Mark and Lisa move down the aisle to exit the church. They *were* happy today, and Nick was glad for it. But he wasn't fool enough to think they'd always be happy. Real life didn't work that way. He didn't make the rule, he just observed it. Real life never worked that way.

The phone at his hip softly sounded. Recognizing the designated ringtone, his gaze collided with Joe and Sam's. Tim turned and motioned with a head nod for Nick to get someplace private.

The whole Shadow Watcher team used the same ringtones and knew Omega One was calling.

High priority.

Omega One was a member of an active-duty task force that didn't exist on paper. It was buried in the bowels of the Office of Personnel Management where it would remain for the duration of its members' commitment to government service, just as the Shadow Watchers once had been. It was during a mission in the Middle East, after the death of Omega One's partner, Jane, that the whole Shadow Watcher team had resigned and departed the military. While Jane had been Omega One's partner, she'd also been Mark Taylor's sister of the heart. That she'd been killed while with them as a subject-matter expert hit the whole team like a ton of bricks. They'd let her *and* Mark down, and every one of them felt responsible for her death. They couldn't have prevented it but, even today, they still felt responsible for not protecting Mark's little sister.

Within two months of leaving the military, the Shadow Watchers had their private security consulting firm, known simply as PSC, up and running. Within four months, they had landed a created-for-them slot on Omega One's anti-terrorism task force unit's payroll. Officially, the team at PSC was classified as subject-matter experts. Consultants. Unofficially, they did what the officials couldn't do politically or legally to accomplish critical essential missions. Their only direct contact? Omega One.

The more things changed, the more they stayed the same.

The church began to empty.

Nick walked down the aisle and out of the nave, through the vestibule, then outside. Squinting against the glaring sun, he continued halfway around the corner of the building. Seeing no one else within earshot, he stopped and then answered the phone. "This is Nick."

"Hey. Wedding over?"

Nick checked his voice recognition app and saw the verification link. *Omega One.* Secure and good to go, he answered. "Just." He watched the grounds with his back to the building; first left, then right, then above.

"Give the groom our congratulations."

"Will do," Nick said, stuffing a hand in the pocket of his slacks. "What's up?"

"I need a favor."

That was code for I've got an assignment for you. "If I can, I will."

"Great, because it's on its way to you now."

"I'm not at my comput—"

"It's not an email, it's a package," Omega One said. "I need for you to accept delivery and hold onto it for me."

Omega One couldn't accept delivery. That meant this matter was CIA-related. It couldn't act on U.S. soil so Omega One was subcontracting the Shadow Watchers to handle the package. "When will it arrive?"

"Imminently."

"Where?"

"Where you'll be in half an hour."

Obscure. *Oh, yeah. Definitely CIA-related.* "No problem," Nick said, expecting it'd be anything but. "How long will I be holding it?"

"Indefinitely."

Great. An indefinite assignment babysitting. *Be still my heart.* "Got it."

"You personally, Nick. Eyes on at all times."

His worry meter fired up and he dropped the silent sarcasm. "All right." Omega One rarely told any of the Shadow Watchers how to do their jobs, and he'd always been just as happy with any of them as with any one of them specifically. That he'd singled out Nick likely meant not only would evasion be necessary but high-tech evasion with deep search and scanning capabilities. "I understand." Unfortunately, he did. "Is the package being retained agreeable to all parties?"

"Not exactly."

Great. The package had no idea who had him or her, or why— yet. He should ask the reason but he didn't want to know. Briefed, he could be put on the spot to explain. Without being briefed, he honestly had no knowledge. That, however, left one question he had to ask for mission security. "Will someone be seeking it?"

"That's a distinct possibility."

"Anyone I know?"

"Oh, yeah. The usual suspects."

NINA. The team's arch-enemy, Nihilists in Anarchy. Nick's skin crawled. He knew that tone, and Omega One knew Nick would know it. "Do we know why?"

"That's a little murky at the moment. We have conflicting reports."

Nick stared down at the freshly mowed grass. Just how much trouble was barreling his way on this? "Chatter?"

"Extensive and discreet," Omega One said. "The Marked Star."

NINA had tagged the package the Marked Star. *Why?*

Footfalls sounded and Nick looked up to see Joe and Sam approaching him. One glance at his face and their expressions tensed. He held up a wait-a-second finger to delay questions.

"Update—" Nick started.

"As soon as I have verified information, I'll be in touch."

"Got it." Now keyed up and tense, Nick disconnected the call and looked at his partners.

"What's up?" Sam asked, loosening the tie he hated but wore today to please Lisa. The Alabama redneck was far more at home and comfortable in sawed-off sleeved shirts, jeans, and flip-flops.

Nick visually scanned the perimeter, the roof, and then dropped his voice. "Inbound package. Half an hour, at the reception."

"Wedding present?" Joe asked, clearly wishing.

Nick resisted the urge to roll his eyes back in his head. "Human. A NINA target."

"Oh, man." Sam groused and stared at the brick wall. "Can't those jerks give us at least a little break?"

"It's not their nature," Joe said. "Scorpions sting because that's what scorpions do, bro." He looked back to Nick. "So why isn't One taking delivery himself?"

"He couldn't." Nick sent Joe a loaded look.

"CIA." Joe worried his lip with his thumb. "So what are we supposed to do with it?"

"Hold it indefinitely," Nick said. "Not us, me. Eyes on all the time."

"This is bad, buddy. Really bad." Sam reached for his missing ball cap to tug its brim down over his eyes. He unconsciously slid into that tell whenever he wanted to shield his reaction to something. Nick had tried to break him of the habit but hadn't had any more luck with the tell than everyone'd had with breaking Sam from cursing.

"Is One trying to prevent an interdiction, or what?" Sam asked.

"That'd be my guess." Joe slid his sunglasses onto his nose and watched the empty street.

"It was mine, too." Nick motioned for them to walk toward the parking lot. "But we're speculating. He didn't disclose his motives."

"Does the package know?"

"I'm not sure. One was vague, but I don't think so." Nick looked from Joe to Sam and frowned. "Extensive chatter. Conflicting reports."

"Early on in the operation, then." Joe unwrapped a slice of chewing gum and popped it into his mouth. It'd been a couple years now, but he seemed as addicted to gum chewing as he had been to the cigarettes that had him chewing gum to quit. How did he make even chewing gum look cool?

Sam sniffed. "Early on or an op that went south coming out of the gate."

"What else do you know?" Looking at Nick, Joe stepped from the grass to the concrete sidewalk.

"They've dubbed the package the Marked Star."

"Star?" Sam asked, clearly baffled. "That's a weird one."

Nick nodded. It was a weird moniker for NINA to hang on a mission. The strangest Nick had heard in a decade.

"Why?" Joe called the question they all wanted answered.

"No idea," Nick admitted, though it grated at him. He hated not knowing details of every mission up front. All of them. "Maybe the package is known in their circle?"

He'd meant NINA's circle, and the stern mask that dropped over Sam's face proved he'd picked up on it. "Or ours."

Joe's gaze landed on Beth and softened. She stood waiting patiently for him beside the open door of her SUV. "One's sure being mysterious."

"Not in the least." Nick spoke softly, knowing the information he was about to disclose would shock them as much as it had him. "He's waiting for authorization to brief us to come down the chain from on high."

"What?" Joe went deadpan. "You're kidding me."

"We have clearances up the wazoo," Sam insisted. "All the way to Pennsylvania Avenue."

Nick absorbed their surprise. He'd been kicked back on his heels about that, too. When it settled, he went on. "We do. Which tells us, this is different."

"Different how?"

The question frustrated Nick. He frowned at Sam. "I don't know...yet."

"Informant?" Joe suggested.

"Double agent?" Sam speculated aloud.

"Omega One could handle either of those."

"Enemy combatant?" Joe stopped moving.

Sam automatically did, too, and then so did Nick. "Being delivered to us on US soil? Uh, no. We'd be on our way to a ship in international waters somewhere obscure."

"Then what do you think it is, bro?" Joe asked Nick.

"Best guess?" When Joe nodded, Nick added, "A high-value target." Made sense with NINA's strange mission name, *The Marked Star.* Surely being marked made the person a target. "Probably interdicted outside our borders. And naturally, NINA wants the person badly."

"No doubt, buddy." Sam stared off in the distance, clearly thinking what they all were. In any language, this assignment spelled big trouble.

"Not a word to Mark." Joe lifted a finger. "He'll postpone his honeymoon, and Lisa will be disappointed and ticked to the nines."

She would be, but she'd never say a word. When she'd needed the team, it had been there. She hadn't forgotten it, and after being sold into human-trafficking twice and being spared twice because of the team's efforts, she wasn't likely to ever forget it. "Agreed."

"See you at the reception." Joe walked away, joined Beth and got into her SUV.

Nick glanced at his watch. "We'd better hustle. One said thirty minutes. If we move, we'll just make it."

Sam elbowed Nick and snagged his keys. "Better let me drive, then."

"Right." Sam's notoriety as a lead-footed speed-demon had been earned. He'd shave eight minutes off the trip. Nick moved around the front-end and got in on the passenger's side, preparing himself for dealing with an uncooperative package.

Indefinitely.

He fell back on the phrase the team had always used to summon that last ounce of strength and courage to make the impossible not only possible but reality. That something you summon when you're spent and have nothing left to give but need more to get the job done. Those words that signal you've maxed out but won't quit—you'll never quit.

Think steel.

Nora stood watch at the Country Club's entrance. The silver-haired senior village mother wore a pink floral dress and clearly had been waiting for Nick and Sam. When they walked in for the wedding reception, she squinted at them, straining to see clearly, and smiled. Her dark red lipstick stained her teeth, and she smelled like violets.

Nick had always had a fondness for violets, and for nearly bat-blind women who adopted and nurtured every stray. "You and Annie did a nice job on the wedding, Nora." They were the village's official wedding planners.

"Annie done most of it," she said about Lisa's mother in a brisk no-nonsense way, then dropped her voice low. "There's a package waiting for you in Receiving, my boy. It's pretty big and, I'm guessing, you're expecting it." She sent him a pointed look. "I didn't mention it to Mark."

Her vision might be sorry but her mind was as sharp as minds get. "Thanks." He looked around, saw only tall columns, marble floors, hallways and French doors. "Where's Receiving?"

"Down at the end of the left hall." She held his gaze, her own steady. "Figured it was important, coming to you here. I got Jeff keeping an eye on it."

Detective Jeff Meyer. Known and trusted by the Shadow Watchers. *Astute, as always.* "Thanks, Nora."

She plucked a thread from the lapel of his navy suit then nodded to Sam. "I'll be saving you some crab cakes." They were Sam's favorites. "Repayment for wearing the tie for Lisa today and leaving your cap in your truck."

"Thanks, Nora." Sam planted a loud kiss on her leathery cheek. "You're the best."

"High time you noticed, I'm saying." She harrumphed, but delight danced in her eyes. "Get going now. I got things to do besides running interference for you boys. And don't be lingering overly long."

"Yes, ma'am." Everyone in the village loved Nora. Everyone protected her, and she made no bones about loving her boys. Namely, Mark, Tim, Joe, Nick and Sam. Mark had brought them to Seagrove Village nearly five years ago and Nora had opened her heart to the whole team and taken them in. Because she'd claimed them, the entire village accepted them as its own. So far, Nora hadn't faltered once in her support.

Nick hadn't known what to do with her steadfastness then. He still didn't know how to process it, but at some point in time surely it would fade. She couldn't really care what happened to any of them. Until then, he accepted her devotion. He didn't count on it, but he appreciated it. She was the first woman in his life who cared whether or not he ate or lived or died. Nick owed her for that. They all did.

Beside Sam, Nick made his way down the left hallway to Receiving. A discreet brass sign attached to the wall beside a wide door winked in the harsh light cast down from the overhead fluorescents. Nick turned the knob and opened the door.

Tim and Joe stood next to a stack of boxes beside a serious-looking Jeff Meyer.

Relief that didn't begin to touch the tension in Jeff washed across his face. "Nick, you made it."

"Yeah, sorry. Nora needed a brief word." Nobody challenged Nora unless it was for her own safety.

"Do we need a sniffer on this box?" Jeff stepped back, revealed a single wardrobe box on the floor. Much larger than the other boxes, it stood out like a sore thumb, and it wasn't the color of normal cardboard, it was white.

Tense, worried, and wary. No doubt Jeff was recalling his being late for the Talbots' wedding last year and walking in on a NINA chemical attack. Fortunately, they'd only suffered one fatality. "Not necessary. Sam's here, and his nose is as good as any dog's that I've ever seen. Thanks for keeping watch on it."

"No problem." He lifted a finger, motioned between himself and the door. "Do you want me to stay or go?"

"Go, by all means." Nick bobbed his head. "Sara's probably waiting for a dance."

"Whew." Jeff headed toward the door. "I was worried this was going to be another...rough wedding."

"No need to worry," Tim assured Jeff. "Totally routine."

"Dang right," Sam said, earning himself a glare from everyone else.

Nora took exception to dang or any other cussing and was determined Sam break the habit. He'd cuss, and she'd spike his iced-tea with jalapeño pepper juice. Nick figured Sam had consumed at least a couple gallons of the stuff. *Hardheaded.*

Jeff missed the tension and departed, then shut the door behind him.

"Sorry." Sam shrugged.

"Never validate," Nick told Sam. "You validate, you plant doubt."

"I know. I know."

Nick rolled his gaze. "Go secure the door, will you?" Nick staved off issuing another rebuke and glanced at Joe. "He's dead from the neck up."

"Sometimes we all are," Joe said, playing the diplomat. "You know as well as I do Sam's brilliant. He's just developed a thing for jalapeño pepper juice in his iced-tea. Some like lemon. He likes the juice." Joe lifted his hands. "You know I'm right. That's the only reasonable explanation for his refusing to remember to clean up his language here."

"Obviously, the juice isn't working," Nick said. "We need something hotter." He bent to check the box. Rocked it, testing its weight. Definitely someone inside. He nodded to the others then backed off and pulled his weapon. He motioned Tim to the left. Joe slid to the right. "Go, Sam."

Sam opened the box.

A woman sprung up swinging and landed a right hook on Sam's jaw. She screamed a string of curses on his head and fought as if her life depended on winning.

"Stop that right now!" Nick shouted.

She stilled, shoved her long hair back from her face, straightened up and stared at him. "Nick?"

Tiny, thin, reddish blonde hair and pale skin with angular features that shouldn't combine to leave a man breathless but did. It'd been a while, but he recognized and reacted to her immediately. "Elle?"

CHAPTER THREE

FOUR YEARS HAD PASSED SINCE HE HAD SEEN HER, AND THE changes in her were stark. Eighteen to twenty-two made a lot of difference in the woman. Her features looked fuller, more honed. Elle always had been a small package of dynamite, but now that fire inside her burned clearly in her eyes and she wore her confidence on the outside. It looked great on her. "What are you doing here?" Nick still couldn't believe his eyes. *She* was Omega One's package?

Elle burst into tears and either hadn't noticed the three guns leveled on her chest or she didn't care. She ran to Nick, slammed against him, wrapped her arms around his waist and held on, babbling bits and pieces of something only she could decipher. He couldn't make out a thing.

Over the top of her head, Nick looked at the guys. They were baffled, curious, and silently speculating.

In their shoes, he would be, too. "Elle Bostwick," he said, then knowing her name wouldn't mean a thing to them, he added, "Daughter of Glen and Daris Howell at AAN." They caught the connection to one of their clients, American Armory Network, and Nick's shoulder shrug. He had no idea why NINA would be after Elle. Her dad? Yes. But Elle? That NINA was after her put knots in

Nick's stomach. "Elle, sh. Wait a second, okay? You can tell me whatever you want, but just wait a second."

"She's *the* Elle Bostwick." Tim frowned.

Nick nodded.

"Who is *the* Elle Bostwick?" Sam asked Joe.

"Singer," Joe said. "A big star."

The Marked Star suddenly made sense.

"Never heard of her." Sam admitted. "Sorry, Elle. No offense, but I only do Country."

That reality bite snapped Elle out of her fear and her confusion. She looked at Nick for an explanation.

"Sam's our resident Alabama redneck," he said. "If it isn't Country music, he's not listening to it."

She nodded. "Devoted fans are a treasure. They don't get more devoted than to Country." She stilled, then swatted at Nick's shoulder. "I should blister your ears—and I might in a minute. I can't believe you did this to me."

His arm stung. "What did I do?"

"Pulled one of your stupid exercises on me to check safety procedures." She swiped her hair back. "How could you do that, Nick? Cut and run on me, and then four years later just grab me like that? You scared me to death. I didn't know what was going on."

"You still don't." He stared at her. When she drew back and stilled mid-swing, he added, "I didn't do anything."

Skepticism flashed across her face, through her eyes. "Then what is this all about? Why am I here? Why are you?" She challenged him, studied Sam, Joe, and then Tim. Finally, she pivoted her gaze back to Nick and let it settle. "You shouldn't have cut and run on me. All your work…for what? Nothing. I could have been killed, and you weren't there."

Nick frowned and held it so she wouldn't miss it. "My job was to give you the tools to protect yourself. I did. It's up to you to use them. I'm not your keeper, Elle."

"I don't need a keeper. But I thought you were my…" Her voice faltered, faded and she lost patience with it. "Oh, never mind. Just never mind." She let him feel her annoyance. "I need a phone." She dangled her fingertips clearly expecting someone to put one in her hand.

No one moved.

When the woman recovered, she recovered. "Who do you want to call?" Nick let her back away, then crossed his chest with his arms.

"Neil St. James," she said. "My European tour manager. I'm going to fire him."

"Why?"

"For hiring a bodyguard who let those apes snatch me off the street and—oh, my stars. I don't know what they did to me. I don't remember it. I do remember waking up in that stupid box." She laid a glare on it that should have the cardboard bursting into flames or disintegrating to ash. "Where exactly am I?" She glanced at the stacks of boxes, the mops and pails standing in the corner. The tall metal shelving packed with smaller boxes. "This—this doesn't feel like London. Everything seems too new."

Nothing in London felt new? Nick debated telling her and compromised. "You're in Florida."

"Florida?" She gasped, opened her mouth to say something, but didn't utter a sound. Her knees folded, she slowly dropped, and sat down on the concrete floor. "I—I need…a glass of water."

Nick motioned to Joe. He was better with women. Maybe he could get past this awkwardness and get some answers from her.

Joe snagged a bottle from Tim's back pocket. "Here you go." He broke the seal, then passed Elle the bottle. "Careful now. I removed the cap."

"Thank you." She looked up at him, decided he was safe, and put valiant effort into a wobbly smile.

Joe was anything but safe, yet women innately trusted him. None of the guys had ever pinpointed why. Some things just are what they are. *Woman magnet.* Tolerable for the times it had come in handy. Nick hoped this would be one of them.

Joe smiled back at her. "So you were in London when they snatched you off the street, eh?"

She looked to Nick. "Can I speak openly to these men you haven't yet introduced?"

He nodded. "Trust them with your life."

"Do you trust them with yours?"

"All the time."

She stared at Nick a long moment, absorbed that, then looked back at Joe. "I was." She took a swallow of water. Her hands shook. "Everything happened so fast. It's confusing. I had this funny feeling about these three guys. They were following me on the sidewalk, so I stopped to look back at them."

"That happens a lot, I expect," Joe said. "Price of fame."

"It does. Paparazzi and well-meaning fans, but this time it felt... I don't know."

"Different?" he suggested.

"Yes." Her gaze slid to Nick. "Dark. Somehow malevolent."

"Were they fans?" Nick asked, clearly certain from what she'd just said that they hadn't been.

"No. Well, I don't think so. They were big guys, like him—" she motioned at Sam "—and they'd been in front of me, but somehow they ended up behind me. Near the corner, they closed in. They weren't actually looking at me, but I know they were watching me. I felt that, too."

NINA. "So these three thugs snatched you?" Nick asked, trying to move this along.

"No, Nick. I didn't see who snatched me. I was still looking at the three guys. They seemed intense, you know? I turned to stare them down and someone smacked into my back. Huge man with arms like this—" She cupped her hands into a wide circle. "He shoved a cloth over my face. It smelled foul. Chemicals of some kind. Then he swung me up off my feet and threw me into a van." She paused to take in a steadying breath. "I never actually saw him. In the van, somebody shoved a scratchy sack over my head. It felt like burlap—same raunchy chemical smell."

"Was he alone?"

"No. It wasn't just the one guy in the van. I heard them talking."

CIA, Nick surmised. "How many voices did you hear?"

"Three speakers. Two altos and a tenor." She looked over at him. "There could have been more of them but, if so, they were silent."

The singer. Of course, she'd slot voices in musical tones. Nick almost smiled. "When was that?"

"Right after the concert."

"In London?" Nick signaled Sam to run a computer check on it, and he stepped away.

"Yes. Royal Albert Hall." She looked up at Nick. "I'm not sure of the time, but it was late. Around midnight." She glanced at Joe and her expression lost some of its intensity. "I often walk after performances. It helps me settle down. You know, the adrenaline rush."

"That's a good way to work through it."

"I enjoy it—normally."

"What day was the concert?" Nick asked, glanced at Sam for confirmation.

He motioned with two fingers.

That this wasn't that same day occurred to Elle. Panic flitted across her face, settled in her eyes. "Excuse me?"

Joe softened his expression and his voice, then repeated Nick's question. "What day was your concert in London, Elle?"

"Thursday." She swallowed another pull of water, laid an uncertain look on Nick that touched protective instincts inside him. "Today isn't Thursday, is it?"

He nodded that it wasn't. "It's Saturday."

"Saturday?" She repeated, anxious and struggling to contain it. "They grabbed me two days ago?" From her expression, she tried but couldn't wrap her mind around that. "How can that be possible?"

"Why is it not possible?" Nick asked, careful to keep his tone level and calm. "You said you were out of it while in the box. So you really can't know how much time elapsed. Getting you from London back to the States—"

"The cloth and sack over my head. It wasn't just those chemicals. They drugged me."

Of course they had drugged her. "Why do you think so?"

She frowned at Nick. "Well, I don't remember a thing about the van beyond getting into it and hearing a little talk. Wait. There was a prick—I remember a prick in my thigh. It burned like fire. Then nothing. Nothing at all until I woke up in the box. How else would you explain it?"

"I'll get the testing kit," Tim mumbled. "There's one in my car."

"I can't explain it yet." Nick nodded for Tim to go. "Something happened, Elle, but we don't yet know what."

She thought about that a second. "No, I guess we don't." Dropping her gaze to the floor, she attempted to shield how much this incident and mental disconnect troubled her.

It was a futile effort. The men standing with Nick were all highly trained to recognize trouble, to read it, and to deal with it.

Nick stepped out of his comfort zone to reassure her. The last thing he needed was for Elle to go postal. He'd seen that happen once before and he wasn't eager to repeat the experience. "Whatever happened, you don't seem to be harmed from it. Do you need a doctor?"

She paused, her mouth dropped open. Clearly, she hadn't considered a physical assault until that moment. It would be atypical, but not alien for NINA operatives. "Elle? Did they hurt you?" He tensed.

"No." She looked Nick straight in the eye. "No, I'm fine."

He let out a breath he hadn't known he'd held. Sweet relief flooded him. "Then you're okay?"

"I am. Really."

"That's good, isn't it?"

Joe shot him a thumbs up, silently praising his effort. It had always been much easier for Nick to see the dark side than to stretch and try to grasp the light.

Elle wasn't impressed. She parked a hand on her hip. "I've lost two days of my life, Nick Sloan. Two days. I have no idea what happened to me, who manhandled me on the street, kidnapped and drugged me, and you say I'm okay and not harmed because I wasn't molested?" She crossed her chest with her arms. "Unbelievable. Time hasn't helped you one bit."

"What do you mean?"

"You're still the same old Nick."

His temper flared. "Well, who else would I be?"

"Wrong tactic, bro," Joe whispered a warning. "Gentle."

Tim obviously agreed and stepped in. "Elle, we'll get this all sorted out, okay? But we need your help to do it." When she nodded, acknowledging him, he went on. "When you were put in the van, where was your bodyguard?"

"Well, isn't that just the million dollar question? I have no idea —which is why I want a phone to fire him *and* Neil." She looked Tim right in the eye. "Normally, he's two steps away in the shadows and, if I turn unexpectedly, I'm tripping over him. He had to have been there somewhere. I just don't recall seeing him. Where he was right then, who knows?"

"Does he have a name?" Sam asked, his laptop on a box in front of him.

"Charles something," she said. "He's new. My regular guard, Frank, refused to leave the States—not that I'd have let him. His wife's expecting any day now. So Neil hired this Charles guy to replace Frank in Europe. Neil will know Charles's last name."

Had Charles been a NINA plant? Had he cut and run? Been bought off? Threatened? Removed? Agitated that he might have been, Nick claimed her attention. "So you remember nothing at all but being in the van?"

She cut a glance his way. "Not exactly. I remember waking up in the box." She shifted to look at it. "It wouldn't open."

"It's not a regular box."

"That explains that."

In his mind, he saw her pushing at its sides, shoving with her feet and getting nowhere. "Why would two groups of men want to grab you off the street, Elle?"

"I don't know. The only person who pulls these kinds of stunts to prove I need protecting is you." She stopped as if something had occurred to her, then leveled an uncompromising and unapologetic look on him, her green eyes sharp, clear and penetrating. "If you really had nothing to do with this, then why am I here—with you?"

Nick looked at the team, who silently deferred to him since he knew Elle. He hesitated, unsure what he should disclose. Elle was a musical protégé. Brains and talent from her father. Grounded and pragmatic like her mother. Yet she was her own woman, and that made her a wildcard he didn't dare to trust. "We don't honestly know."

His response surprised her. It surprised the team, too.

She dropped her gaze to her hand. Her eyes widened and she gasped. "Oh, no. It's gone." Upset, she twisted to search the box.

"What's gone?" Nick asked. "What are you looking for?"

"My ring." She frowned. "It should be easy to spot. It's an amethyst the size of a small walnut."

"Are you sure you had it on when you were abducted?" he asked.

"Positive." She glanced back at Nick over her shoulder. "It's an antique my dad gave me to celebrate the European tour. I've never taken it off."

The light dawned. "Big stone, eh?"

"Special stone—and big, in a gold setting. A gorgeous antique," she said, sitting back on her haunches. "It's not here." Disappointment rippled through her tone and she blinked fast and hard.

NINA. Nick shot a look at the guys, and saw the worry he felt reflect back at him in their gazes. They all had reached the same conclusion.

NINA was after the ring. The CIA had snatched her to get it before NINA could. Which meant NINA would come after her, and its operatives would keeping coming after her until they got her and it.

Indefinitely.

CHAPTER FOUR

SOMEONE JERKED THE RECEIVING ROOM'S HALLWAY DOOR OPEN.

Peggy Crane, the director of Crossroads Crisis Center, ducked her head in. "What's keeping you guys?" She quizzed the team of men the size of small mountains as if they were school kids, not at all intimidated by them. "Lisa's upset. She thinks she's somehow offended you and you're boycotting the reception and not dancing with her like you did Tim's Mandy at her wedding because of it. You're shunning her." Peggy frowned her disapproval. "I know that's not so, but if you boys put the bride in tears because you're lollygagging and—" Her gaze lighted on Elle. "You're...*Elle*?"

Elle smiled at her. "Hello."

Peggy glanced from her to the guys. "What's going on here?"

Nick cleared his throat and stepped forward. "Elle's a friend of mine," he said, hoping she wouldn't dispute him. "I—we wanted to surprise Mark and Lisa. Elle graciously agreed to come to the wedding and sing for them."

Elle glanced at him with confused daggers, but she didn't dispute him.

Peggy smiled, then looked at Elle's clothes and her smile faded.

"You always look so elegant but you wore jeans and a wrinkled shirt to a wedding?"

"I left my tour in a hurry," Elle said, her face flushing. "My luggage hasn't arrived. That's why we're here. We're waiting for it."

"Mmm." Peggy didn't buy it but, to her credit, she didn't question Elle. "Well, then. Let me see what I can do." Without a backward glance she disappeared through the propped-open door and then closed it behind her.

"Thank you." Nick turned to Elle. "I appreciate your——"

"Discretion?"

He nodded.

"So who got married?" she asked.

"Mark Taylor."

"The CEO of your firm," she said, revealing she knew more about them than Nick realized. "And who are all of you—Sam, the Country music loving, Alabama redneck aside?" She swept the team with her gaze.

"Joe."

"Tim."

"Me," Nick said, "you know."

"No last names," she noted. "Your colleagues, I take it."

Nick nodded.

Elle pinned him with an unwavering gaze. "Who was that woman, and why did you lie to her?"

"Peggy Crane. She's the director at the crisis center where the bride works." He met Elle's gaze and held it. "And I didn't lie really, I just didn't disclose anything else because I don't want to put anyone here in unnecessary jeopardy."

"Uh-huh." Elle stewed on that a long minute. "Does that include me?"

He hiked his chin. "It does."

"Okay, then."

Vintage Elle. He'd liked that accepting part of her four years ago, and he appreciated it now. She asked no uncomfortable questions he didn't want to answer. Just accessed the situation, accepted what he offered, and moved on. Smart woman.

Peggy returned carrying a hanger draped with plastic. "It's Lisa's going away outfit."

"You took the bride's clothes?" Elle frowned. "I can't wear her going away outfit, Peggy."

Nick rolled his eyes. "You don't have a lot of choice."

Elle frowned at him. "Lisa probably spent weeks picking this out. "It's special, Nick."

"Well, it's that or your rumpled shirt and jeans."

"Oh, for pity's sake." Elle frowned at him. "Go get me a table-cloth and something I can use as a tie or scarf."

The guys looked at him as if they questioned her sanity.

"Would you move?" Elle shook herself and told Peggy, "A drapery tie will work."

"You're going to wear drapes?" Nick asked her.

"Hey, it's like Scarlett in *Gone with the Wind.*" Sam guffawed. "Yeah, baby. The South's rising again."

"Sorry to disappoint you, Sam." Elle laughed, soft and tinkling. "No drapes, just the tie."

"Well, it ain't that big a leap from drapes to a tablecloth. Maybe you're half Southern. At least, honorary Southern."

"I'm humbled to be honorary." Elle managed a little laugh.

Its familiar tinkle chimed in Nick's ears. He'd always associated her laughter with a tinkle, and she laughed often. It grated at him. It wasn't the sound. It was that he liked the sound. Warm and pleasant, it floated over his skin and kind of seeped in and spread through him. He liked the sensation, and he vehemently disliked liking it.

Peggy again returned, holding a white tablecloth and a peach rope tieback in her hand. "I hope the color's okay. I looked for something dark—for contrast—but everything is peach today. Lisa loves peach and cream."

"Peach works great," Elle said. "Goes with my hair."

It kind of clashed. Her hair was reddish-blonde. Long and curly. It framed her face and made her eyes seem enormous. Elle wasn't classically beautiful, but throw all her distinct features together and she looked beautiful. She looked stunning. Even at eighteen she had commanded a room. People watched her move; she intrigued them. It wasn't anything she deliberately did; it was that star quality, that x-factor people talk about. Some claimed it was mystical. Nick never bought into that. It wasn't mystical at all. It was just Elle. She, not that star stuff, for reasons he had never been able to explain, left him breathless.

Joe stepped closer. "She adapts well."

"Yeah," Nick agreed. "She's hardheaded but flexible."

"Seems pretty reasonable to me." Joe looked at Nick.

Nick had thought so, too. Once. "Don't cross her."

"Ah." Joe waited for details.

"Remember when I went to LA to design AAN's security system for her dad?"

"Yeah, a couple years ago."

"Four. Elle was eighteen and had a crush on me," Nick mumbled, watching her and Peggy fashion the tablecloth and loop the tie until it made an X crossing her chest. "I didn't act on it."

"She got hardheaded then?" Joe asked.

"Oh, yeah." The tassel dangled at her slim waist.

"It looks good, Elle." Tim didn't seem surprised. "You've done this before."

Elle smiled. "Clothes go missing pretty often. Craig, my manager here, says the staff sells them."

"Why do people steal your clothes?" Sam looked totally confused by that.

"She's a star, Sam," Tim explained. "Some people collect things that belong to stars."

"But her clothes?" Sam could care less about stars or their things.

Tim nodded. "Kind of like you with a Civil War relic."

That, Sam got. "Humph. Surprised the hotels put up with that."

"They don't like it," Tim assured him, "but they have a rough time stopping it."

"They do try," Elle assured Sam. "Mostly, they're successful, but every now and then, someone manages."

Nick watched her interacting with Peggy and the team. Elle

31

seemed totally at ease, which considering her circumstances was nothing short of a miracle. Maybe having her here indefinitely wouldn't be as bad as Nick had worried it would be. Looking at the woman still took Nick's breath away. He had to remind himself to breathe and blink. But he'd focus and get beyond that nictitate, winded predisposition. Odd, but the other guys seemed immune to her. Not one of them seemed the least bit affected or star-struck.

The first time Nick had met her, she'd been working for her father and not singing. He'd been as tongue-tied as a boy talking to a beautiful girl for the first time in his life. She'd pretended not to notice. Her beauty he could handle—even then. It was her disposition that rattled him to the marrow of his bones. Sunny and gracious, like warm breezy air—at least, she had been until he'd started imposing security measures on her to keep her safe. Then she'd morphed into a fire-spitting dragon.

The ferocity of her rebellion had shocked her father and dismayed her mother. It hadn't surprised Nick at all. But, in fairness, people rarely surprised Nick. He'd learned the lesson of discreet observation from his stepmother, Jacinda, one of the most beautiful women he'd ever seen in his life. She'd shocked him. But only once. After that incident, he always expected the worst from people. When you expect the worst and get it, what else is left to surprise you, or to disappoint you, or to knock you to your knees?

"How's that?" Elle asked, backing away from Peggy and patting the folds at her stomach flat. "Will it do?"

"It's amazing." Peggy studied the handiwork. "I've made do on a lot of things in my life, but none of them looked like a gown." She smiled. "Lisa's going to love this. It'll go down as one of her best wedding memories for all time."

"Oh." Elle stilled. "I don't have my guitar."

"The musicians have one," Peggy said. "Will it do?"

A sideward glance at Nick, then Elle smiled at Peggy. "If it has strings, I'll play it."

"I don't care what she says," Sam insisted, "that woman's definitely from the South."

"Whatever." Tim let out a shuddery sigh. "Let's go then before Lisa cries and Mark hunts us down."

"Good idea." Peggy nodded, her dark bobbed hair swinging against her chunky necklace. "They get upset and Annie will have our hides."

"Who's Annie?" Elle whispered to Nick.

"Lisa's mom," he whispered back.

"And upset Annie, and you upset Nora," Sam said on a gravelly grumble. "No crab cakes."

The group started toward the door. Elle stepped in beside Nick. "I'm going to do this. But then you've got some explaining to do."

Wise enough to take a win when one dropped in his lap, Nick nodded and held his tongue.

The reception was in full swing but Elle's entrance created a predictable stir.

Sam aside, everyone in the village recognized her.

She smiled warmly and walked right up to the bride and groom. "Lisa and Mark. Congratulations." She gave them a joint hug. "I'm a friend of Nick's, and I wanted to wish you a long and joyful marriage."

"Elle!" Lisa squealed. "I can't believe you're here."

"I'm here, and I apologize for crashing your wedding. Nick wanted to surprise you and thought you might enjoy a song. I'd be happy to—"

"Crash it? Are you kidding? We're thrilled you're here, and I'd love to hear you sing." Lisa smiled at Nick. "What a surprise, Nick. " She gave him a quick hug. "You're awesome."

Elle held her thoughts on that. "What song would you like to hear?"

"Anything you like," Mark said.

"New Dawn," Lisa said over him. "If you wouldn't mind. The first time I heard it, it spoke straight to my soul, Elle."

"Thank you for that." Elle blushed prettily. Clearly, the song was special to her. "New Dawn it is, then." She clasped Lisa's forearm. "I'm so happy for you."

Why did she say that? Nick wondered. She didn't even know Lisa or Mark. But Elle sounded sincere. Even a jaded cynic could see her authenticity. How did she do that? Why did she do it?

Whatever Elle's reason, Lisa and Mark liked it. They liked Elle.

"People skills," Joe whispered from beside Nick.

"What?"

"You were wondering why she said that to Lisa." Joe shrugged. "People skills."

"How did you know what I was thinking?"

"I could see your confusion, Nick. You wear it like a sleeve on your jacket."

"Coat." He shrugged snippy at having his thoughts invaded and at being called out. "It's not a jacket, it's a coat."

"Your coat, then." Joe moved away.

"And stay out of my head."

"Keep it off your sleeve, bro."

Elle crossed the broad floor and stepped onto the stage. The musicians clearly were ecstatic to meet her. They spoke briefly and her easy laughter carried back to Nick. That grating, irritating tinkle. He had to give her credit, though. She'd been through a lot and yet rolled with the punches and just took to the stage like she'd planned to be there, in that spot, in this room with these people, all along.

He respected that. He didn't know exactly what it was. He did know he didn't have it, and he wasn't sure he wanted it. But it suited Elle and he respected it.

Maybe if he watched her he could learn to project whatever she projected that made people open and friendly to her. That skill could come in handy in his line of work. It wouldn't be easy for him —alien to his nature, actually—but it wasn't impossible to learn to interact on a less than formal footing with people. He'd already proven that with the team. They were his family. Well, as close to family as he got.

The music started and Elle began singing. The room went silent.

Expressions altered, softened, enthralled. She'd captivated and enchanted them.

Fascinating. Definitely a handy asset to have in one's personal toolbox, and not impossible at all. Provided he kept her out of NINA's clutches.

And alive…

Sara Jones, co-owner of the successful software company, SaBe, caught Lisa's bouquet, setting off a flurry of speculation and good-natured teasing about her and Detective Jeff Meyer. According to Lisa, Sara and Jeff had been a couple for about as long as Joe and Beth, Sara's partner. Elle watched them together, and the hint of a smile curved her full lips, her mood a little wistful. Just once, to have a man look at her with that—

"Elle?" A silver-haired, senior woman whose bright red lipstick stained her teeth walked up, holding the hand of a gangly blonde girl about ten.

"Yes?" She turned to face them and smiled a greeting at the child. "Hi, there." The girl waved.

"I'm Nora," the older woman said. "I understand you're here with one of my boys."

Ah, Nora. The village mother everyone adored. "Yes, with Nick." Elle said, opting for the simple rather than explaining what she didn't yet understand herself.

"Nick?" Nora seemed surprised, then her gaze turned sharp. "Well, then. No flittin' around like some stars do."

"I'm not one for flitting." Elle wasn't positively sure that flitting was even a word, but Nora had to be talking about a woman who flits from man to man. At least, Elle hoped that's what the woman meant by her remark. She hadn't heard the term before.

"Glad to hear it." The look in Nora's eyes steady, turned flat. "You be good to him, Elle. My Nick's had enough."

Her Nick? Enough what? How did Elle respond to that? A sixth sense warned her with that kind of warning in Nora's tone, she had to be worried, and that meant only honesty would do. "So have I, Nora. An absolute gut full."

"Well, I'm sorry to hear it but glad you ain't all glitz and glamour. My Nick needs a woman with substance." Nora stared at her a long second and, from the look that lit in her eye, she truly understood just how honest Elle had been with her. "Fine, then. I'm saying we understand each other."

Elle didn't understand Nora at all, though her meaning and intent were clear enough. She was in full-fledge protect-him-mode. Not that Elle deluded herself for a second that she had the power to hurt Nick. She didn't. She never had. "Neither of us want to see Nick hurt, Nora. If that's what you mean, then, yes, we understand each other."

"Glad that's settled. Now." She tugged the girl's arm, drawing her closer. "This young lady wants to meet you." Nora glanced at the girl. "Lizzie Montgomery, this is Elle. Lizzie's a big fan of yours."

"Hi, Elle." Lizzie's voice sounded faint, reverential.

Humbled, Elle lifted her hand. "It's good to meet you, Lizzie." She was a pretty girl, but the haunted look in her eyes reminded Elle too much of her own. "I'm in the mood for a good chat. Would you two mind if we got some food and grabbed a table? I'm starving." She pressed a hand to her stomach. "I feel as if I haven't eaten in days." Could be true. She had no idea. That rattled her.

The normalcy in that admission had Lizzie's feet out of the clouds and back on the ground. "I get that way sometimes. Mom says it's because I'm growing."

"Is your mom here, too?"

"No. She, um, couldn't make it." The haunted look returned. "I'll, um, get some napkins."

Nora sighed.

Elle worried. "Did I say something wrong?"

"No, not at all. Lizzie's mom, Sue Ellen, had to take an unexpected trip. She'll be gone a few days and she left Lizzie to keep me company." Nick joined them and Nora dropped her voice. "Her mother didn't want Lizzie exposed."

"To what?" Nick asked.

"No idea." Nora laid a flat look on him that spoke volumes. "Probably has something to do with her brother and an intervention." She blinked. "I ain't met the man but I heard he has…issues."

Elle watched Lizzie. She clearly missed her mom. "Where's her dad?"

"Near as I can tell, she ain't got one. Never met him. Never seen him. Never heard a word about him."

Growing up, how many had thought that same thing about Elle? Feeling a bond with Lizzie, she kept her thoughts to herself.

They got their food and sat down at a table, then Elle engaged Lizzie in conversation. She was bright, funny, and when she forgot to be sad, she seemed thoughtful and sweet. Nick didn't have much to say, but he didn't miss a thing. That could be good. Elle had no idea what his plans were for her, but he was less likely to toss her out on her elbow to fend for herself with Lizzie around. Two groups of men bent on abducting her… she wanted protection and answers, and since she'd ended up here, Nick likely had them or he could get them—if he would. That was the big question. *Would he?*

For the next hour, Elle and Lizzie talked about music and fashion and dogs. Then about school and their favorite subjects—math for them both—and smoothies, a favorite they also shared, though Lizzie preferred chocolate and Elle strawberry.

Nora talked with them, seeming to enjoy the conversation, though as time wore on she looked a little peaked. Elle excused herself and went the restroom.

On her way back to the table, a woman she hadn't yet met bumped into her, passed her a begonia. "I enjoyed your new song, Elle."

"Thank you."

The woman's smile faded. She leaned close, and her tone turned serious. "Take care. These days, you never know who's watching you or why," she whispered, then rushed away.

"Wait." Elle called out after her, instinctively certain her words weren't idle. "Wait."

But the woman kept going, hastening her steps.

Surprised and not sure how to react—should she go after the woman?—Elle watched her rush straight to the exit and leave the building. Did the woman know something, or had hers been an innocuous, general comment after all? Was even wondering just Elle jumping at shadows? Reacting because of what had happened?

The woman couldn't know what had happened, of course. Yet her intuition warned even now the words were deliberate. The woman shared a message. Elle's intuition had been right on the street in London. She'd been wrong about dying in the van, but the incident had cost her two days of her life that remained a mystery to her. Too much odd had happened to ignore the woman's warning— if that's what it was. It's what it felt like it was, but in her present state, she couldn't be sure.

Nick had more experience at deciphering. Letting him know she could still be at risk could encourage him to help her. Of course, she had to tell him. How could she not? Bent on immediate disclosure, Elle walked back to the table, purpose in her step. "Nick, I—"

Nora stood up and swayed on her feet.

"Nora!" Elle grabbed her arm to steady her. "Are you okay?"

Nick stood at her side. "Sit down, Nora, and tell me what's wrong."

"Don't be fussing, Nicholas. I ain't checking out. I'm a wee bit dizzy is all." Nora sat, then dragged in a steadying breath.

Lizzie licked at her ice-cream spoon. "She has the flu."

"The flu?" Elle looked at Nora. "Why are you here?"

"No choice. Annie and I had too much to do for the wedding." Nora sat down and exhaled a deep, stuttered breath. "It ain't the flu —I wouldn't deliberately infect anybody else. But I don't feel perky, and that's the truth."

Nick motioned to Sam. "Get Annie. Nora needs to go home to rest."

"What I need," Nora said, looking at Nick, "is for you to take care of Lizzie for me for a spell. Just until I feel better."

Nick opened his mouth to object, but Elle cut in. "Of course, Nora." She looked at Nick. "Your boys will take care of her for you."

Nick pulled Elle aside. "We can't take her with us. It's not safe."

"You're a security specialist, Nick." Elle smiled at him. "Make it safe."

Nick shot a worried look at Sam, Joe and Tim—all of whom surrounded Nora and bombarded her with questions about her well being.

Nora patted Sam's forearm. "I knew I could count on my boys."

Nick's mouth flattened to a slash. That sealed it. All of her boys would rather face a firing squad than to let down Nora. Nick looked at the guys. "I'm going to need some help."

They nodded in unison.

Sam told Nora, "Annie's getting her purse and keys. She'll be here to take you home in just a minute, okay?"

Nora nodded.

"You're sure you don't need a doctor?" Joe asked. "Lisa's gone but Harvey Talbot's still here. Why don't I call him over to take a quick look and make sure—"

"Don't you be bothering Harvey. I don't need nobody poking at me, Joseph. We're going to have a normal, non-eventful wedding in this village today if I have to . . ." She glanced at Lizzie and turned the subject. "I just need some rest and I'll be fine."

Annie rushed over and bent to Nora. "Oh, Nora. I told you not to overdo today." She looked at Nick. "She's been feeling poorly since yesterday. I told her to stay home, but would she listen to me? No."

"You through talking about me like I ain't even sitting here, Annie Harper?"

"I am."

"Then let's go." Nora stood and swayed.

Sam scooped her up. "Put your arm around my neck, Nora. I'll carry you to the car."

Nora winked, clearly reassuring the child and her boys. "Lookie here, Lizzie. I got my own white knight. Ain't that grand?"

"If he don't drop you on your head."

Sam looked affronted. "I won't drop her."

"Course he won't," Nora said. "Lizzie, stop being so cynical."

"He ain't even got a horse. How can he be a white knight without a horse?"

"He's got a white truck. Well, I think it's white under the mud."

"It's white," Sam assured her.

"A truck ain't a knight's horse, Nora."

"It is, I'm saying. Now button it up."

"But it ain't the same."

"It is cuz I said so, girl, and that's that."

"Don't—" Elle whispered and put a staying hand on Lizzie's arm. "You can't win. She loves them."

The girl raised her brows but didn't utter a sound. When they stepped away, she whispered to Elle, "White knight, my left foot." Lizzie grunted. "Sam tricked her. Dr. Talbot's waiting at the car."

"They want to make sure she's okay, that's all. They love her, Lizzie."

"I know when she says 'that's that' nobody argues with her."

"You can't fight them all and, if you upset Nora, you're going to have to."

"Which is why I didn't." Wisdom shone in Lizzie's eyes. Wisdom and mischief.

"She smells like violets." Elle crooked her head. "I've never smelled violet perfume."

"Sometimes she smells like lavender. That's when she's missing Scotland, she says."

"Is Nora from Scotland?"

Lizzie nodded. "She talks about it all the time. Well, when she's in the mood."

"You spend a lot of time with her, then?"

"While my mom's at work."

"Lucky you."

"She's really smart. People don't get it, but Nora knows everything."

"I think you're pretty smart, too. You do get it." A kindred spirit. Elle staved off a smile. "You are okay about coming with us until Nora feels better, right? I apologize, Lizzie. I should have asked you first."

"It's fine." She nodded. "Nora's not going away forever, is she?"

"No, just resting until she feels better."

"Promise?"

The plea in that request squeezed Elle's heart. Lizzie already feared her mom wouldn't come back and now she worried about Nora.

And apparently, Nick picked up on that, too. "Nora will be fine, Lizzie. And so will you."

"Okay."

"And you're right about Dr. Talbot waiting at the car," Nick told her. "Jeff's going to get Nora into the house, unless the doc thinks she needs the ER. If he does, he'll tell Jeff."

Elle smiled. "Excellent. All the bases are covered then."

Lizzie twisted her lips, thinking. Finally, she said, "Nora'd have to be half-dead to go to the hospital without a fight. But I don't think she needs it. She's worn to a frazzle, pure and simple—that's what she said. I figure, she just needs rest." She looked up at Nick. "Thank you for taking care of her."

Sam returned—and shot Lizzie a look, daring her to find fault with his execution of his knightly duties.

She ignored him, asked Elle, "What's that?"

Elle looked to the table. "Oh, that's a begonia." The scent filled her nose. In all the ruckus over Nora, she'd forgotten about it. "A lady gave it to me." Elle looked at Nick.

"What lady?" he asked. "Can you point her out?"

"She left. I don't know her." He'd introduced her to nearly everyone in the room, but that woman hadn't been among the guests then. Lizzie stepped away to talk to a girl she clearly knew well. "She was about the same age as Annie," Elle told him. "A Louis Vuitton fan."

"Louis who?"

"Never mind," Elle said. "She wore a blue dress."

He persisted. "Did she say anything to you?"

"She enjoyed my new song."

"Is that it?"

The tension in him washed over Elle in waves. "No." She leaned close. "Take care, Elle. These days, you never know who's watching you."

"Oh, man." Nick whispered. "We need to go—now."

"Why?"

"You're in danger here." He spotted Lizzie and called out. "Lizzie." He motioned her over.

"When she said that, I got a funny feeling," Elle admitted. "I came to tell you, but then Nora…"

Nick interrupted, agitated and not hiding it. "The flower carries meaning."

A signal, or something? The muscles in her torso clenched all at once. "What is it?"

Dread filled his eyes, his voice. "Beware."

CHAPTER FIVE

ELLE HALF-TURNED IN THE PASSENGER'S SEAT OF NICK'S SEDATE sedan. The air-conditioning felt delicious in the hot car. "You buckled up, Lizzie?"

"Yes." She darted her gaze anxiously from Elle to Nick. "Where are we going?"

"Good question." Elle smiled. "I don't know." She glanced at Nick. "Where are we going?"

Clearly, from that forced lilt in her voice, Elle would also like an answer. Nick pondered, then gave her one that should stifle more questions he wasn't yet prepared to answer. "PSC has a lodge north of the village." He diverted focus. "There's an arcade in the basement, Lizzie."

"I like games."

"Sam does, too. There are plenty of them—and other things you'll enjoy." At least, Nick hoped she would. The guys really enjoyed their time at the Lodge—when they weren't being shot at, of course. But none of them were little girls.

"It's remote?" Elle asked in the direct manner he'd come to expect from her.

Not at all diverted. Best he could do was accept it, and answer what he could. He draped his arm over the steering wheel and nodded.

"So it's remote, isolated and easier to protect than in a popu- lated area like the tourist-filled village."

Before he could answer Elle, Lizzie popped a similar question, only she was even more blunt. "Is it safe?"

Odd question for a kid, and a little insulting. Would he take them there if it weren't safe? He swallowed the irritated bubble and didn't press her. She'd earned a little leeway with everything going on in her life lately. He needed to learn more about that—and he would, in due time. But right now wasn't it. He had to focus to be sure they didn't pick up another tail. "Yeah, it's safe. I designed the security myself. You don't have to worry."

Elle dropped her voice so only he could hear. "Is there a reason Lizzie might worry?"

"Seems like," he said and shrugged, signaling Elle he presently didn't know any more than that.

"Did Sam check it, too?" Lizzie sounded small, vulnerable. "Does he say it's safe?"

Nick thought Lizzie hadn't much liked Sam but, like him or not, apparently his opinions carried weight with her. Probably his size. Big man. That likely inspired trust in a little kid. Made her feel safe around him. "Actually, he did—and so did Mark and Ted and Joe."

"I like Joe."

No surprise there. Nick grunted. It was a rare female who didn't like Joe. He had a gene other men were missing or something. Even young girls like Lizzie weren't immune to his charm.

"Joe's a good listener," Elle said, glancing back at the girl. "Nick's very good at designing security systems, Lizzie. He checks everything over and over and then checks it again. I'll bet his system is perfect."

"Is it?" Lizzie asked Nick. "Perfect, I mean?"

Elle's praise surprised him, though he'd have traded it all for one Joe kind of comment. "Nothing's ever perfect," he honestly admit- ted. "But everyone looked hard and no one found a flaw in it, so I guess it's as good as systems get." He pulled out of the resort and turned left onto Highway 98.

"See, Lizzie. No one found a single flaw, and they're all very good at finding flaws. It's their job. So this place is safe." Elle motioned to a cluster of flowers near the base of a stone fountain marking the entrance to a gated community, *Sea Breeze*. "Oh, look at those irises. Aren't they gorgeous?"

"Uh-huh. I like flowers."

"Me, too. What's your favorite?"

Tapping his earpiece—the guys had been silent—Nick marveled at how easily Elle adapted. She accepted she'd been warned and, even after all she'd been through, she made small talk to comfort a scared kid. Impressive woman. But then she'd always been impressive. That was the problem with her. Beauty and leaving him breathless, he could handle. But her character and compassion? Impossible to blow off.

"I forgot the name of them," Lizzie said.

Traffic was heavy. It would be on a warm and sunny summer afternoon. The beach with its white sand was a huge draw that made the village a beacon to tourists. Frankly, Nick preferred being there in winter when Seagrove was a sleepy little village. Peaceful and calm...and NINA wasn't there, stirring up trouble.

"What do they look like?" Elle asked.

"They're pink. That blue pink not red pink," Lizzie said. "And they grow in bunches that look like cotton candy. I love cotton candy."

Elle laughed.

That chiming tinkle grated on him, seeped under his skin, and that irritated Nick more. The woman unnerved him. Why did he let her get to him? How could he not let her get to him?

Clueless on that, he glanced into the rearview and spotted a green Chevy he'd seen just outside the gate at the club. His attention riveted. It could be a coincidence, just a car that happened to be going in their same direction. Highway 98 was the main thoroughfare in the village... Still, he kept an eye on the car, and checked further back in traffic, spotting Joe on his Harley and Sam in his mud-spattered white truck. Relieved that they were close, Nick gripped the wheel. Sam hadn't wasted any time catching up to them. That, too, was telling on just how much weight they put on the "beware" warning.

Joe's voice came through Nick's earpiece. "You've got a tail, bro."

"Green Chevy?" Nick murmured.

Elle must have heard him and quickly said something to cover his voice so Lizzie wouldn't notice. "They've been to the beach." She pointed to a cluster of people crossing the street, wearing flip-flops and swimsuits and hauling rafts and brightly colored beach bags. One man dragged a wheeled cooler.

"Yep." Joe said. "It's falling in right behind you now."

"Picked it up just outside the club." Nick glanced back.

"Red light!" Elle said sharply.

Nick hit the brakes.

The green sedan rammed into the rear of his car.

Lizzie screamed.

Elle glimpsed her, the people in the sedan—a woman and a man driving who had dark-hair and glasses and sat half slumped over the steering wheel. Was he unconscious? "Lizzie, you okay?"

"I'm scared."

"Are you hurt?" Elle persisted.

"No."

She pivoted to look at Nick. "What about you?"

"Okay." He held his forehead.

"What's wrong with your head?" Elle asked. "Did you hit it?"

"Yeah." He shook his head as if to clear it. "I'm a little woozy. Just need to close my eyes a second and I'll be fine."

The woman got out of the car behind them and ran up to Lizzie's window. She motioned and Lizzie lowered the glass. "Is everyone all right?"

Lizzie raised onto her knees. "Nick's woozy."

"Is your driver unconscious?" Elle asked.

"No, he's fine." She began backing away.

Elle could see the man still slumped. He was definitely not okay.

"Nick..." Blood tricked from between his fingers. "Nick, you're bleeding." She pressed the handkerchief he held over the cut harder to stem the flow. Lizzie said something to the woman and she back to the girl. Elle felt grateful. She'd really rather Lizzie not focus on the blood. "Move your hand and let me see."

He grumbled. "It's a...scratch."

Elle looked. "It's more, but it doesn't need stitches." She pressed the handkerchief back in place, plucked some tissues from a box on the console and dabbed at the blood trickling down his fingers.

"Lizzie okay?" His gaze collided with Elle's.

Elle looked back, checked. The woman was heading back to her car. Lizzie was on her knees, staring out the back window. Following the woman visually, Elle stilled. The woman shoved the driver of her car over and got into the driver's seat. Recognition lit. "Hey, it's her. Nick, it's her."

"Her who?" He didn't open his eyes.

"The lady at the reception who gave me the begonia."

The green sedan backed up, pulled up onto the median dividing the highway, then sped away, leaving half its tires on the asphalt and churned smoke in its wake.

"Why'd she do that? Is that man with her dead or something?"

"No, Lizzie," Elle assured her. "She told you he was fine. Everything is fine."

"She ain't driving like everything's fine."

Elle couldn't disagree so said nothing.

Sam and Joe pulled up next to Nick and screeched to a stop. "Everyone—"

"We're all okay," Nick said. "No thanks to me. I got distracted."

"Not your fault, bro." Joe disputed him. "I watched it. The hit was deliberate."

The beachgoers stood gathered on the side of the road watching. From their high-pitched comments, they agreed. The green sedan's driver never hit the brakes. He wanted to hit them.

Sam pulled out his phone and reported the incident. Elle thought he'd been calling the police until Sam said, "No, Tim. Intentional."

Joe stepped between Sam and the car, then spoke to Nick. "You okay to drive?"

"Yeah. My head's clear now."

"Get to the Lodge. Too exposed out here. We'll catch up."

Nick nodded, told Lizzie to buckle up, and took off.

When he turned off 98 and headed north, Elle finally stopped rattling inside and found her voice. "Do you know what that was all about?"

"Not yet." Nick spared her a glance. "But it's likely that accident is what you were to beware of—at least, I hope it was and there isn't something more coming."

"These people, whoever they are, aren't through with me, are they?"

Smart and she cut to the chase, not dancing around on heavy topics. He respected that about her and found it immensely appealing. He hated that as much as her laughter. The last thing he needed was to find anything else about her appealing. "Not yet."

Her expression crumbled. "If I'd known, Nick, I never would have involved Lizzie. I—I—"

"You didn't know." He had, but hadn't told her. If anyone was to blame, it was him. "We're okay." He said it and hoped it proved true. He and the team would do everything in their power to make it true, but what had happened to Mark's pseudo-sister Jane proved definitively that there were no guarantees. Sometimes you can do everything right and still fail. Still, Elle's distress ripped at his heart.

She didn't quite meet his eye. "I should have considered it possible, and I didn't." She folded her hands in her lap, laced her fingers and squeezed. "I thought if Lizzie were with me, you wouldn't kick me to the curb again—"

What? "I have never kicked you to the curb."

"You left me."

"I finished the job I was hired to do and went home. I wasn't with you, so I couldn't have left you much less kicked you to any curb, Elle."

She stiffened. "I wanted you to stay. You knew I wanted you to stay." Pain flooded her voice. "You didn't even say good-bye."

He hadn't. And it'd been deliberate. If she'd asked him to stay, he doubted he'd have had the resolve to go. Not that he'd ever admit it to her. Only by sheer force of will was he able to admit it to himself. "You were a kid—my client's daughter. Think about that."

"I was eighteen."

"Exactly." He frowned. "Thank you for proving my point."

"Whoa." Lizzie chimed in. "Are you two married?"

Elle sputtered.

Nick groaned.

"Are you?" Lizzie persisted. "Because you sound—"

"No, we're not married." Elle snorted. "We're not. . .anything."

Great. Now she was frosted. Nick started to defend himself, then thought better of it. Some arguments, no matter how logical or reasonable, a man just couldn't win. He clamped his jaw shut and seethed at the injustice. And he had to put up with this.

Indefinitely.

Omega One's assignment rang in Nick's ears. His own *think steel* followed.

Remarkably often, the team's phrase worked, giving them that last little push they needed to make the impossible happen. But with Elle?

Was there enough *think steel* in the world to get through this with her?

Not at all sure, Nick hunkered down, checked the rearview, and just kept driving.

CHAPTER SIX

Everyone in the car eventually settled down. The adrenalin rush wore off and all that had happened to Elle since Thursday when she'd been abducted replayed in her mind. Who was after her? Why? And what had happened to her during those two missing days?

Obviously she'd traveled from London back to the States. But it was unnerving to remember nothing of it. Those men clearly had administered some kind of amnesia drug. But what kind? What side-effects did it have? Any lasting impact? That, she didn't know and wouldn't know until the tests Tim did on her blood came back from the lab. To be living her normal life, just walking down a side-walk one minute and thrust into danger and this drama the next rattled her to the core. Ending up here with Nick rattled her just as much if not more.

She'd trusted Nick from the very beginning. That was rare for her, and while he'd been reserved and distant, at least now she thought she had an insight as to why. She was younger than him and he'd viewed her as a kid and the boss's daughter.

Ironic. Her whole life she'd wanted to be recognized as her parents' daughter, and the one time she actually is, it's an impediment. And, of course, Nick being Nick, he didn't need three strikes against her to count her out. He was more than satisfied with one, much less with two. Someone had burned him badly long before she'd come along.

Elle gazed out the window. Trees lined the two-lane road. They were twisted and gnarled pines mostly, with a few magnolias and a stray oak or two tossed in. The road dipped and rose, gentle hills. This was Florida but it didn't look like the sandbar state she'd imagined it. It was quite lovely, actually. Lush and green.

Twenty-five minutes after the northbound turn, Nick slowed down and made a right onto a dirt path she missed seeing from the paved road. How he'd sensed it there, she had no idea. Must have clocked it on his odometer or something. "Are we there?" she asked him.

"Almost."

He drove another five or six minutes down the smooth path. That it wasn't rutted from weather surprised Elle. A lake appeared on her right, and they crossed a little wooden bridge. It didn't feel full of thumps like a wooden bridge should. Nick and the guys had somehow reinforced it. Knowing Nick, it lifted or sank or twisted away to prevent anyone crossing it that he didn't want crossing it.

They crested a little hill and what she supposed was the lodge came into view. "Is that it?" It looked more like a house. A big house. Three floors with a broad deck on the second floor and a columned porch that wrapped around three sides on the bottom floor. Upstairs, dormer windows flanked an A-frame, green metal roof with a stone fireplace shooting straight through its center.

"That's it."

"I thought you were talking about a hunting lodge," Elle said. "More like a cabin."

"It's a little bigger."

"A lot bigger. Three floors?"

"Four actually. The bottom can only be seen from the back. Walkout basement."

Surprised, she looked around. A broad expanse of green lawn in front of it, broken only by a concrete helicopter pad. Woods to the right and back. A lovely covered gazebo on a boat dock down at the lake. And pretty close to the house—"Is that a creek?"

"It is. Goes through the woods and feeds into the lake."

"Very pretty." It was lovely. Apparently Nick and his associates were successful at PSC. Far more so than she'd been led to believe when she'd told her mother she was going to find Nick and convince him that he would be lucky to have her—an intention Elle never acted on due to the incident that changed her life forever. Her mother had objected, of course, alleged Nick would be intimidated by Elle's family and money and it would be unfair to put him in that position.

Elle nearly had laughed in her mother's face. Nick didn't do intimidate, first of all, and beyond that, Elle had never been recognized as family by her family. Her parents hadn't even given her their last name. What about putting their own daughter in *that* position? Her mother'd had no compunction doing that. Unfortunately, her father hadn't either.

The old resentment roiled and surfaced. She tamped it down, buried it. And buried knowing they must have really been ashamed of her, disappointed in her, to deny she belonged to them. "Who owns this place?"

"Technically, PSC."

"Who owns PSC?" She knew, of course. But she wanted to know if he'd trust her enough to tell her.

"We all do—the team, I mean. Equal shares."

He did trust her. At least, with that. Relieved, she pressed further. "Does anyone live here?"

"Me, more than any of the rest. I like my privacy." He shrugged. "The guys come out, and now and then their families join them. Otherwise, it's just me."

Why did he feel the need to be alone so much? What made him crave isolation?

He pulled the car between two columns and a garage door that looked like siding and not a door at all lifted. He pulled in and shut down the engine. Closed the door behind him. "Lizzie, wake up. We're here."

She roused and rubbed at her eyes. "I'm up."

Nick showed them around.

Elle had expected the furnishings to be sparse and stark with lots of sharp edges, but the main floor was an open and inviting gathering room with lots of glass and light and a broad expanse of warm woods. A long bar with stools defined the kitchen. In the center of the gathering room stood two separate sitting areas. The first was filled with plump warm brown leather sofas, one curved, one straight, and littered with comfortable textured pillows facing an enormous flat-screen TV. The second sitting area was in a nook near the entry. A large recliner and a rocker were placed near a free-standing gas stove. Sunlight streamed in from the far wall windows and a staircase leading up to the second and third floors occupied a third wall.

On the right, she paused, not sure what she was seeing. It was a long bank of oversized screens. Three of them. A slim desk stretched out before them, but the screens appeared to be windows with sunlight streaming in. At least, at first glance. "Your techie station, I take it," she said to Nick.

"More or less."

Cryptic. Definitely a techie station, if not his main one.

"Where's the arcade?" Lizzie twirled looking for it.

"Downstairs." Nick pointed to a passageway between the kitchen and seating area. "You can go down. Light switch is on the left. Don't touch the weights—or the darts—and stay out of the spa unless an adult's with you."

"Whoa." Her eyes stretched wide. "All that's down there."

Nick frowned, clearly not trusting the gleam in Lizzie's eyes. "Maybe we'd better come with you."

Elle seconded that thought with a healthy nod. "Definitely."

They spent the next fifteen minutes with Lizzie *oohing* and *ahhing* over located treasures, then broke away to explore the rest of the house.

He showed Elle and Lizzie two bedrooms on the second floor. "You can stay here. Next door to each other. You'll share a center bath."

"Where will you be?" Elle asked.

"Downstairs. There's a bedroom there."

"Where's Sam gonna be? Out on the porch?" Lizzie pointed out the long window to the deck.

"No, he'll be upstairs. Joe, too."

"Where's the stairs?" Lizzie asked, eyeing the long door to the deck with skepticism.

"End of the hall," Nick said. "I'll show you on the way down."

The rooms were a good size and both had doors onto the second-story deck. Hers was decorated in sunny yellow and Lizzie's in pale green. Soft colors, lots of little touches of comfort, like the quilts draped over the edges of the beds. On a hunch, Elle turned to Nick. "Nora and Annie help decorate these?"

"Actually, they did. Lisa and Mandy, too."

"Very nice, Nick."

"Thanks." He cleared his throat. "I'll leave you two to settle in for a bit. When you're ready, come down and we'll see if we have any luck identifying the people who rammed into my car." He paused. "Oh, don't open the doors onto the deck. You'll trigger the alarm."

Relief washed over Lizzie's face. "If somebody tries to come in, it'll go off, too?"

"Loud enough to wake the dead." Nick nodded, then thought that probably wasn't a wise thing to say to a kid. "Well, really, really loud." He turned and went out into the hall. "If you need anything, just press the button."

"What button?" Elle asked.

"Sorry." He sounded a little flustered. "There's a panic button beside your beds." He looked at Lizzie. "Don't touch it unless you're in danger and need help right now."

She nodded.

He went on, stepping close to a narrow wall just outside the bathroom they shared. "See this?" He pointed to a little black dot at waist level. "It's an intercom. Press it and talk. Someone will hear you."

"That's kind of cool." Lizzie's blue eyes danced. "I didn't even see it until you showed it to me."

"An intercom comes in handy when there are four floors. Beats having to hit the stairs to check each one when you're looking for someone."

Nick paused, pushed some button on his watch, then said. "Sam and Joe are here." He made for the hallway. "See you downstairs in a bit."

His footfalls faded on the stairs. Elle absorbed all she'd seen. Equipped as it was, the Lodge seemed more like a fortress than the getaway Nick claimed. Elle looked at Lizzie and she at her.

"We must be in a whole lot of trouble," Lizzie said, wide-eyed and swallowing hard.

Elle had the same feeling, but she wanted Lizzie's insights. Kids had special gifts on that kind of thing. "Why?"

"Because if we weren't, Nora's boys wouldn't think we needed all this."

Elle's stomach fluttered. She didn't want to scare Lizzie, but she refused to lie to her. "We probably are in a lot of trouble. But I'll tell you something. If you're a person in trouble, this place—with these guys—is *exactly* where you want to be."

She swiped her hair back from her face. "My mom said that, too."

Elle frowned. "Then why did she leave you with Nora?" Why hadn't she left Lizzie with Nick and the guys?

"So they'd watch over me." Lizzie lifted her arms. "Nobody tells Nora no. Especially not her boys."

Elle got it now. The quickest route to PSC was through Nora. "I think you and your mother are very smart cookies."

Lizzie twisted her mouth, and the look in her eyes was far too old for her years. "Not as smart as we needed to be or we wouldn't be in trouble."

Wise answer, but one she could honestly dispute. "That's not always true. Sometimes we see trouble coming and sometimes we don't." Today, no one knew that better than she. The injustice of it settled inside her, and Elle frowned. "I'm in trouble, and I have no idea in the world why."

Lizzie recognized the offer of a bond of trust between them, and accepted it. "Me neither."

"What's that?" In the great room's kitchen area, Lizzie knelt on a stool and leaned over the breakfast bar, pointing at some brown, soupy food in a crockpot.

Sam frowned at her. "Beats me, but I ain't eating it."

"Why not?"

"Mandy cooked it."

Nick cleared his throat.

Tim clapped him on the shoulder. "No problem, Nick. I love my wife and will always love her, but truth is truth and she can't cook any better than Lisa."

"Mark's Lisa can't cook?" Elle asked.

"No self-respecting dog will eat her food."

"Sam, that's harsh." Elle frowned.

"It might be, but it ain't no lie."

"It's honest." Tim nodded. "If you value your stomach, keep both those women far, far away from the kitchen—but don't mention it."

Elle bit back a smile. "They're touchy about it?"

"Naw, not a bit," Sam said. "It's just pointing out a flaw ain't the way to a woman's heart, if you know what I mean. And they overlook a lot of flaws in us. So fair's fair."

"Ah, I see." Boy, did she, and it amused her.

"I have a theory on that business," Joe said, sliding a hip onto a stool at the breakfast bar next to Lizzie.

"On what business?" Sam asked.

Lizzie snarled at him. "Lisa and Mandy cooking. Can't you keep up?"

Before Sam could snarl back at the girl, Joe intervened. "I think they don't like to cook and they don't want to cook, therefore they can't do it."

Tim cocked his head. "I don't know, Joe. I've seen them both make the effort."

"Have you really? Or have you seen what you expected to see?" Joe lifted a finger in Tim's direction. "Both of them are smart, skilled, capable, and determined. Do you really think if either of them wanted to cook, they couldn't? Seriously?"

"I never looked at it that way." Tim frowned. "It's possible."

"It's probable," Sam agreed.

"Well, if they don't like cooking and they don't want to do it, what's wrong with that?" Lizzie asked.

"Not a thing," Tim said. "I cook and so does Mark. It works out fine." His expression softened. "But we don't rub their noses in it because—"

Lizzie cut in. "That's just rude."

"It is. Everybody doesn't like doing something." Elle grinned. And rubbing salt would be a sure-fire path to women being in wickedly bad moods. Smart men would studiously avoid that. "So is anything in there salvageable?" She nodded to Mandy's pot, her stomach growling. "I've been without much to eat for a few days and I'm hungry."

Sam shrugged. "Mark usually cooks when we're out here, but he's on his honeymoon." He hooked a thumb toward the door. "I'm worse in the kitchen than Mandy and Lisa together, but I can run get some pizzas."

Nick told Elle. "The fridge and freezer are stocked. I'm passable in the kitchen, if you want to risk it."

Elle liked to cook, and she liked to eat. "Mind if I snoop around?"

"You really need to look at some pictures," he said. "You, too, Lizzie."

"Of what?" She twisted on the stool, swiveling it.

"To see if we can find one of the lady at the wreck."

"After we eat, Tim," Elle said. "We can't focus if we're starving."

Tim nodded. "Let's see what we can do then."

Elle went to the fridge and pulled out lettuce, tomatoes, onions and bell peppers. "Nick, here's the stuff for salad."

"Sam's better at slicing and dicing."

"Here, then." She passed off the stuff to Sam. "Lizzie, help him with that."

She bounded off the stool. "Where's the salad bowl?"

"Second cabinet, top shelf," Nick told her.

She looked up at Sam. "I need a boost."

He hauled her up. She opened the cabinet and retrieved a bowl. "Got it."

Sam put her down on the floor. "You could use a few pounds. You're light."

She cranked back her head and looked up at the giant. "You're handy to have around. At least, until I get taller."

Oh, yeah. Elle watched Sam and Lizzie. The child appreciated his size. He made her feel safe. What exactly had made her feel unsafe? Elle wondered, but didn't ask. Lizzie already had said she didn't know why she was in trouble, but Elle had an inkling she knew more than she'd said, or maybe more than she thought. "Nick, do you have salad dressing?"

"In the fridge."

Elle checked and found three jars. "They're all expired."

"What now?" Nick said.

"We make our own." She pulled out some ingredients, went in search of spices, and then mixed together a vinaigrette and a pseudo-ranch. "That'll do."

"We need boiled eggs," Lizzie said. "I can't swallow salad without boiled eggs cut up in it, Elle."

"Boil some." Elle passed Lizzie the carton, and then spotted half a roasted chicken in the fridge. "You have plans for this?"

"No." Nick frowned. "It's not expired. Bought it yesterday."

"Great. Put on some rice and, Tim, you find some vegetables."

He headed for the pantry.

She cut up the chicken and pulled out a skillet, then added a little oil. "Is there any pineapple in there, Tim?"

"Yeah, and green beans and corn."

"No corn. Just the pineapple," Elle said. "Nick, clean some carrots, will you?"

He got busy next to Sam at the sink.

She rummaged through the freezer. "Eureka!"

"What?" He looked at her.

"Snow peas." She smiled. "We've got a meal."

"Great." Tim grinned. "And it's not burned."

Nick grunted. "Refreshing change, eh?"

"You don't act like a big star," Sam told Elle. "You act like a normal person." His face went red. "I mean, you seem at home in the kitchen."

"She likes to eat." Nick dumped the pineapple into the skillet. "Really likes to eat."

Elle laughed. "I do."

Lizzie frowned at Sam. "Don't act goofy. Everybody eats."

Sam motioned with a huge hand. "Set the table, you pint-sized tyrant."

Lizzie grabbed a stack of plates someone had put on the counter. "Tyrant." She paused, then told Sam. "I don't know what that is, but I don't like the way you said it."

Elle let that pass and whispered to Nick, standing at her side, watching the steaming skillet. "I take it word is out that I'm missing."

"Actually, it's not. Joe's been in touch with your manager and bodyguard, but they've kept it out of the press."

"How?" She'd had commitments, and neither Neil nor Charlie impressed her as that savvy.

"Laryngitis or something. I'm not sure." Nick's gaze slid away. "Joe's...resourceful."

"I have the feeling ear-blistering was involved." She stirred. The carrots were done. "After dinner, I'm calling my parents."

"That's probably not a good—"

"I wasn't asking, Nick," she said softly. "I call my father every other day, so I'm already overdue. I'm not letting him worry." He would. Her mother? Well, maybe she'd noticed Elle hadn't called, and maybe she hadn't. It depended on what was on her calendar.

"Okay, then." He gave in gracefully. "Call. But say nothing about the incident and especially not about where you are now."

Their phone could be monitored. "Got it." Elle turned and lifted her voice so everyone could hear her. "Dinner is ready."

After a boisterous meal, they all sat around the table until Elle said, "It's after seven. Let's get the dishes done and look at those photos before Lizzie falls asleep sitting up. She's had a busy day."

"We'll do the dishes," Joe said, already gathering plates. "Fair repayment for a good meal that's not charred."

Elle smiled. "Fair enough." She turned to Nick. "Which phone do you want me to use to call my folks?"

"Mine."

It was secure. Vintage Nick. Always thinking defense. She held out her hand.

He passed her his phone and she walked through the nook, past the recliner and gas stove, then stood near the windows. Staring outside, she dialed her parents' home in Los Angeles.

Her mother answered on the third ring. "Hello."

"Hi, Mom."

"Elle," she said, sounding breathless and more than a little annoyed. "Your dad's been calling me every hour to see if you've phoned yet."

Definitely not happy at her day being constantly interrupted. "Where is he?"

"Washington. I have no idea why." Static crackled. "How's London?"

Elle hesitated, saw Nick two steps behind her, sitting in the recliner so he could listen while pretending not to hear a thing. "London is good. The audience seemed to really like *New Dawn*."

"New what?"

"My new song." Just once couldn't she at least fake an interest in Elle's work? Just once?

"Oh. Well, that's wonderful, darling."

"You seem distracted." Even more so than usual, which meant she might or might not remember Elle even called. She'd have to phone her father herself.

"I'm in the middle of my massage."

She was always in the middle of something. The pit of Elle's stomach hollowed. She could have been killed and her mother remained totally oblivious. Maybe she didn't have that mother's intuition women supposedly had. Or if she did have it, she didn't recognize it for what it was. That was highly possible. Either way, Elle felt abandoned yet again.

No one could make her feel like an intrusion just by existing the way her mother could. The worst part was her mother had no idea what she was doing. She never had, which made it impossible to expect more from her or to resent her for what she lacked.

It is what it is, and she is who she is. Love her anyway. "I'll leave you to it, then," Elle said. "You're fine. I'm fine. Everything's fine."

"All right, dear." She paused, then added, "Do phone your father. His obsessive calling is driving me crazy—and, Elle, please make a reasonable effort to stick to your phoning schedule so you don't worry him."

Resentment steeped in Elle. It's a little hard to not inconvenience others when you're kidnapped off the street, drugged, and you lose days of even knowing what planet you're on. She wanted to say it all. The words burned her throat and tongue. But she didn't utter a sound. Since she hadn't told her mother a thing about the incident, she couldn't fairly hold her accountable for not expressing any concern. That wasn't right. "I'll do my best, Mother." Elle hung up and glanced at Nick. "She's busy at the moment. Getting a massage."

He nodded, but the look in his eye said he'd picked up more than enough to grasp the strain between her and her mother, and maybe Elle's resentment, too, though she hoped not. Letting go of all that, she dialed her dad.

He answered on the first ring. "Elle? Is that you?"

"It is. Sorry I'm late calling. I got...delayed."

"No problem. I wasn't worried yet. Neil hadn't called, so I felt sure everything had to be fine. Otherwise, he or Charles would have phoned."

Neil hadn't called because Joe likely had threatened him into not calling. "What are you doing in DC? I thought you weren't due to go for another month." Two weeks actually, but something about his reaction, his tone—all of this—didn't feel right.

"I decided to come out early and get it off the schedule."

It was all she could do to keep her jaw from dropping. Her father never went to DC without dragging his feet until the very last possible second. He detested DC and almost any place else outside his lab and testing facility. Something was definitely wrong. "Is everything going okay?"

"Absolutely. We exceeded expectations, of course. That always puts them in a good mood."

"Well, I hate to wreck your good mood, but I have some bad news."

Nick jumped to his feet, motioned for her not to disclose her circumstances or location.

Elle put up a restraining hand, mouthed, "Don't."

Nick stilled, but clamped his jaw and the look in his eyes chilled to ice.

"What kind of bad news?" her dad asked.

"I'm afraid I lost my ring," she said. "One minute I had it on, and the next it was gone."

"Oh, Elle. You had me worried something happened to you."

She sought a response that was honest and true. "I'm fine."

"That's all that matters, then."

She tensed. Something was definitely wrong. Her father would ordinarily be talking about insurance adjusters and filing claims and police reports. Instead, he doesn't even ask a single question? Beyond odd and headlong into bizarre. What was going on here? She pushed, digging for information that would make his reaction make sense. "I told you I was concerned about wearing a diamond that big all the time."

"It's jewelry. Isn't jewelry meant to be worn?"

He didn't dispute her. "Yes, but…" He didn't know. *He didn't know!* Her heartbeat jacked up, thundered, pounded in her chest, in her temples. What did this mean?

"I'm sure you reported it. We'll deal with the rest when you're back home."

The bottom fell out of her stomach. She swallowed hard, struggled to keep her voice steady. "Of course." Her throat bone-dry, she worked to steady her tone. "When will you be going home?"

"In a few days. I've got field study results to go over with the people here, and you know how that goes."

She knew too well how those briefings went. She'd handled a lot of them while working with her father. "Good luck with it," she said. "I've got to go now but I'll call again in two days."

"All right, dear. Be careful over there."

"You be careful, too." She hung up the phone, rattled to the core.

"Is everything all right?" Nick asked.

She refused to lie to him but did she dare to tell him the truth? Unsure, she shrugged and passed him his phone. "Thanks." Glancing at the brown sofa, she spotted Lizzie. Droopy-eyed and snuggled down. "Lizzie's fading fast. If you want us to look at photos tonight, I'd say now's the time."

Lizzie sighed for the tenth time in as many minutes. "How much longer do we have to sit here, Elle?"

Elle glanced over to the child seated beside her before a computer screen the size of a TV. "Until we find her."

"Why? She didn't hurt us. She just asked if we were okay. Why do we need to find her?"

"Because she damaged Nick's car." And fled the scene of an accident with an unconscious, injured driver in her car, and she'd warned Elle to beware. "When she came to your car window, what exactly did she say?"

"I told you." Lizzie tapped the cursor to advance to the next line of photos. "She asked if we were okay."

"That's it?" Elle took over on the cursor.

Lizzie twirled her hair with her fingertip, stopped suddenly and squealed. "Stop, Elle. Stop."

Elle stopped advancing the photos. "That's her—the lady who gave me the begonia."

Tim sputtered a swallow of iced-tea. "That's impossible."

"It's her." Elle looked back at him, then to the others, settling her gaze on Nick.

"It's not her," Lizzie said. "She's not the lady from the wreck, either."

Elle reacted to the certainty in Lizzie's voice. Doubt took hold. "Seriously?"

"Oh, yeah." Lizzie nodded to add weight to her claim. "She looks like her, but she's not."

"Well, that's a relief," Nick said, his voice dripping sarcasm.

"Why?" Elle turned in her seat to look back at him.

"Because that's Mandy. Tim's wife."

Lizzie frowned at Tim. "Then you have to know the lady."

"Why?" he asked.

"Because she looks just like her."

"She does," Elle agreed. "The lighting was dim, but she did look like Mandy, Tim."

"Well, not just like her," Lizzie said. "The lady was older. I saw her in the light when she opened the door to outside."

"You saw her leave?" Elle asked.

Lizzie nodded.

"And she looked like Mandy only older?"

A flash of the woman walking out into the sun filled Elle's mind and came into sharp focus. "You're right, Lizzie." Elle recalled the woman clearly now. "She's about twenty or twenty-five years older than Mandy. But age this photo, and you've got her."

Tim looked thunderstruck. So did Nick. "What's wrong?" Elle asked. Had she said something goofy? Missed the obvious?

Nick let his gaze drift to the other guys. All of them looked intense, worried, and a little confused. "Nothing's wrong."

Elle stood up and called Nick outside onto the porch. Near a rocker, she leaned a shoulder against a column. "You know more than you're saying on this."

"I do," he admitted. "But, at the moment, there's nothing I can share."

"Who is she?"

"I'm not sure—and that's as honest as I can be. If she's who I think she is, then we're okay."

"And if she isn't?"

"Then we're clearly not." He leaned against the rounded column, facing her. "I don't have the answers you're asking for, Elle. When I do and I can, I'll tell you what I know."

"Well, don't mess around." Her nerves jangled.

"Why? What's happened?"

There it was. The moment of truth. She had to trust him, or not. All in, or all out.

Innately, she did trust him, and equally important, whatever was going on with her kidnapping and being shipped back to the States and this strange woman with the begonia and then the intentional ramming of the car was bigger than she could handle alone. That decided it. "Because I don't know the identity of the man in DC I talked to on the phone." She lifted her gaze to meet his. "But he was not my father."

"What do you mean, he wasn't your father?"

"There's no sense in screaming at me, Nick. I meant just what I said." Elle glared back at him. "His reaction·to me on everything was off. So I said something about the ring being a diamond. He didn't dispute me."

Nick stilled. "You said it was an amethyst."

"It was." She nodded. "And since he gave it to me, he'd know that." She worried her lip with her teeth. "He should have picked up on the discrepancy and asked me for our code word, but he didn't. Whether that was because he couldn't or he didn't know to do it, I'm not sure, but my instincts are telling me he wasn't my father." A rush of worry had her eyes stinging. "Nick, do you think something's happened to my dad?"

"I don't know," he said honestly. "But we'll find out."

"I should have told you right away," she admitted.

"Yes, you should have. I trust you won't hold out again."

"I won't." She hugged him and held on. He didn't hug her back, but he didn't let go, either. And he smelled good. Like fresh air and pineapple. "Thank you." She'd needed that hug. Elle had learned early to hold herself together and roll with the punches, but she'd never learned to do so without it taking an internal toll. Nick didn't say anything but she innately knew he sensed that about her—and her end of the conversation with her mother likely affirmed it to him.

"You go on inside now. Let me brief the guys and make a call. See what I can find out."

"Do I want to know to whom?" Curious, she'd asked, but she held no hope for an answer. Nick had secrets. And he kept them to himself. He had four years ago, and he still did.

"No." He nodded toward the door. "You really don't. It wouldn't mean anything to you anyway."

Elle paused, her hand on the knob. "Please don't make me sorry I trusted you."

"That, you never have to worry about, Elle." The shield in his eyes slipped for a second. "I promise."

Praying he was right, she went back into the Lodge.

Elle challenged Lizzie to a game in the basement arcade.

"You're on." Lizzie scooted off the sofa and, when they cleared the steps, Nick nodded to Sam, who went to the computer, depressed the keys, and the guys waited for the screen to appear in what had looked like a window. Twelve frames appeared on it. Various shots of the property and lodge, four of which were on the inside, including one in the basement, where Elle and Lizzie sat side-by-side playing Sam's favorite, NASCAR Racing.

"Lizzie drives like a maniac." Sam said, a twinkle in his eye. "She's spunky, that kid."

"Just don't cut her loose on the street in anything motorized." Nick frowned.

"Well, what's up?" Tim said, clearly expecting a briefing.

"The woman they identified is easy enough," Sam said. "She had to have been Mandy's mom."

Nick stood behind Sam. Olivia Dixon—Liv—and Mandy did look a lot alike. The resemblance was strong. In the dim light at the reception, Nick could see anyone confusing them. Olivia was CIA and had infiltrated NINA years ago. She'd been walking the line between the two for decades. "But why was Olivia there? She had told Mandy she wouldn't be seeing her again. NINA didn't like close association between Shadow Watchers and their operatives."

"We're not Shadow Watchers anymore." Sam said.

"Technically, no, we're not," Joe said. "But we'll always be Shadow Watchers to NINA." He sat down in the recliner. "We cost them a lot of money, disrupting their revenue streams. They're not going to just let that go, bro. It's bad for business."

"Joe's right." Tim rubbed at the back of his neck. "NINA is one of the worst terrorist groups in the world. Add their funding of political objectives to their activities and they can't afford to just forget anything—ever. They let anything slide and people stop fearing them. Their organization can't function without fear."

"Elle called her parents," Nick told them. "Heavy tension between her and her mom."

Tim tensed, hand in his slacks' pocket. "Did she tell her mother what happened in London?"

"Not a word. I asked her not to, but I also asked her not to call and she insisted on doing that anyway." Nick wasn't sure what to make of it. "Her mom said her dad was in DC. She called him," Nick told the others, then quickly briefed them on the conversation. "She told me she didn't know who the man she spoke with was, but he was an imposter."

"Whoa." Sam sat down on the sofa, braced his arms on his knees. "Why is she so sure he wasn't her dad?"

"He gave her the ring."

"We know that, Nick," Tim said.

"She had a funny feeling, so she tested him. Said the stone was a diamond. He didn't correct her or ask for her code word."

Joe frowned. "They have a code word?"

"Apparently." Nick nodded. "She said he should have asked her for it, and he didn't."

"Why do they have a code word?" Sam looked back at Nick.

"I don't know. But she was really upset that he hadn't asked her for it. She's worried about where her dad really is and what's happening to him."

"To me, that seems more odd than them having a code word," Tim said, dropping onto a stool at the bar. "Lots of parents have a code word with their kids. They might have started that when she first started school or something."

Nick sat down beside him. "Her dad's whereabouts and what's happening to him, and her worrying about him, is not as odd as you might think."

That got their attention. "I'll fill you in on why as soon as I talk with Omega One," Nick added. "Someone's got that ring—the CIA or NINA—and I think we need to find out who."

"You think the ring is the reason NINA grabbed her," Sam said. "Well, tried to grab her."

"Would have grabbed her if the CIA hadn't gotten to her first," Nick amended. "And we need to find out about her father."

"That, too." Joe nodded. "I agree. The two might be connected."

Nick would bet on it. His instincts were humming it. "Let's get to it. You know what to do." Nick pulled out his cell and stepped outside onto the porch, leaving the guys to run some intense background work.

Omega One answered, sounding half-asleep. "Yeah."

"I got your package."

"Good. Everything okay?"

"Okay is a relative term. The package is intact, though an item was removed and is now missing," Nick said, staring out at the trees. He waited for Omega One to say something.

"We're aware of that."

"So we have it?" The CIA must have taken possession of the ring in the van. What was special about it?

"Not exactly."

Bad news. "Our adversary has it?" NINA. Oh, yeah. Something special, all right. Knots formed in Nick's stomach and his muscles clenched.

"Unfortunately."

"When did that happen?" Elle specifically said the ring was taken from her when she was in the van.

"During interdiction. Apparently, we had it and…the chain of custody was broken."

"Is there reason to believe it is in the custody of our adversary?" If NINA had the ring, then why were they still after Elle? That made no sense.

"It's possible." One paused, then added. "We're not sure yet."

Someone was looking into it. Olivia? A gentle breeze rustled the leaves, carried the scent of mowed grass and pine. Crickets chirped and frogs croaked in the near wood. Normal nighttime sounds he'd come to enjoy at the Lodge. "We might have encountered that person."

"Oh?"

"Yeah. Leaving the delivery location, we had an intentional traffic accident. I didn't see the individuals, but two witnesses have identified one of them—more or less."

"Anyone injured?"

"No. Everyone's fine." So One hadn't refuted that Olivia was involved. "Clear to disclose?"

"Just a second." A couple seconds passed, then a couple more. "Okay, go ahead."

Scrambling the signal. "Olivia Dixon. They identified Mandy, only the woman, they said, was older. At the reception, the same older woman issued a warning to the Marked Star and gave her a begonia."

"Beware," One said, repeating the meaning of the flower. "Sounds like her."

"So is this a good or a bad thing?"

"I wish I knew."

That was the answer Nick expected, but one he still hated to hear. Even One wasn't sure what Olivia was doing. "What do we do about the father who is or isn't the father?"

"If he isn't her father, it raises the question of where her father is and why someone is doubling as him."

"If he is her father, not sharing the code word is apt to be a signal he's in trouble."

"Either way, we have enough to warrant checking it out, especially considering his...interests." One said. "I'll work that angle from this end. I don't have to tell you that the dad being in question is a really bad sign."

His interests all required security clearances at the highest levels. Information not only NINA would kill to get but would bring a fortune on the black market. Doubt about an imposter stepping into his shoes was a very bad sign. "Yeah. Or worse." Nick turned toward the door. "Keep me posted. Some context on why the package is here and how it connects in all this would be helpful."

"As soon as I can."

"Rush them. If my neck's on the line, I want to know why." Nick ended the call and then went back inside. The guys looked at him, their faces expectant.

"The woman could be Olivia," he told Tim, since she was his mother-in-law. "One didn't refute me, but he also didn't know if it being her was a good or bad thing."

"In other words," Tim said, "he doesn't have a clue what she's doing."

"That pretty much covers it." Unfortunately, that was common problem when an undercover agent was working both sides of the fence.

"What about Elle's dad?" Joe asked.

"One's handling that aspect from his end." Probably best considering he remained unable to offer them full disclosure.

Sam frowned. "Why would NINA be interested in a singer and her father?" He looked to Nick for an explanation. "They always have a reason for everything, but this one stretches beyond my imagination."

Nick fought and lost the battle raging within. "Because Elle isn't just a superstar singer. And her dad isn't just your average dad."

Tim straightened, stiffened in his seat at the bar. "Who are they?"

Elle stepped into the room. "If you want to know something about me, just ask." She sent Nick a sympathetic look. "Sorry to put you on the spot like this."

"You want to explain?" he asked.

"No, frankly, I don't want either of us to have to explain," she said, walking to the fridge and grabbing a can of cola. "But if it has to be done—and apparently, it does—I'll do it."

The guys all sat down on stools at the bar. Elle stood in the kitchen. "I feel like some cookies." She glanced past their confused expressions. "Nick, do you have the ingredients to make cookies?"

"Yeah. Oatmeal raisin or chocolate chip?"

"I like them both," she admitted. "You choose."

"I vote chocolate chip," Sam said.

"Second that." Joe smiled. "I love chocolate chip."

"Chocolate chip it is, then." She began measuring and dumping ingredients into a huge metal bowl. "You guys know my dad founded and owns AAN—American Armory Network. You probably don't know that he designs the systems."

"All of them?"

"Almost," Elle said, beating the eggs in the bowl. Her hands were shaking. "You definitely know—from your former . . . line of work, of course—many of his designs are dual use."

She referenced their active-duty days as Shadow Watchers. "Dual use. Military and civilian applications," Nick said.

"We're aware of that," Tim interjected. "We've used systems he's developed from time to time."

She sent Tim a level look. "You use systems he's developed every day of your life. We all do. You just know more about the systems with military applications."

Tim held his silence. So did the others.

Elle blended in the sugar and flour. "His military systems' designs have been successful, but he's been beyond successful with his commercial applications."

"She's being modest." Nick rolled his gaze. "He's got fistfuls of patents and more money than Gates."

"Maybe. Even I don't know how much, but it's a lot," Elle said. "I'm his only child, so I'm an heiress."

"Is that why you were kidnapped?" Sam kept glancing at the stairs.

"Lizzie's gone to bed, Sam," Elle said. "I tucked her in before coming back down."

"Okay." He slid off the stool and keyed in a series of strokes at the computer keyboard. An image of Lizzie sleeping soundly in her bed appeared on the screen.

Protective. Elle liked that. "Anyway, to answer your question, I don't know if it's why I was kidnapped. But it might be."

"What else could it be?" Sam sat on a stool and twisted so he could watch Elle and the screen. "The star thing?"

"Maybe. But maybe not." She hesitated, then went on. "I worked with my dad from the time I could walk."

"Shuffling paper and stuff?" Joe asked, elbow on the bar, chin propped in his hand.

"Early on, but mostly as his assistant, until I…outgrew the position."

Nick stopped dumping chocolate chips into the bowl. "You *outgrew* the position of being your dad's assistant?"

She nodded. "When I was seventeen."

"Neither of you told me that when I was there." Nick frowned. "You've got to be kidding me."

"Not kidding, believe me." She set the oven temperature, then began spooning the dough onto cookie sheets.

"Wait a second." Nick washed his hands at the sink, then tore off a paper towel to dry them. "You were working there with him when I met you. You were eighteen then."

"Yes, I was."

"Yet both of you led me to believe you were his assistant."

"You assumed it." Her face burned hot. "And we let you."

"Why?" Sam, not Nick, pushed for clarity.

Elle so didn't want to talk about this. So didn't want to relive it. But it would be unfair to them not to, so she girded her loins and told them. "Over the years, I'd cultivated a real knack for development. Systems, in particular. By the time Nick came to us, I had an assistant of my own."

Nick just stood there, stiff and silent and a little stunned. She hated that. Truly.

Joe pressed her. "Elle, are you a singer or an engineer?"

"Actually, I'm both." She popped the cookie sheet into the oven and set the timer. "I became a mechanical engineer at seventeen."

"Seventeen?"

She nodded, answering Joe. "I had a little more than a knack for it. I was pretty good at it."

"Yeah, I'd say." Sam guffawed. "College grad at seventeen. Wow."

Elle shifted uncomfortably. "Singing and songwriting was always a passion, but I never intended it to be a profession. Well, not until later." She worked up the courage to look at Nick. He still hadn't moved, and his expression had sobered even more. How that was possible, she had no idea. "I know," she told him. "You thought I was an artsy kid with a crush on you. Not a mechanical engineer and an artsy kid with a crush on you."

His face went red. Clearly, that's exactly what he'd thought. "You should have been honest with me, Elle. I was trying to protect you."

"My dad forbid it—for good reason. I couldn't disagree without breaching a confidentiality agreement, so I didn't. I'll take the hit for that." She sighed her frustration, a spoon mid-air. "But honestly, Nick. Didn't you ever wonder why he was so adamant about every little security detail? Didn't you wonder why he went off the rails when I was out of sight for even a minute? I did drop you countless clues."

"I picked up on them." He shrugged. "But everything your father touches is classified. You're his daughter and an heiress to a fortune. He feared that the company, he and your mother, his designs and, most of all you would be targets for everything from kidnapping to industrial espionage."

Nick had no idea just how right he was about her father's fears. Her mother was just as bad in her own way. "Hmm." Elle checked the cookies. Not done yet. She adjusted the timer, adding another minute.

Tim mimicked Joe, propping his elbow on the bar, his chin into his upturned hand. "So you were an engineer and dropped designing systems to go pro in music."

"Yes." She didn't elaborate. She couldn't. Not that she'd be eager to even if she could.

The old guilt washed through her like a raging tsunami. She stiffened against it. Nick hadn't said another word. He was clearly still stinging and thoroughly ticked off that she and her father had deceived him, and because he had every right to be angry, she couldn't offer a defense. Because she couldn't, and she felt the weight of that guilt, she couldn't make herself look at him.

The timer went off.

"Ah," she turned her back to them all, grabbed an oven mitt and got the cookies out of the oven.

Something ripped behind her. Startled, she jumped.

"Wax paper," Nick said, his jaw nearly in spasms from his clamping down on it.

The look in his eyes disabused her of any illusions. This conversation might be postponed by chunky chocolate chip cookies fresh from the oven, but it was far from over.

Elle's stomach fluttered then flipped. For her, the events that prompted her move to music would never really be over. She'd gotten better at coping, but ever letting go?

Couldn't happen. That was a pipe dream.

Some things you do change your life forever, and no matter how much or how often you wish you could take them back or change them, you can't. Done is done.

All you can do is to try to live with them.

CHAPTER SEVEN

Sunday, June 7ᵗʰ, 8:00 a.m.
The Lodge

"Where'd these clothes come from, Elle?"

"I'm not sure." She looked at the clothes she'd spread out on her bed. "When I woke up, they were in those bags, outside the bedroom door." Four empty shopping bags rested near the foot of the bed. "There are several outfits for you."

"For you, too." Lizzie touched the fabrics. "Soft." She looked at Elle, her worry in her eyes. "If they got us all this stuff, we're going to be here for a while."

"I hadn't thought of that." Elle sat down on the edge of the bed. Shorts and tops, two dresses, underwear, shoes, and even cosmetics. "I hope Nick didn't pick these things out." *Too personal.* Her cheeks went hot.

"I'd bet he didn't." Lizzie lifted a pink print top and pair of capris. "They'd all be black."

Elle couldn't disagree. "He does bend toward the gloomy side." How many hours, months, in the last four years had she speculated on why?

"He's broken." Lizzie held up the capri pants. "These are my favorite. I love pink."

Shock rippled through Elle. "What do you mean, he's broken?"

"Nora says somebody hurt him real bad. He's broken inside from it."

Elle couldn't disagree with that either, even if she wished hard she could. The idea of someone hurting Nick like that…it hurt her. Truly, hurt her. He was such a special man. "Did Nora say who or what they'd done to him? Anything else about it?"

"Yep." Lizzie paused, holding a yellow sundress up and looking in the mirror. She twirled to face Elle. "She said, 'the man needs loving, Lizzie. You think some things are broken so bad they can't be fixed, but love can fix just about anything—'specially people.'"

"Do you think she's right?" Elle felt a little silly asking a ten year old that question, but Lizzie wasn't an ordinary ten year old. Her eyes were as haunted as any adult's Elle had ever seen, including her own. And repeating Nora…there was much to be learned from her.

"Nora's always right." Lizzie clutched the sundress to her chest, looking vulnerable and hopeful more than certain.

"What's wrong?" The pleasure of the pretty dress had faded, and worry twisted Lizzie's face.

"Nothing."

"That's not true. I can see it," Elle said. "You can trust me. We can talk about anything and I won't say a word. I promise." Elle remembered how she'd longed for someone, anyone, to talk to about her troubles. But she didn't dare do it when she was a child, and she hadn't since…

"I'm worried about my mom."

"Why?" Elle patted the edge of the bed, for Lizzie to join her.

She sat down, and went still. For a long moment she didn't say anything.

"It's okay, Lizzie." Elle let the truth shine in her eyes. "I had secrets, too. I still do. I know how to keep secrets."

She whispered, low and gruff. "She's not at an intervention for her brother."

"Where is she?"

"I don't know, but she's not there."

"How do you know?" Elle asked. "I mean, surely she'd tell Nora so she could get in touch if she needed to do it." What if something happened to Lizzie and she needed medical treatment or something?

Lizzie lifted her chin. It quivered. "My mom doesn't have a brother."

"Oh." So she hadn't told Nora the truth. Whatever her reason, it must be awful.

"It's just her and me, and she's in trouble. That's why she brought me to Nora."

"So the guys would watch over you."

Lizzie nodded.

"Do you know what kind of trouble she's in?" Elle couldn't imagine.

"No." Lizzie looked down at the carpeted floor. "Something happened, though. Something bad, like when we were in trouble before." She risked looking at Elle. "That's why we came here and her name is Sue Ellen and mine's Lizzie. It used to be Megan."

What in the world? Elle wasn't sure what to say so she played it safe and simply nodded.

"I don't know what happened then, either, but these bad people came after my mom. They blew up her car at our house and we had to run away. We came here because the man helping us said nobody could find us here, only…"

"You think the bad people did find your mom and that's why she left."

Anguish filled Lizzie's face. "Yes." She sucked in a staggered breath. "My mom wouldn't leave me unless she was more scared not to leave me. She wouldn't."

The fine hairs on Elle's neck stood on end. Inside she shook. It wasn't possible. It wasn't…unless it was possible. She had to know. "If that's the case, I'd say your mom is very brave, and you have to be brave, too."

"She said so, too, but it's hard."

"Yes, it is." Elle remembered the fears she'd felt, the conflicts at keeping secrets. How she'd envied the other kids just getting to be kids. That was a luxury she'd never known, and it appeared Lizzie hadn't either.

"Before, my mom worked for the government."

A sinking feeling struck Elle like a blow. Another connection. "Doing what?"

"Studying papers. Lots and lots of papers." Lizzie turned to face Elle and whispered. "She used to go on trips and talk to people about stuff they were building."

Oh, no. No. Elle fought to keep her voice steady, calm. "That sounds exciting." This couldn't be. Couldn't be! "Um, where did she go?" Elle asked, praying hard she wouldn't get the answer she expected.

"The desert. She went there a lot. I think the desert is cool, don't you? It looks like there's nothing in it, but it's full of all kinds of stuff."

"Definitely."

"Utah and California, too. She liked California best because it had ocean and mountains and desert."

Contract negotiator. Project manager. During Elle's time with her dad's company, she'd worked with plenty of both. "You said your name was Megan." The sound of her name sent chills through Elle. "Um, what was Sue Ellen's name?"

Lizzie dropped her voice even lower. "Jaycee Cole—but I can't tell anybody that. We could get into a lot of trouble. The man told us to forget those names and those lives. But you can't just forget your whole life."

Elle's heart nearly stopped. Her mouth went dry and she had to work hard to keep her voice from shrieking and her shock hidden. "No, you can't." *Witness protection.* This was Jaycee's daughter, and they'd been relocated with new identities. Shaky at wrapping her mind around that, Elle slumped, stiffened against the waves of disbelief gushing through her to keep them from turning to panic. "It's just about impossible."

"We try hard, and we were doing pretty good until mom left."

Lizzie, wide-eyed, blinked hard. "I—I'm not doing so good without her."

Elle clasped Lizzie's trembling hand. "I know it's rough, sweetie, and I really do understand." Boy, did she. So much so that it broke her heart to think of Lizzie and Jaycee going through this… whatever they were going through right now. "My life hasn't been that much different." Elle wanted to weep, to rage, to crawl into a hole and stay there. Jaycee and Lizzie's challenges weren't their fault, but they certainly suffered the fallout…

She crushed the sundress to her chest. "I don't know what to do."

Elle frowned, thought of Lizzie and not herself. There'd be time for that later. "Why are you so worried about your mom right now?"

"She was scared like before. Sick with it. She never does that, Elle. Well, she did then and she was like that just before she left me with Nora, but my mom don't scare easy. This is bad like that was bad."

"What exactly is this? Do you know?"

Lizzie gave Elle a negative nod. "She wouldn't tell me."

Can't tell what you don't know. Jaycee had been protecting Lizzie, though it likely didn't feel that way to the child. "So she left you with Nora where you'd be safe—"

"I think she did it so the bad people would follow her and leave me alone and so I'd be safe. But she's not safe, Elle." Tears spilled down Lizzie's cheeks. "I tried to tell Nora, but she was so busy with the wedding and not feeling good that she didn't really listen." Lizzie gulped and her tiny shoulders heaved.

Wanting to comfort her, Elle curled her arms around Lizzie and pulled her close. Her whole body shook like trees in a stiff wind.

She mumbled against Elle's shoulder. "Nobody believes kids anyway." A hint of hopelessness tinged her tone.

Elle hated it, and disputed it. "Some don't believe kids, but Nick will."

"No, he won't. Neither will Sam. I thought about telling him, but he won't listen, either." She frowned. "He thinks I'm a tyrant."

"He was teasing, and they will believe you." Elle pulled back, forced conviction into her voice that Lizzie couldn't miss. "Lizzie, these men know what it's like to be in trouble. They know what it's like to have to keep secrets. And if you think they will blow off what you tell them because you're young, you're wrong."

"How do you know?"

"I—I…" How did she know? Unable to answer specifically, she added, "I just do. You learn to read people, and I read them pretty well. They will hear you, and listen to you, and they will believe you. I promise."

"Promise?"

Elle nodded. "Your mom needs help. You've got to tell Nick so he and the guys can help her."

"I want to, but I can't. The man said we could never tell anyone."

"You can tell Nick. He and Sam and Joe and Tim are… Well, people can tell them things they can never tell anyone else."

"How come?"

"Because they know things nobody else knows."

"How come?"

"I don't know. But they do."

"So it's okay and people tell them secrets? Really?"

"They do all the time." Elle couldn't get anymore specific. She didn't know anything more specific. She clasped Lizzie's shoulders. "Listen to me. They can help your mom and, most importantly, they will help her. She needs them, Lizzie."

Lizzie looked skeptical but hopeful. "You pinky swear I can trust them?"

"Yes, Lizzie," Elle said softly, lifting her finger and hooking it with Lizzie's. "You can trust them all."

"Do you trust them?"

"I do." Elle nodded, adding weight to her words. "I wouldn't pinky swear otherwise."

That satisfied her, but another doubt reared its ugly head. "But why would they help me?"

Elle smiled. "Because that's what they do."

"That's what my mom said." The affirmation comforted Lizzie. "But I don't have any money to pay them."

"You don't need any." Elle stroked Lizzie's face. "I have gobs of money and we'll use every penny of it if we have to, but I know Nick Sloan, and I'm telling you, Lizzie, he doesn't care about the money. He cares about you. And the rest of the guys are like that, too, or Nick wouldn't be partners with them."

"He cares about you, too."

Did he? Uncertain, Elle held her silence.

"He does. He watches you when you're not looking. You can tell when you see that."

Elle let that news settle into her hungry heart. "He cares about me—a little bit." A lot less than she cared about him, but that's the way it always had been. "But for you, any of Nora's boys would move mountains."

"You think so?"

"I know so." Elle lifted her arms. "Doesn't Nora nurture everybody?"

"Uh-huh, but I ain't Nora."

"Course not, but these men are special to her."

"Everybody's special to Nora."

"Well, that might be, but why do think only they are *her* boys?"

Lizzie dried her eyes and drew in a sharp breath. "Because they're like her."

"That's right." Elle nodded. "You tell Nick. The sooner he knows, the sooner they can help your mom."

"I will—in just a second." Lizzie stood up and sniffled. "I need to do something first."

She ran toward their shared bath, stopped, then came back and snagged the yellow sundress. "I need this." She ran through the bath and on into her room.

Elle waited but curiosity got the best of her. *What was she doing?* Shuddering inside, reeling from their talk, Elle entered the bathroom and peeked into Lizzie's room.

The child was kneeling on the floor beside her bed, her eyes closed, her hands folded. Her lips moved but she kept her silence.

Praying for her mom. For courage.

Elle backed up a step and pressed her hand flat over her abdomen. Her stomach had so many knots in it she feared she'd be sick. Jaycee and Megan Cole were Sue Ellen and Lizzie Montgomery. Elle heard it, believed it, but still could barely grasp it.

Nick would come through for them. The team would come through for them. Elle didn't doubt that. But when they discovered the truth, they surely would kick Elle to the curb like yesterday's trash.

Because whatever this fix was Sue Ellen was in, it was Elle's fault.

How in the world could Elle explain that?

Secrets. She couldn't explain it. She'd never be able to explain it. Tears burned the backs of her eyes, stung her nose.

If Nick hadn't hated her before for deceiving him about being an engineer with her dad's firm, as soon as Lizzie told him her story and he put all the pieces together, he would hate Elle with unbridled passion the rest of his days.

The most horrible part was, she deserved it. And even his worst would be a fraction of the hatred she felt for herself about it.

As she left the bath, she spotted the black dot on the wall and remembered the cameras. The surveillance camera downstairs, where last night they'd all watched Lizzie sleeping.

Part of Elle, the cowardly part, hoped the guys had observed the conversation between Lizzie and she. Elle wasn't at all convinced Lizzie would open up to Nick or Sam—Nick clearly intimidated her with his stern disposition—and Elle couldn't tell them. She'd promised. Yet they needed to know. Sue Ellen's life could well depend on them knowing and helping her.

Oh, don't make me break a promise to her. Please, don't make me have to do that.

Elle dressed quickly in the bath and then called for Lizzie. "You ready to go downstairs?" The sooner, the better. Less time to change her mind.

"Yep." She joined Elle, wearing the yellow sundress and white sandals. "I figured it couldn't hurt to look like a scared kid—mainly cuz that's what I am."

"Ah, I see. You're making it hard for them to say no, they won't help you." Elle was on to her.

"That, too."

"Lizzie, you don't have to worry. They won't say no. It won't even occur to them that they could say no. They aren't those kind of men."

"She's right, bro." Joe looked pleased with himself. "We're not those kind of men."

They weren't. Nick poured himself another cup of coffee. "No one says a word. We saw and heard nothing."

"The kid nailed you, Nick." Joe sat down on the sofa.

"That ain't no lie." Sam nodded in agreement.

"I said, not a word." Nick's temper flared. Bristling at hearing her description of him, he tried to forget it, but her words grated at him. *Broken.* Broken?

"Don't get fired up, bro. Elle trusts us all because of you," Joe reminded Nick. "That's a good thing."

"She reads people well." Nick recalled her sense of the three men following her in London. "You heard her instinctively react on the street in London."

Joe nodded. "Most ignore their instincts in those situations."

"And pay huge for it." Nick thought back. Elle's instincts had been sharp four years ago during his security tests, too. She hadn't surprised him then, but she had impressed him, and that was nearly as difficult to do.

"We can't say anything about any of what we heard to either of them?" Sam frowned his obvious disagreement with that decision and tugged his ball cap down until its brim shaded his eyes. "You're gonna put the kid through relaying all that again?"

Nick lifted his chin. "Yes, I am."

"Why?" Joe lifted a hand, let it drop onto the arm of the sofa. "Seems unnecessarily cruel."

Nick kept his temper in check. He wasn't just being bitter because she'd nailed him. He wanted to be, but he couldn't do it. "Nothing cruel about it."

"*Seems* cruel, then," Joe persisted. "And unnecessary."

Nick frowned and held it so Joe wouldn't miss it. "If Lizzie tells us herself, it establishes trust between her and us—in addition to her trust with Elle. She needs people to trust. It also gives us the opportunity to learn more from her. You know all this. It's basic interrogation technique. And both of you know we need more than we have to do her mom any good."

Sam wanted to argue; that was clear from the set of his jaw. "I see what you're saying, buddy," he said, pointing at Nick, "but you make her cry again, and we're gonna have a problem."

"My objective isn't to make Lizzie cry," Nick said from between his teeth. "I want to ease her worries and to help her mother."

"Wait. I see it now. Sam, we need to lighten up." Joe stood up and got between Nick and Sam. "He recognized it right away. I just got it. When Elle and Lizzie were talking, Nick saw what I saw."

"Yeah, I saw it, too. A crying kid and an uncomfortable adult trying to comfort her."

"Not just uncomfortable. There was more," Joe said, letting his gaze glide to Nick. "Elle knows a lot of something that she's not eager to talk about. If Lizzie has to cry a few tears to get Elle to talk to us, then so be it. Tears aren't all bad, you know? They can be therapeutic." Joe clapped Sam's shoulder. "If she cries again, you can get her an ice-cream cone or something. How's that? Maybe she won't be ticked off at you any more for calling her a tyrant."

"The kid's worried sick about her mom and you're thinking an ice-cream cone's gonna make anything better?"

"Works for you, most of the time," Joe said. "Well, ice-cream and raging like a maniac for a while." Joe lifted a hand. "Let her yell at you. Kills two birds with one stone."

"Shut up, Joe."

"No sense of humor at all." Joe rubbed his chin. "Maybe you are dead from the neck up."

Sam shot Joe a killer glare. "Dead enough to save your sorry backside more than once—and to wonder why I bothered."

"You don't mean that, bro."

"No, but right this second, I wish I did."

Sam was gifted and insightful with a nose beyond compare. Nick knew it immediately, and Joe had learned it within hours. Still, the whole team hammered Sam about being dead from the neck up. Like a stump. Course, they hammered each other about that, too. It was a running thing between them. Now if an outsider said it, there'd be consequences, but needling each other helped alleviate stress and, on missions, they always had a lot of stress. The team had all kinds of decompression valves. A perk of the business they were in.

Elle and Lizzie came down the stairs and into the gathering room.

Sunlight streaked in from the windows and lit Elle's smiling face. Nick's breath caught then swooshed out of his lungs. Irritated by that, he frowned. How did she do that to him? Why couldn't she stop doing that? *Broken. Unloved.* Humiliated.

"Are we interrupting something?" Elle asked, clearly picking up on the tension in the gathering room.

"Nothing at all. Sam's just threatening to take me outside again. He gets grumpy if he's not fed early in the morning. His sugar runs low." Joe smiled. "Don't you two look gorgeous this morning?"

"Thank you for the clothes," Lizzie said.

"Yes, thank you." Elle smiled. "You did well on guessing our sizes."

"Joe's the ace at that." Nick nodded, giving credit where credit was due.

"Well, thanks. I'll reimburse you as soon as… well, as soon as I can." She licked her lips and studied Nick. The look in her eyes went suddenly serious. "Lizzie needs to talk with you about something important. All of you, if that's okay."

"Course." Sam walked up to Lizzie and looked down at her. "What's up, half-pint?"

Lizzie opened her mouth to talk but no sound came out. She tried again but remained mute.

"Lizzie?" Sam's tone softened. "You okay?"

She burst into tears.

Sam shot Nick a look that would melt steel, then scooped up Lizzie and patted her back. "Hey, I don't know what all these tears are about but I wish you'd stop them."

"Why? Cuz you don't like to see girls cry?"

"That ain't no lie. I don't like seeing anyone cry," Sam said. "But I hate seeing you cry."

She pulled back and looked at him, eye to eye. "Why do you care if I cry?"

"Because I know how brave you are, and anything that upsets you that much, upsets me."

Lizzie's tight jaw went slack. She worried her lips, then admitted the truth. "I'm not brave. I'm scared, Sam."

"Well, here's the thing. Even the bravest of the brave gets scared sometimes."

"Not you."

"It ain't often, but it does happen. Now Nick, he's scared most of the time. That's why he's so grouchy."

Nick cleared his throat, warning Sam off.

Sam smiled.

Lizzie burrowed deeper into Sam's shoulder. "He don't look scared. He looks really mad."

"Naw, he's just thinking hard. He always looks like that when he's thinking hard."

"What's he thinking about all the time?"

"All kinds of stuff," Sam confided. "Nick's real smart."

She nodded. "You're not scared of him?"

"Nick?" Sam laughed. "Not a bit."

That relieved her. "Guess I won't be either, then."

"Course not." Sam nodded toward the recliner. "What do you say about us going and sitting down in that big chair over there and you can tell me what's got you scared?"

"I'm not supposed to tell."

"Secret, eh?"

She nodded.

"Well, I guess you need to know then that we're the official secret keepers."

"What?"

"It's true, Lizzie." He dropped his voice. "We keep all kinds of secrets for all kinds of people."

"Even ones people aren't supposed to tell anybody else ever?"

"Even those."

She looked at him openly skeptical.

"Think about it, Lizzie. We fix things. How are we going to fix them so people ain't scared if we don't know what's broken or why they're scared? That don't make sense—and you're a sensible girl. Smart, too, so you know I'm telling you true, of course."

"I do. But I could get in a lot of trouble, Sam. Big trouble."

"Well, now. That's quite the puzzle." He dragged a hand through his beard. "Will there be more trouble if we just talk? Or more trouble if we don't?"

"I don't know."

"Hmm…Well, let's talk 'til you do know, and then we'll decide."

She thought a second. "That seems sensible."

"It's settled then. And no more tears, okay? They scare me." He bent his head close to her ear and whispered. "That's one of my secrets you can't tell."

Lizzie shot him a doubtful look. "Nah-uh, you ain't scared of nothing."

"Uh-uh. Tears make me shake in my boots." He held up a hand. "Promise."

She leaned over and looked down. "You're wearing flip-flops."

"Right now, and they definitely ain't made for shaking."

"Sandals either." She lifted her foot for him to see.

"There it is, then." He moved to the chair. "Okay, half-pint. Let's talk…"

Elle watched Sam with Lizzie, then told Nick. "He's very good with her."

"He's half kid," Nick muttered. "That helps."

"So while they talk, what do we do?" She asked, surmising Nick was still stinging from what he'd overheard of the conversation with Lizzie upstairs. The way the guys were acting, they'd definitely heard every single word. More than anything else, Sam's tenderness with Lizzie proved it.

"We wait," Nick told her.

Joe passed her a cup of coffee. "No cream or sugar, right?"

"Right." He remembered. "Thanks." She took the cup, looked back at Nick. "What are we waiting for?"

"Sam to call us over for advice."

Elle nodded. So they'd let him handle whatever, then seek their advice, and then they'd all be invited in on the conversation. Wise, and not so overwhelming for Lizzie, who did seem to have a special fondness for Sam. At first, Elle thought it was because he was big and that made her feel safe. Now, she wondered if Lizzie didn't sense the protective streak in him that ran as wide as his back was broad. Either way, she appreciated the little respite. She had a decision to make and it was a hard one.

She could let them find out the truth on their own-- the probable costs of that would be her booted out on her foolish elbow to face only heaven knew what alone—or tell them what she'd just discovered and suspected and spare them the trouble of unearthing it themselves. That could soften them a little toward her so they'd keep her around and help her and Lizzie.

If Elle could be as brave as Lizzie and work up the courage to reveal it all.

Elle had become accustomed to seeing cool reserve in Nick's deep gray eyes. That was hard, considering her feelings for him. She'd been crazy about the man from first sight. But to have him look at her with condemnation?

She wasn't sure she could stand it. Even his anger at her forced deception about being her father's assistant had been hard. He'd definitely taken it personally. She could only imagine his reaction at what she had to tell him now.

Her insides shaking, she emptied her cup and then poured herself another coffee. Steam lifting from the cup, she glanced over to the big chair. Sam and Lizzie were still talking. He nodded, frowned, and sighed. Muttered, sputtered, and stroked at his beard. Twice, she'd heard him say, "Well now, ain't that something?"

Elle sat down at the bar, sipped from her cup. He wasn't rushing Lizzie. It would be a while.

Nick came up behind her. "Hungry?"

She couldn't swallow a bite. Not with all this hanging over her head. She didn't have a lot of options. She didn't dare return to London. Didn't dare go to her parents. Didn't dare go home. And she wasn't sharp enough on events to face her kidnappers alone. One group, she had no idea who they even were and the other group, she'd spent four years trying to forget. "Not even a little bit."

Nick sat down beside her. "You surprised me last night—about the engineering."

"I'm sorry. I couldn't tell you."

"Yeah, you said your dad insisted."

"Confidentiality agreement, actually." She nodded. "I didn't like not being totally honest with you, for what it's worth. I tried to convince him, but…" Her voice faltered. "Just so you know."

"I understand." He said it, but whether or not he actually believed it, she couldn't tell. "It's just that people rarely surprise me," he admitted. "You did."

He sounded more intrigued than angry. That was encouraging. "I'm sorry it was in a bad way."

"Not bad, really. You might cross your father, but you could hardly go against your boss and lose your clearances, could you?"

"No, I couldn't. Not either of them really. Not on that. But I could have fought harder. It's just that . . ." She shouldn't say it. She really shouldn't say it.

"What?"

She looked into Nick's eyes. "My parents have always kept a lot things private. They raised me to live that way, too. It was my normal."

"I gathered that."

Surprised, she cocked her head. "From what?"

"They refused to give you their name, Elle."

Resentment feathered on the edges of panic. "You know that?"

"I know Bostwick is your maternal grandmother's maiden name, and it's what's on your birth certificate. My only question is why would your parents do that?"

A question she'd spent more than half her life contemplating and most of it resenting. "Do you want the truth or their sanitized version?"

"I always prefer the truth."

So did she. "When it comes to me, they're paranoid, Nick."

"They have reason to be."

"I know." She did. Half the nuts the world would love to get their hands on what her father and she produced. The other half wanted his money and would be more than happy to use or abuse her to get it. "But having your own parents deny you as their child...that's not fun."

"It hurt you a lot and for a long time."

She held her silence.

"I imagine it still does hurt you."

Something in his voice snagged her ear. Something that struck her like empathy, not sympathy. "Were you denied by your parents, too?"

He hesitated, and she let him off the hook. "You don't have to answer, if you'd rather not. I certainly understand. It's hard to think about and nearly impossible to talk about with anyone, even yourself."

"My mother left my dad and me. I was six." He didn't quite meet her eyes, focused on her chin instead. "I went to school one day and, when I came home, she was gone. We never heard from her again."

"I'm so sorry." Abandonment. The boy he'd been must have been mortified. Terrified. Was that what hurt him? Broke him?

"My father remarried in short order." A little tremor strained his voice. "I couldn't find any evidence of him bothering to divorce my mother first. But a couple weeks after my mother left, he and Jacinda married."

Weeks? Clearly, there'd been no divorce. "Was she good to you?"

"Good? That's a relative term, isn't it?" He hiked a shoulder. "She didn't lock me in a closet, but she hated me on sight and she never let me forget it."

"Why? You were just a little boy." And how had she reminded him?

"Because I existed." The look in his eyes turned deadpan flat. "She was beautiful. I never trusted her, but I respected her—at least, I did until I overheard her convincing my father that I had to go."

"Go where?"

"She didn't care where, so long as it was away from them."

Indignation swelled in Elle. "I hope he set her straight."

Nick paused a long beat, then answered. "Not exactly."

His own father didn't stand up for him? "What happened?"

"He beat me to within an inch of my life for making Jacinda worry, said if she left him too, it'd all be my fault and he wasn't having it. Then he shipped me off to boarding school."

"You've got to be kidding me."

"Not kidding," he said, the distant look in his eyes warning her he was reliving the incident in his mind. "I didn't see either of them again until after I graduated from college."

"No." Her chest went tight, ached for the abandoned boy he'd been, the betrayed son who could trust neither his mother nor his father. "Your mother, either?"

"Never heard from her again." He shrugged. "I went to see my dad right before I enlisted in the military. Jacinda wouldn't let me in the house. She said to come back the next morning. So I got a motel room and went back to their house the next morning."

It hadn't gone well. That much was evident. "Was your dad there?"

"No. Neither was Jacinda." Nick stiffened. "In the middle of the night, they'd packed up lock, stock, and barrel and had taken off for parts unknown."

"They just left? Without you seeing them? Without your dad knowing you were there?"

"They left. He knew I'd been there. The neighbor next door heard them arguing about me in the driveway. He didn't want to go away and Jacinda didn't want him to see me again. She won." The look in Nick's eyes turned bitter. "That's the thing, Elle. In my life, people never stay. They make promises and vows , but then they leave. They always leave."

What he said broke her heart. But it also infuriated her. "Nick, did Jacinda tell you it was your fault they were leaving?"

"My father did. In a note he taped to the back door. He was pretty ticked off at having to give up his house and job."

"What was his job?"

Nick shrugged. "I'm not sure. He was gone all the time. That much I know."

"Haven't you ever looked to find out?"

"Why? They didn't want me in their lives and I sure don't want them in mine."

"I'd want to know."

"Why?"

"I just would." Elle tilted her head. "A part of me would always wonder if it was my fault. The more I could find out, the more I'd know whether or not it was actually my fault. Either way, I'd want to know."

"That's because you care."

Elle touched his forearm. "I think you care, too, Nick. I think you hate caring, but I think you still do care."

He opened his mouth to respond but closed it again without uttering a sound.

"So their leaving was your fault, too."

"According to my father."

"Unbelievable." The fury in Elle burned deeper. "And Jacinda said—what?"

"Nothing. I never saw her again on that last trip."

Relief at that flooded Elle. The woman had done more than enough damage. "There was another trip?"

"Almost." His voice came out sharp, firm. "I called once before, during my junior year of college. I didn't want to be alone on Christmas." He looked away. "Always before, someone was around at boarding school. But that year, everyone had plans so it'd be just me. I called my dad to see if I could come for a visit."

Tension coiled tight in Elle. "You'd never asked before."

"No, never." He stared at the coffeepot. "At first, I was angry at being sent away and I wanted my dad to miss me. I had all these elaborate plans for when he called and said I should come home for a visit. I wouldn't be able to make it. I wanted him to feel as alone as I felt. He couldn't of course. He had Jacinda. But I was a hurt kid and didn't think she could replace his son then."

"Only he never called."

"No, he didn't. Not once."

Elle felt the full weight of Nick's isolation. It was different than her own, but relatable. Which childhood had been worse? She had no idea. Shunned was shunned, regardless of the reason. "So when you called about the Christmas visit, what did your dad say?"

"He wasn't there. Jacinda told me no, and not to ask again. She never wanted to see my face again. I was the reason my mother had left, and if I came back, Jacinda would leave my father, too."

"And, of course, her leaving would be your fault."

"Yes."

"She told you that you weren't loveable."

"She didn't use those words, but--"

"She didn't have to use them. She made herself clear." Elle tamped down her anger, though she'd like five minutes in a dark alley with Jacinda. What kind of monster did that to a child? "It's not true."

He sighed.

Didn't the man he'd become realize that? "It's really not true, Nick." Elle covered his hand, squeezed it gently. "You can refuse to look at me all day, but it doesn't change the facts. Jacinda lied. You're loveable. And, for the record, I didn't abandon you."

"I just left first," he said. "But it's not the same thing. You were a kid."

"No, I wasn't a kid. I'm not sure I've ever been a kid. That's a luxury we all don't get to enjoy. You didn't and neither did I. The reasons are different, but the results are the same." She paused and dug deep for courage. "And, for the record, I'm not a kid now."

Something she couldn't identify flashed through his eyes, but when he spoke, a sharp edge honed his tone. "Elle, don't." He squeezed his eyes closed a second, then reopened them. "Don't do this, okay? I know you think you have feelings for me, but you don't. Not really." He set his cup down on the breakfast bar, sighed, then looked back at her. "I intrigue you. Probably because guys fall all over themselves around you and I don't. "

"That's not true."

"It is. I saw it myself in LA." She started to protest but he held up a staying hand. "It's just intrigue, not genuine feelings. You and me… We're different. Really different. We don't mix." Before she could say anything, he went on, dropping his voice, making it more gentle. "You're like sunshine, you know?"

"Yes, I am. I choose to be even when I don't feel like it. And you're like rain." She smiled. "Together we cover it all and kind of balance each other out. Isn't that the way it usually works for couples? Ying and yang and opposites attract and all that?"

"Stop it." The shields lifted in his eyes. "There is no couple. There is no we."

"Of course, there's a we." She didn't laugh. She wanted to but couldn't. He so didn't see her for who she was, or have a clue what was in her heart. But the injured boy, the broken man inside him, wouldn't, would he? "You might not like it. You might not want it. But there is a we, Nick, and I won't let you deny it. You don't get to dictate my feelings because you're afraid I'll leave you, too. That's what this is about."

"I knew it. I knew I'd regret telling you." He shook his head. "I don't know why I did it."

"Maybe you needed to talk about it." Oh, she hoped the reason was more than that, but she didn't risk believing it.

"I've never needed to talk about it. Who wants to even think about it?"

He had a point. "I know. Same here on my parents." So he'd never spoken of his past with anyone until now. Interesting. Neither had she. "I'm glad you did. I'm glad I told you, too."

He stilled. "You haven't told anyone else?"

"Never." She thumbed the rim of her coffee cup. "But it's been good. It helps me understand you better and me better. I like that."

"Don't even try to understand me," he told her. "Nora was right. I'm broken. I've been broken my whole life."

"You don't have to stay broken."

"I do." He let the shields in eyes fall for a moment. "It's all I know. It's all I've got."

"No, it isn't. Maybe it was at one time, but not now." She lifted a hand. "Now you have partners and friends, the people here and in the village. You have Nora and…and, for what it's worth, you have me."

His gaze snapped back to hers. "No."

"Afraid so." She gave him a trembling smile. "You've always had me, Nick."

"Don't be absurd."

"Why is that absurd? Are you insulting me again? Trying to tell me you know my mind better than I do?"

"No. It's absurd because you don't even know me."

"You'd be amazed how well I know you, and how much we have in common."

"Don't do this, Elle. You've got everything. Me… I've got a cobbled together life that works better for me than my life ever has worked for me. It's not much to someone like you, but it's everything to me."

She pushed at her cup. "Why are you so sure me caring about you will destroy what you've got? I just might make your life better, you know? Given a chance, I'm sure I could."

He stared at her, his eyes full of hunger and longing and fear. "You don't want me. No one ever has. It's the idea of me, some fantasy you've spun like one of your songs that you want, and it doesn't exist."

"That's not only unfair, it's untrue."

"It has to be true."

"Why?"

He stared at her, silent and tense.

"I asked why it has to be true, Nick. It's a fair question."

"How could it possibly be anything else? Nothing else is rational."

The man had no idea of his appeal. Not the first clue. "It can be and is true. I hate to break it to you but rational or not, my thoughts and opinions are mine. You don't get to dictate or legislate them." Since when were feelings rational?

"I'm not trying to dictate or legislate anything. I'd never do that. I just…" He took the heat out of his voice. "I know how it would end, Elle."

"You *think* you know and you're afraid."

"Wouldn't you be?"

"Yes, of course. But, honestly, more than anything, I'm amused. Not only do you not see the man I see in you, you don't see the woman I am, standing before you. You think I'm not scared?"

"Why would you be scared?"

She laughed, that tinkling chime that grated on his last frayed nerve. "Why not?"

"I told you, I'm the one broken."

"So am I," Elle said. "That's what's amusing. We're all broken, Nick. No one escapes childhood unscathed." She covered his hand with hers on the edge of the bar. "It's not that we don't break. It's that we live and heal in spite of those breaks. The breaks don't define us—everybody's got them—it's what we do in spite of them that defines us."

He sat back against his seat and stared at her. "That's—"

"Nick. Joe," Sam called out. "Me and Lizzie need a little help over here. Can you guys come and tell us what you think?"

"And there it is. " Nick slid off the stool. "The summons."

"Does that include me?" Elle asked Sam.

He looked to Lizzie, who nodded. "Yes."

"You sure about me, Lizzie?" Nick asked.

Again, she nodded. "I ain't scared of you anymore, and Sam says you're real smart." Lizzie motioned with a flailing arm. "Come on, Nick."

He didn't smile, Elle noticed, but for the first time in a long time, he looked as if he wanted to smile.

That small gesture of her deliberately including him gave Elle hope. Nick needed to belong. He needed to know he mattered. She could show him he he mattered to her because he did. And she would show him… if when she told him what she had to tell him, he didn't ban her from his life for good.

Unfortunately, that could go either way.

CHAPTER EIGHT

Sunday, June 7th, 9:30 a.m.
The Lodge

STILL RATTLED FROM HIS TALK AT THE BAR WITH ELLE, NICK joined the group. They discussed Lizzie's issue and her fear for her mother. Sam, whose stomach growled, sped up the process by briefing Nick, Joe, and Elle while Lizzie sat woodenly, watching them, gauging their reactions. The poor kid looked as tense as a cracker about to snap.

Nick hated that, but he still stood by his decision to proceed so that she came to trust them on her own. Kids need to know for themselves who they can and can't trust.

No one held more proof of that than he and maybe Elle. He knew there were issues, especially between her and her mother, but he hadn't known how deeply they'd impacted Elle. Her resentment of her mother oozed from Elle's pores. Her resentment of Jacinda had run just as deep.

He hated loving that more than her laughter.

But she had a point about his father. Maybe he'd do a little digging and see what turned up.

During the discussion, Elle seemed altogether too nervous. She knew what they were doing, and unless he was one-eighty out—and he rarely was one-eighty out on anything—she also knew they had overheard the original conversation upstairs between her and Lizzie. She should have deduced by now they were going to help the child and her mother—her instincts had been on target about that—so why was Elle beyond on edge? Her hands weren't steady and, from her shoulders' rapid rise and fall, her breathing was fast, and her eye movements darted. None were good signs. She'd seemed more at ease when they'd been airing their family's forbidden dirty laundry at the bar. More confident and comfortable. That was the worst sign.

Whatever she was holding back was worse than the family secrets. She seemed as afraid as Lizzie, and Nick didn't like seeing her like that anymore than he liked seeing Lizzie upset. What he didn't understand was why Elle was upset? What could she be hiding that was so bad she feared it?

Yes, she'd been through a lot in a short period of time, but she'd been fine. In true Elle fashion, she'd rolled with the punches and accepted what was in front of her. At least she had until the conversation about Lizzie's mom had started between her and Lizzie. On the monitor, he'd seen Elle react, stiffen and fight to hide shock. Now, in the group discussion, she looked a blink from tears, and that surprised him as much as her attempts to convince him he was loveable. *Absurd woman.*

"Okay, half-pint." Sam set her down on the floor. "I think we've got all we need to get started on this mission. Why don't you go downstairs and practice your NASCAR driving—you need more time behind the wheel, and that's a fact. We'll get the help party up and running."

"I can help you."

"Great," Sam said. "I'll call you when we're ready. We have some basic stuff to do first."

She stared at Sam. "In other words, you guys want to talk it all over now."

"Yeah," Sam said without apology. "So we can develop the best strategy. That's normal procedure for secret keepers. It's sensible."

She watched him a long second, decided he was talking straight with her, then said, "Okay." She headed to the stairs and went down.

The sounds of screeching tires on the NASCAR video game floated up the stairs. Elle shuddered. Reckoning time had arrived. She stepped into the fray. "Um, before you get too deeply into anything, there's something I need to share with you—some history on Lizzie's mom that might be helpful. It could be pertinent to everything going on, considering recent events."

All eyes turned to her. She avoided Nick's and took a gulp of water from the glass on the table beside her.

"You know them?" Nick asked, a quiver in his voice. "Lizzie and her mother?"

She forced herself to meet his gaze. "It's complicated."

Staring at her, he sat down on the sofa then folded his arms. "Complicated? There's nothing complicated about it. You either know them or you don't, Elle."

"It *is* complicated," she insisted, taking in a ragged breath. Joe looked most open. Sam had tugged his cap brim down over his eyes, and Nick looked as if the wrong word would have his jaw splintering. "First, I want to say that I didn't not tell you," she said, lifting a hand. "I just realized what I know, and this is the first opportunity I've had to share it."

"When did you just realize whatever it is you know?" Nick pushed.

"When talking to Lizzie upstairs. You heard us."

Nick didn't respond to that either way. "Okay. So share."

Testy and, for some reason, as nervous as she. "I already told you I was an engineer at AAN and I had a knack for developing systems." She paused, and when Nick nodded, she went on. "Lizzie's mother was a government negotiator on one of AAN's contracts. An outside group tried to force her into giving it details on the system being developed." Elle hesitated, choosing her words carefully. Classified information was still classified and the line she was walking was a thin one she didn't dare cross. "It played hard-ball," she said, avoiding details on the group, the system, and every-thing else possible. "Long story short, the group bombed the negotiator's car at her home and she ended up unemployed, and her and her daughter were forced into witness protection."

That created a stir and Sam shoved his cap back on his head. "You didn't think this was important enough to mention sooner?"

"When?" Elle lifted her hands. "While you were talking to Lizzie?"

"Calm down, Sam." Nick looked at Elle. "So you realized Lizzie is this negotiator's daughter and her mother is in trouble?"

"Lizzie says she is, and I believe her."

"You thing this group is after her again?"

"I think this group is relentless. If it found her, yes. Whether or not it did, I don't know, but her leaving Lizzie with Nora to get her under your protection says it's possible."

Nick didn't agree or disagree. "But Lizzie doesn't know you knew her before, correct?"

"I didn't know her before. I knew her mother. But I knew of Lizzie, of course." Elle tried to be as specific as possible. "I—I can't help but think with me sent here and her mom gone… " Was there a connection? Unsure, Elle admitted what she was sure of. "I don't know what to think."

"Who was the group that strong-armed her and bombed her car?"

Elle looked at Joe, who'd asked the question. "I can't tell you that."

"Can't or won't?"

"Can't." Oh, boy. Dangerous waters here. "It's, um, classified."

"But you do know?" Sam pushed anyway.

She nodded.

"Why do you know?" Sam stood up, clearly not trusting her and letting her know it.

She couldn't blame him. The name of that group was held close in tight circles.

"Sit down, Sam." Nick looked from him to Elle. "The group was NINA."

Wave upon wave of shock ripped through Elle's body. Her knees folded and she sank down onto the sofa cushion beside Nick. He knew about NINA. He'd been out of the military for a long while now, but... oh, no. *Were they NINA?*

No , no way. He and PSC would never be a part of NINA. They were part of the force opposing NINA. She tested that theory, and all the puzzle pieces fell into place. She met and held Nick's gaze and nodded.

"How did you come to know all this about Lizzie and her mother—not who they were but what happened to them?" He frowned. "Did Lizzie tell you that, too?"

Confirmation. They'd all listened in on the morning conversation. "No. She didn't have to tell me. I knew because I was there when it happened."

"There?"

"At AAN."

"I'm missing a step here," Sam said, growing short-tempered.

"Tell him, Elle," Nick said.

She forced herself to look at Sam. "I was there because it was my design, Sam. I developed it and I hold the patents on the system NINA was after." Elle swallowed a threatening sob. "Lizzie and her mom were nearly killed because of it. Because...of me."

Nick leaned forward on the sofa. "And you've carried that guilt with you every day since the attack at their home happened."

Joe nodded. "Which is why you left engineering and went into music."

She nodded.

"You should have told me right away, Elle." Nick stood, paced a short path before the sofa. "NINA is after you for that design. If it finds you, now it also finds Lizzie."

"I didn't know. It's not like I knew her on sight, I didn't. It wasn't until she was telling me her story about her mom that I put the pieces together." She turned on Nick. "Do you really think I would intentionally put that child's life in jeopardy?"

Joe leaned back. "Okay, so all this happens and you walk and get into music. Did you know where Lizzie and her mother were located?"

"No. And I couldn't look for them without alerting NINA."

"Makes sense." Joe pursed his lips. "So you changed your name, dropped Howell and went by Bostwick for additional distance?"

Nick, stone silent until then, spoke up. "She's never gone by Howell."

Joe looked to Nick to explain but he offered nothing more.

"My parents didn't give me their name," Elle admitted. Shame and humiliation, the old wondering what was wrong with her, why they were ashamed of her and the thousand other flaws in her that might have spurred them to make that decision, reared its ugly head. No parent kept even their name from their child, robbed her of her identity and place in her family, to protect her. "I've always been Elle Bostwick." Elle steeled herself, then admitted the rest. "Very few people know that I'm my parents' daughter. Maybe six, but no more. Even people at AAN think I'm a distant cousin."

"What?" Joe frowned.

"They thought they were protecting her," Nick said. "It was stupid and selfish but it is what it is. Let it go."

Joe sat back down and spoke not another word.

Elle could have kissed Nick. Admitting all this was hard enough, but admitting her own parents shunned her cut too deep for any defense.

"Something's up," Sam said. "No game noise down there."

Joe moved to the monitors. "Nothing going on down there."

"You see her?"

"No, I don't."

"She's too quiet. It ain't natural." Sam hauled himself to his feet. "I'm gonna go check on her."

Elle shifted to the edge of the sofa and rubbed at her face, more from nervousness than need. "Thank you, Nick."

"No problem." He cocked his head. "They're not judging you, you know."

"Aren't they? Aren't you?" She smiled but there was no warmth in it. "Surely you're wondering what about me is so awful that my own parents want to deny to the world I exist."

"Me? Remember who you're talking to, Elle." He cleared his throat. "It's not like it was for me for you. Your dad loves you so much he forfeited his place in your life to keep you safe. Not to get rid of you."

Tears welled in her eyes. "I would rather have taken the risks and belonged."

Sam thundered up the stairs. "Grab your weapons."

"What's going on?" Nick jumped to his feet.

"Lizzie's not downstairs playing."

"But she didn't come up here," Elle started. "Maybe she went to the bath—"

"No!" Fear, stark and raw, deepened every fine line in Sam's face. "The door to the outside is open. Lizzie's gone!"

At the door to the Lodge, Nick held up a hand, blocking Elle, but looked past her to Sam and Joe. "Locked and loaded?"

Both nodded, their weapons drawn.

Pulling out his own from its holster at the back of his waist, Nick looked at Elle. "Stay close to me and be as quiet as you can. Don't call out to her. Don't talk, and don't make any unnecessary noise."

Elle bobbed her head, signaling she understood, her eyes wide with fear.

Fear, he felt down deep in the pit of his stomach. "Any word, use A protocol. Let's move."

They went outside. In a series of silent hand signals, he motioned Sam to go left, toward the wood, then Joe to the right, around the house to the backside. He nodded toward the lake and bridge they'd crossed when coming in, and he and Elle moved in that direction.

On the far side of the helicopter pad, the grass gave way to natural ground, sandy and uneven. Elle slipped on a stump root.

Nick caught her elbow and kept her from falling. "You okay?" he silently mouthed.

She nodded that she was fine.

They moved on, winding down toward the water, the little rock-strewn creek. Water moved downstream at a lazy clip. Beyond a thicket of squat fat bushes, she snagged Nick's shirt and tugged. He looked back at her, and Elle pointed.

Lizzie sat alone on the bank of the creek among downed branches, digging her bare toes in the sandy dirt. "What's she staring at?" Nick whispered to Elle. He sent up a series of bird calls.

"I don't know," Elle whispered back, scanning the broader area but seeing no one. "The bird calls—A protocol?"

Nick nodded, but didn't look at her. He too scanned a grid. Slowly, methodically, meticulously. Nothing stirred, no unusual sounds echoed over the water to him. And no strange scents assaulted his nose.

They crept toward Lizzie in stealth-mode, moving gingerly tree to tree, bush to bush, hunkering low to obscure them as much as possible. In the thicket, he paused and again opened his senses. The only sound was of the summer breeze. The water on the rocks. Lizzie humming, staring at something he couldn't see. Nick stopped suddenly. "What's she looking at?"

"I don't know." Elle whispered. "It's in her hands, I think."

A bird call sounded to his left. Moments later, another came from his right. Sam and Joe were in position. He looked to Elle and motioned that they were moving in.

"Lizzie?" Nick said, drawing near. "Are you hurt?"

"No."

"What are you doing out here?" Elle asked. "You were supposed to be downstairs, not outside."

Lizzie cupped her hand into a fist. "I saw the lady through the door. She tapped on the glass and waved for me to come."

"The lady?" Worry streaked up Nick's back. "What lady?"

"The one from the wreck." Lizzie dusted the sand off her skirt. "The man was already here."

"Here?" Nick's worry meter shot off the charts. "At the creek?"

"Uh-huh."

"What man are you talking about?"

Lizzie sighed. "The one from the wreck."

"I didn't see a man at the wreck."

Elle frowned at Nick. "He was driving. You hit your head, remember. He was passed out and the woman came to the car then got behind the wheel of their car and took off."

"Where'd they go, Lizzie?" He scanned nonstop, but saw nothing.

"They had a boat down there—at the dock." She pointed toward the gazebo.

Why hadn't that shown up on the monitors in the house? Anything like that should have shown up. "Sam!"

He ran up, paused and looked at Lizzie. "You okay, half-pint?"

"I'm fine."

"Don't take off like this on me again."

"I didn't take off."

"I didn't know where you were. You scared me, Lizzie."

"Sorry."

"Sam, check the boat dock and the monitors there. Something's wrong with them."

"On it." He took off in a trot.

"What did the lady want, Lizzie?" Nick asked.

"She asked if we were all okay. I told her yeah, and the man was kind of mad. He didn't say anything. Then the lady gave me this and said she thinks it belongs to Elle." Lizzie held out her hand and in her upturned palm lay Elle's ring.

"Your amethyst, I take it?" Nick asked her.

Elle squealed her delight. "Yes!" She laughed that grating tinkling laugh. "Thank you, Lizzie."

"The lady gave it to me for you. I didn't do anything."

Nick's gaze collided with Joe's. *NINA*. "Let's go. We need to get you inside. Joe, scout and see what you can find."

He turned and disappeared into the woods, which is where Nick would have made egress had he had to choose.

Nick scooped up Lizzie. "Listen to me, both of you," he told Lizzie and Elle. "We need to get you inside where you're safe. Move quickly."

He took off toward the Lodge in a near run, Lizzie bouncing on his hip, Elle at his side. On the porch, he set Lizzie down. "Stay here."

He disappeared inside, checked the monitors, the windows and ran a perimeter check, then retrieved Lizzie and Elle and took them down to the basement. "You can't tell anyone what I'm about to show you. It's a secret keeper's secret, and I'm trusting you. Got it?" Lizzie nodded.

At the wall, he pushed a sequence of stones. The stones split open, revealing a door. "This is a bunker. You'll be safe here. No matter what, do not come out until I come back to get you."

"All right." Elle swallowed hard, touched his sleeve. "Be careful, Nick."

"I will." He motioned them inside. "You'll find what you need in there. Just remember, stay put until we know everything is okay."

They stepped into the bunker, and he pushed the stone sequence.

The door slid shut.

Nearly two hours later, the guys had checked every inch of the property, briefed Tim, Omega One, and Joe then joined Nick in the gathering room.

Hot and sweaty, Joe had stripped down to a t-shirt and jeans. His face was still flushed. He downed a glass of water and refilled it at the kitchen tap. "They took a boat down a quarter mile. Found it docked there. I figure they borrowed it from the owners. On shore, I found four-wheeler tracks and followed the trail to a public park. Four wheeler was left behind there. I took some samples from it, but if we pick up anything, I'll be shocked. It reeked. Doused in bleach.

Lots of fresh tire tracks in the park, so no way of telling which vehicle was theirs. Bottom line, they're long gone."

"How did they get past our security here?" Nick asked. "Did you see any signs of damage?"

"None," Joe said, unwrapping a fresh piece of gum. "Who are these people? NINA or CIA?"

"We're nearly positive the woman's Olivia so they could be either," Nick said. "We didn't even know there was a man—well, Lizzie and Elle did, but Elle thought he must be insignificant because we never mentioned him and we were all about the woman. He could be either."

Joe swallowed a few more gulps of water. "Don't beat yourself up about the security breach or the man, Nick. There's no time for it."

Valid point, and Nick had been beating himself up about both. "Where's Sam?"

"Pulling some diagnostics on the system to see what failed."

"If anything."

"Something failed, Joe. The woman knocked on the door downstairs, for pity's sake." Nick still couldn't believe it. The computer station in the gathering room stood empty.

"Sam working in the lab?"

"Yeah."

"We'd best get up there and see what he's found."

Nick followed Joe up the stairs to the third-level lab and spotted Sam at the computer. When he heard them entering, he turned to face them. "It's a loop," he said. "They spliced in a long loop on us. That's why we didn't pick them up."

Nick frowned. "That explains the monitors, but the alarm should have triggered. It didn't."

"They created a backdoor into the system and disarmed it. Left tracks, too."

That had to be deliberate. They wanted Nick to know they'd been there. As a warning? Or flaunting in his face he'd been outwitted? "Did you trace them?"

"Yeah, I did." Sam rocked back in his high-back seat. "Worthless. Takes me on a false trail."

"To where?"

"Across three continents then to a dead-end."

"What dead-end?" How could Sam be sure of that already?

"It's to Omega One."

One had been compromised? Nick's jaw went lax. "These hackers know what they're doing."

"Best I've seen outside of you." Sam tugged at his cap. "Has to be intentional, buddy. Olivia wanted us to know NINA created a breach. She had to be signaling Omega One that they'd breached his system, too."

"Sure sounds like it." Nick agreed, but that too raised more questions.

"I get the heads up part of this," Joe chimed in. "Liv would let us know about the breaches here and especially to One. But the incident with Elle makes less sense now." Joe slid a hip onto the edge of the computer desk. "Actually, none of this with her makes sense. Why would NINA kidnap her to get the ring and then give it back to her?"

Nick thought that over.

Sam thought out loud. "The CIA snagged Elle before NINA could get to her. So apparently it had the ring and apparently it wanted Elle to have it back." Sam stroked his beard. "NINA never got her or the ring."

"Doubtful it's that cut and dry," Nick said. "The CIA could have just returned the ring to Elle. Instead, it gets the ring to Olivia and she returns it to Elle, breaching our security with a NINA operative in tow?" Nick guffawed. "Not likely the CIA did that—especially here, revealing the location of our Lodge. One wouldn't compromise us like that, and the CIA sure wouldn't compromise us or One."

"I agree, bro. But the chain had to be CIA to NINA to us. Maybe the CIA didn't cue Liv, so she acted on her own."

Working both sides, she might have. She had before. "Maybe.

She warned Elle to beware," Nick said. "And she signaled us that our location was known to NINA and our system was flawed."

Sam disagreed. "So Olivia gives up One to NINA." He guffawed. "No way, bud."

"Way," Nick said. "If NINA already had it and she wanted One to know it."

Sam stilled. "I'd buy that."

Joe hooked a thumb in his pants' pocket. "Which brings us back to the ring. They both want it, so why give it back to Elle?"

"I've been thinking about that," Nick said, pacing a short path across the lab. "They had it, but didn't find anything in the ring, or they found something and have no idea what it is or what it means."

Joe locked gazes with Nick. "Then Olivia had to signal NINA's knowledge of our location and One's. If there is something special about the ring—"

Nick nodded. "They think Elle might know what it is and what it means."

"Whoa. That makes it certain they'll be back for her."

It did. The scenario unfolding in Nick's mind infuriated him. "The return makes perfect sense if the CIA wants NINA to come after Elle again—and it could. One said she'd be with us indefinitely. Maybe that's why."

"So you're saying it's not the ring, it's her?" Sam asked. "Man, I thought it had to be the ring or they'd have kept Elle out of the country."

"We don't know the answer to that yet. It could be both." Nick frowned. "The key question isn't about the ring, though."

"What is it about?" Joe asked.

"Was Olivia here as a clandestine CIA operative, or as a senior NINA operative?" Nick rubbed at his neck. He didn't like the questions coming up. All of them, no matter how he looked at this, put Elle in greater danger. "And," Nick went on. "Was the man with Olivia CIA or a NINA operative?" Their grim expressions turned bitter; they too saw the escalation of risks to Elle. "That's step one."

"What's step two?" Joe hooked his sunglasses on the front neckline of his t-shirt.

"Is there one?" Nick asked.

"Yes," Joe said.

"Dang right," Sam added. "Anytime you ever say step one, you always have a step two."

"Do I?" Nick asked.

"I said always."

"Well, there is a step two." Nick admitted. "We need to examine that ring."

"I thought it wasn't about the ring." Sam removed his cap and ran a frustrated hand through his hair.

"Never said that," Nick told him. "I said, we don't know yet. Could be Elle herself, the ring, both or none and more. We need more information than we currently have to make that determination."

"I agree." Joe nodded, hooking his thumb in his pants pocket. "NINA never does anything without a reason. The CIA doesn't either."

"Exactly," Nick said. "Whichever had and returned it did so for a reason. And we need to find out what that reason is—and whose side the man with Olivia is on. That will tell us which hat—CIA or NINA—she was wearing when coming here, though I suspect the answer is both hats." That worried Nick most of all. For Olivia, Elle, the team and One.

"System back to safe again?" Joe asked.

Sam nodded. "The new backdoor is shut tight and locked."

"Did you poke around for other vulnerabilities?"

"I did."

"Find anything?"

"Nothing." Sam looked Nick right in the eye. "You didn't miss anything, Nick. They punched through a wall and created a new backdoor. Pure and simple."

"Yeah, well, do something to reinforce the walls to keep it from happening again—the more painful for them the better."

"Got it. Stiff consequences."

"Crippling consequences." Nick frowned. "I'm going to go get Lizzie and Elle out of the dungeon."

"Time to look at more pictures," Joe said, then stood up. "They'll love that."

Not surprisingly, Joe was on target. They needed to identify the man with Olivia. "Elle will want to eat first," Nick predicted. "The woman eats when she gets scared, and she was terrified by Lizzie going missing."

"I imagine her stint in the bunker hasn't done much to calm her down."

Nick glanced at Joe. "Not touching that."

"Me, either," Sam said. "It's a sucker bet."

"Hope the freezer's got plenty in it." Joe said.

"It's full." Nick headed toward the hallway door.

"I hope she shares." Sam grunted. "I'm starving."

Recruiting everyone but Sam for kitchen duty, Elle directed them through making a salad, spaghetti, and garlic bread. While the others were busy on that, she rummaged through the freezer and found frozen blueberries, so she threw together a cobbler for dessert.

Her insides still rattled. When in the bunker, Lizzie relayed every word the man and woman had said to her. He had been stone silent and looked mad, which worried Elle. The woman had been casual and chatty. Lizzie hadn't feared her at all, and that worried Elle more than anything.

Lizzie needed fear to protect her, and Elle had done her best to instill it. That directly opposed the nurturer and comforter in her, but this woman, whoever she was, wasn't safe, and Lizzie wasn't safe interacting with her.

They gathered at the table and ate their meal. Nick watched Elle closely the entire time, pretending that he wasn't paying undue attention. The breach worried him. But then it would. He'd designed the security system and it had failed. Likely, he was beating himself up inside because, well, that was Nick. Which meant she had to lighten up the tension. Her being worried and showing it would just make him feel more guilty, and nothing good could come of that. Nick hadn't had much to smile about in life, and now she understood why. But he had almost smiled earlier today. She'd liked it, and she didn't want him reverting to all gloom and doom.

Elle swallowed a bite of hot bread. "I was thinking maybe we could go fishing later. I saw some rods down in the basement." A rack filled with them hung on the wall.

Lizzie brightened up. "I never been fishing." She looked at Sam. "Will you show me how?"

"I can do that, half-pint," he said. "But we need to find out about the man before we go. Work first, then fun."

She nodded.

Elle laughed. "Sam, you've got cobbler in your beard."

His eyes twinkled. "Saving a bite for later."

Lizzie rolled her eyes at him. "That's gross."

He dabbed at his beard with a napkin.

From the corner of her eye, Elle watched Nick. He didn't smile, but he didn't look as if the weight of the world sat on his shoulders anymore, either. He did still seem a little… apart and distant. Of course, he hadn't had many family meals.

That thought made her sad. He hadn't had any really, not from the time his mom left. He'd grown up in a boarding school. Alone in a room full of people. And now, even with his closest friends, at least a part of him still felt alone in a room full of people.

"Elle?" he asked. "You okay?" He placed his napkin on the table.

"I'm fine." Bittersweet, she smiled, then deliberately brightened. "Especially since Lizzie didn't try to snitch that bite of cobbler Sam was saving for later."

"Eeew!" Lizzie pulled a face. "That's worse than gross."

Elle laughed in earnest. And Nick's eyes flickered amusement.

Her laughter no longer irritated him. The realization hit her like a ton of bricks. It'd always irritated him, which is why she'd laughed so often. He probably thought she did it to needle him but she hadn't. She'd done it to anesthetize him to it. Anything done often enough comes to seem normal. Laughter should be normal. Amused wasn't far from normal, and when he'd let them out of the bunker and she'd thrown herself into his arms, he hadn't just stood there and tolerated her hug. For the first time, he'd closed his arms around her. He hadn't hugged her back, but he'd more than endured her holding him. That was progress.

Feeling as if she'd conquered Everest, Elle put down her fork. "If we're going to get to fun and fishing, we'd best get busy and get our work done."

Elle and Lizzie again sat before the computer screen in the gathering room and looked at photos. Nick stood behind Elle, sounds of Joe and Sam working in the kitchen breaking the silence.

"Why are you showing us photos of thirty-year-old blondes, Nick?" She looked back over her shoulder at him. "The woman looks like Tim's Mandy, only older."

Each of the thirty-seven photos he'd shown her had been of Olivia. She had passed their inspection, scrutiny, and intense observation. That was incredible really. When you factored in that both Elle and Lizzie had expected to see Olivia, it was decidedly remarkable that they hadn't recognized her even once. "It's standard procedure," he said. "To clear your mind of preconceived expectations." He reached over, brushing her question aside, then clicked the mouse. The photo advanced, and this one was of the organist at Tim and Mandy's wedding.

Lizzie folded her leg and propped it under her free one, nearly bouncing on her chair. "I know her!"

Nick paused. "You do?"

Lizzie's head bobbed. "I was at the wedding. I saw her."

"Oh, I see." Joe and Sam wrapped up in the kitchen and joined them.

"Whose wedding was it?" Elle asked.

"Tim and Mandy's." Nick advanced the photo. This one looked like Olivia. She wasn't impersonating anyone. It was rare to see a photo of her as herself, but Tim had provided him with one via email. Nick's gaze clashed with Sam's, but both men remained silent.

"That's her." Elle looked back at them. "That's the woman at the wreck."

"Lizzie?" Sam prodded. "What do you think?"

"It's her, Sam." Lizzie went knees on the chair and looked up at Sam. "It's the lady who knocked on the door and gave me Elle's ring at the creek."

"You're sure."

She nodded. "I'm definitely sure."

"Okay then." Nick cleared the screen. "Now let's look for the man." He intended to make this part of the process much shorter. Little required confirmation. When Lizzie had described the man, all three of them—and Tim, who was tied up on another case today but joined them by phone—drew the same, immediate conclusion. Still, they had to offer reasonable alternatives to the man they suspected. Just to verify his identity beyond a reasonable doubt.

Six photos appeared on the screen. All were male, dark eyed, and wearing thick black-framed glasses. All looked straight ahead but none wore the same expression. They looked enough alike to be related, if not brothers. One, Nick felt certain, was the man who'd been at the Lodge with Lizzie.

Elle hadn't seen him at the Lodge, but she had gotten a partial look at the man at the wreck. "Do you see him, Elle?"

Disappointment shafted through her voice. "Honestly, I can't tell. The man was out like a light and slumped over the steering wheel. I didn't get a clear look at his whole face."

"No problem." Nick looked at Lizzie then nodded at Sam.

Sam nodded back, silently acknowledging his cue. "Well, half-pint, do you see him?"

"Wait," she said. "I see him, but I want to be real sure I don't make a mistake." She continued to study the photos, one by one, slowly soaking in every detail.

"Yeah, I'm sure." She looked at Sam. "He's this one." She pointed to a man on the screen, top row, third slot. "Even his glasses are the same. One side has a silver screw in it. The other side has a gold one. See?"

That surprised Nick. "You remember the screws in his glasses?" Most people ignored them. Oh, they'd remember someone wore glasses, but often couldn't tell you a thing about the shape or color."

"Not the lenses," she said, "other than they were thick. His vision must be really bad. But I remember the frames and the screws. The lady bumped into him and knocked them off his nose. The sun hit the frames and made them sparkle. That's when I saw one screw was silver and the other one was gold."

Olivia's bump had been intentional. Something she didn't want him to see... like the return of the ring. Maybe. "When did that happen?"

"When the lady told him to take a walk. He didn't like that, and he flipped his arm like this—" she lifted her arm in a *whatever* motion "—and she bumped into him and knocked his glasses off his face. They landed right by my foot. I picked them up and gave them back to him."

"What did he say?" Sam asked.

"Thank you." Lizzie shrugged. "That's it." She shot Elle an apologetic look. "I told you he didn't say anything, but he did say thank you. I forgot that until just now."

"No problem."

Nick looked back at Elle. "Do you see anything in him that doesn't fit with what you saw at the scene?"

Elle studied the photo again. "No," she finally said. "Nothing jumps out at me. It could be him, but I can't be sure."

Nick glanced at Sam, and they shared a loaded look Elle clearly didn't miss. "Who is he?" she asked.

Joe tapped Lizzie on the shoulder. "Hey, let's go downstairs and rig up the fishing rods. You can practice casting into a cup so when we go to the stream, you'll be ready."

"You guys want me out again," she told Joe.

"Yep."

"Okay." She slid off the chair. "Casting. What's that?"

"It's how you get your line in the water."

"Got it."

Chatting, the two disappeared downstairs.

Elle pinned Nick with an unrelenting gaze. "Who is that man?" She lifted a warning finger. "And don't even try telling me you don't know. I can see that you do in your face—and so does Sam."

"We know him," Nick told her. "He's a well-documented NINA operative. They both are. She's known as Phoenix."

"And him?"

"He doesn't have a code name. At least, not that we know of."

"You've got this. I'm going to report in." Joe excused himself.

Elle brushed her hair back from her face. "So you don't know much about the man who was here?"

"Actually, we know quite a bit about him." Nick sat down on the chair Lizzie had vacated. "His name is Paul Johnson. He worked for a man known as Gregory Chessman. Chessman was a honcho in the village for a while. A philanthropist, or so people thought."

"NINA?" Elle guessed.

"Oh yeah. A mid-level honcho." Nick studied her face. "We busted him. He's in Leavenworth now. Actually," he amended, "we busted Paul Johnson, too. He was in prison for about a year, but he was released." Nick could have added that Johnson nearly had been busted a second time by the Shadow Watchers but he'd skipped the country and hadn't surfaced again until now.

"Why did they let him out? I don't get it."

Neither did Nick, though he knew Jackal, Chessman's replacement, had bought Johnson out of prison. The Shadow Watchers knew it, Omega One knew it, but neither of them could prove it without divulging information that couldn't be divulged without stiff consequences. Evidence walked. Which meant, in the highest circles, the honchos on their side determined Paul Johnson was more valuable to them on the outside than in jail. They knew he'd return to the fold and no doubt wanted to expose as many NINA operatives as possible by letting him. "Who knows why the powers that be do the things they do?"

"Well, it's clear they messed up this time. " She lifted a frustrated hand. "He's right back with NINA."

Which had been the plan. Get Johnson back into the NINA fold and see who he exposes and what happens. He could tip them on as yet unknown operatives or on NINA's next target. "Appears so."

"But you're not sure," Elle whispered.

"In my line of work, you can rarely be sure anything is what it appears to be."

Elle twitched, clearly afraid, obviously terrified, and confused. "Nick, what are we going to do? NINA knows where we are."

"Yes, it does."

"I don't understand any of this. It seems illogical. Why would they kidnap me to take my ring and then ship me to you and send my ring back to me?"

Sam returned, stood nearby. "That's the million dollar question right now, isn't it?"

"It's bizarre." Flustered at not being able to figure it out, she grunted. "Extremely bizarre."

Nick addressed them both. "It only seems bizarre because we haven't yet figured it out. What I know is NINA never does anything without a purpose. Historically, it doesn't take unnecessary risks and it never leaves witnesses."

"Lizzie," Elle said, pressing her hand to her stomach. "They'll try to kill her?"

"They didn't," Sam said.

"No, they didn't," Nick says. "Which means they're behaving in a way that's contrary to their normal operating procedures."

Elle's eyes stretched wide. "Which means we have no idea what they've done, are doing, or will do."

"I'm afraid that's true," Nick admitted. "At least, not yet."

"Elle," Sam said. "You told us your dad gave you the ring."

She nodded. "To celebrate the European tour."

"Is there anything odd about it?"

Lifting her hand, she studied it. "Not that I know of. He didn't say anything or even hint that it was anything more."

"We need to look at it," Nick told her. "If you don't mind."

"Not at all." She slid the ring off her finger and dropped it into Nick's palm.

He closed his fingers around it. The metal was still warm from her skin. "Sam and I will be in the lab. There's a reason this was returned to you. We need to find out what it is."

"What should I do?"

Nick saw her worry. He hated it. "Rest. Write a song. Do something relaxing."

"Okay if I bake?" Elle stood up. "I'm in the mood for oatmeal raisin cookies."

The woman was scared.

Sam grinned. "Great. I love oatmeal raisin."

Elle smiled back. "Guess we'll need a double batch then."

Heading upstairs, Nick heard Sam on the stairs right behind him. "Buddy, I'm giving you fair warning. You don't go after that woman and I'm going to."

Nick stopped on the steps, glared back at Sam. "Touch her and die."

Sam laughed. "I thought that was the way of it."

"What?"

"You're as crazy about her as she is about you."

"Don't be stupid, Sam."

"Stupid? It's as clear as the nose on your face, bud."

Was it? It couldn't be. That'd be impossible. He'd never let anyone get that close. After Jacinda? No, no way. "You're wrong."

"I ain't wrong, but whatever." Sam tugged at his cap's brim. "I'm just saying. If you don't want her, move over."

"No." Nick snarled, unsettled and freaking out inside. He wouldn't move over, but want her? He'd have to be crazy. Sam opened his mouth, and Nick lifted a staying hand. "Shut up, Sam. I'm asking you to just shut up—please."

"Please?" That wiped the smile right off Sam's face. Compassion flooded his eyes. "Okay, buddy. I got it now. Not a problem."

Nick feared Sam did have it. He probably understood the conflict and turmoil in Nick about Elle a lot better than Nick understood it, and that griped Nick to no end. He passed Sam the ring. "You get started. I'm going to call Omega One."

"Put the pressure on him. Is Liv being Liv or NINA? We need to know. Do we bug out or stay put?"

"Joe's probably dropped the hammer on him already, but, yeah, I will." Nick grimaced. Why Omega One had them flying blind didn't make any more sense than most of what was going on here. Actually, Nick stiffened, this whole case had the hallmark signs of a classic setup.

Only years of experience with Omega One convinced Nick that it wasn't. Anyone else, and maybe. But Omega One would take a bullet for any of the Shadow Watchers. They had taken bullets for him. He would die before crossing them, just as they would for him. One was steadfast and loyal to Jane and so was Mark. The team was loyal to Mark. No way would One cross the team. Nick paused at the foot of the stairs. Though to keep secrets, One had to be under enormous pressure. Powerful pressure. But from who and for what?

Those were the questions. But Nick had no answers. He walked out onto the porch to make the call. The more he thought about everything, the more certain he became that One was counting on Nick to figure that out.

He wasn't telling them more because he couldn't.

But he was making Nick aware that the team needed to know more. For Elle? Lizzie? Her mother? For the team? For Omega One and his team?

Maybe for all of them. Nick pulled out his phone. Or maybe for even more.

CHAPTER NINE

Sunday, June 7th, 3:00 p.m.
The Lodge

NICK DIALED THE SECURE NUMBER, CHECKED THE CONNECTION to assure himself the scrambler was properly activated, and then waited for Omega One to respond. He stepped down from the porch and walked an erratic path out on the grounds. If NINA had made it to the downstairs door, they might have bugged the porch. Joe had swept the area and declared it clean. Nick would sweep it again but, until then, he'd keep his distance.

Omega One answered. "Hello."

"Get somewhere you can talk and call me back. I'll be waiting."

"What's wrong?"

Neither Joe nor Sam had reached him yet, which meant he'd been out of reach on something and, whatever it had been, Nick had interrupted. "We've had an incident."

"Three minutes."

The line went dead.

Elle stuck her head out the door. "Want a cookie?"

"In a minute. I have an urgent call." He hiked the phone.

She smiled. Pretty woman, in jeans and a t-shirt. In a tablecloth. It wasn't the clothes, it was the woman. He held off a sigh by the skin of his teeth, wishing he could get her out of his head and . . . everywhere.

Setting the cookie on a napkin on the porch railing, she pointed to it, then went back inside.

Okay, so she got to him. She was smart, pretty, kind. And being around her made people feel good. It was as if she had this magnetism that was unseen but felt, and it drew people to her. Not just people. Him.

He snagged the cookie and bit down on a bite, wishing he were immune. He'd thought he was, in part, other than to her laughter. He couldn't even lie to himself that he was immune to it. Oddly enough, it didn't grate at him anymore. Maybe it never had. Maybe he wanted it to grate at him because she was so upbeat all the time, so flexible and able to morph to fit her circumstances like shifting was no big deal. But Sam being interested in her had envy and worse beating on Nick like a battering ram. No way could he stomach that.

Irritation wouldn't spark that kind of reaction. If Nick had been asked, he would have insisted nothing could get that kind of rise out of him.

He would have been wrong. His gut reaction to Sam saying he was going after her proved it.

So what was this with her? Even Nick couldn't tag exactly what she did to him much less how it made him feel. Or could he? He opened his senses and what he felt stunned him. "Oh, no." He muttered, stilled. "Impossible."

He cleared his emotions. Shut down and rebooted, then reassessed. That same flood washed through him.

The impossible was possible.

Forcing himself, he faced it head on. These feelings... The truth slammed through him.

Not just possible. Fact.

He liked the way she made him feel. And he no longer hated liking it.

Dangerous. Foolish. Crazy.

"Worse." He dragged a hand through his hair. She'd get through this and go home. Back to her friends and her world, back to her life as a star.

And if he dared to not hate, to let himself care, he'd be left behind with a broken heart.

That was *not* going to happen.

The phone rang.

Grateful for the interruption, he answered, still chewing the cookie. "Yeah."

"What incident?"

He ran a quick security check. *Omega One.* Nick relayed what had happened with Olivia and Johnson showing up at the Lodge and returning Elle's ring through Lizzie, then asked, "What's this about?"

"I don't know. I wish I did, but I don't. We had the ring," he said. "They got it off her in the van. But the chain of custody is murky and the ring was never logged in. The guys agree they had it, but no one knows who had it or what happened to it."

"That's insane."

"There's an investigation going on to determine what happened."

"NINA never touched her, One."

"So I'm told. Look, I'm not saying saying this is logical. I'm saying it's what's happening."

"Who's investigating?"

"Hip Pocket's hamster."

Great. Hamster was a worthless yes man who answered to Hip Pocket, One's counterpart and a gutless wonder. "Why would they put him on this?"

"Good question," One said. "Unfortunately, I can't answer it. But we both know what it means."

They did. Hamster would pencil whip the paperwork Hip Pocket told him to pencil whip, and it'd all turn yellow with age before a word came out about it. All the leaks could prompt all the Freedom of Information Act requests in the world, and they wouldn't change a thing. This whole incident was, for all intent and purposes, buried—and the honchos intended for it to stay buried or they'd never have assigned it to Hip Pocket. "Well, it stands to reason then that someone there gave the ring to NINA."

"I hear you. But I don't know it, and I can't prove anything."

And that admission told Nick plenty. Omega One's reluctance to reveal mission-essential details in this case had nothing to do with security clearances. They had the clearances required all the way to the administration. Yet One wasn't withholding. He didn't know anything, and what little he did know, he'd been ordered not to relay. They'd muzzled him. Squelched and gagged him. "Specific Confidentiality Agreement?"

"Signed, sealed and delivered to all interested parties."

And One was as ticked off about it as Nick would be. His stomach curled. "If someone there got the ring to NINA, Olivia intercepted it and returned it."

Silence.

On track. One didn't cough. If Nick had been one-eighty out on what One knew had happened or believed had happened, he would have coughed. "So she's either signaling that the ring is insignificant or that they weren't after it. They were after Elle."

Again, One remained silent.

"Do you have anything you can tell me that might help?"

"The case has been pulled. I'm out of the need-to-know loop. They're handling it upstairs."

The fine hairs on Nick's neck stood on end. "Why?" They'd never before pulled a case from One. What was going on here?

"I don't know."

They'd pulled the case and not even told him why? Worry crept through Nick. In all the years they'd worked together, he'd never heard of anything like this happening. "What about Elle's dad?"

"No info on him. None."

They'd taken that upstairs, too. "Is Lizzie's mom in trouble?"

"My guess is, yes."

"Where is she?"

"I don't know."

"They take that case, too?"

"It's all one case."

"All of it?" Elle, her dad, Lizzie's mom, Lizzie—all one case?

"All of it." One sighed, his frustration palpable. "Think broader. That's all I can tell you."

Verification enough for Nick. "Do I still report to you?" Nick stared out beyond the stream, to the leaves blowing in the tops of the trees. The Shadow Watchers had always reported only to Omega One.

"Hip Pocket wants you to brief him. I reminded him that our contract prohibits you from engaging with anyone except me. So report to me and I'll relay."

In other words, One didn't trust Hip Pocket. One wanted Nick to keep him out of the loop so he couldn't relay anything significant. Now Nick understood. Omega One wanted insulation for Elle and Lizzie. Insulation and protection, and he didn't trust Hip Pocket or Hamster to provide it. He trusted Nick and the team. "Got it."

"Watch your back."

One definitely didn't trust what they were doing, but he was powerless to stop them. "Always." The warning was as extraordinary as the entire handling of this mission. From One's tone and what he didn't say, he was worried. Not concerned or uneasy. Worried. And that worried Nick. Considering the missions they'd been on during their careers, this should be a calk-walk. Instead it seemed to be a death-trap.

He disconnected the call and shoved his phone into its holder at his waist.

Joe walked out, off the porch, and down to Nick. "I take it that didn't go well."

"We're on our own," Nick told Joe. "Hip Pocket yanked the case from Omega One and ordered him to execute a Specific Confiden-tiality Agreement. There's a break in the chain of custody on the ring. And everything we report to One he has to relay to Hip Pocket."

"Which means One doesn't want to know a thing." The look in Joe's eyes went deadpan flat. "We being set up to take a fall?"

"Not yet." Nick stilled, not at all surprised the question had crossed Joe's mind. "But it's all one case, Joe. Elle, her dad, Lizzie and her mom—and her mom is in trouble. One doesn't know why or where she is, though."

"Tim's trying to track her down now. I spoke to him a few minutes ago."

"He's been working on her whereabouts since Lizzie talked to us."

"She was his other case?" Joe asked.

"I didn't want Lizzie to worry." Nick nodded. "One said something else. I asked him if NINA had been after the ring or Elle and Lizzie."

"What did he say?" Curiosity burned in Joe's eyes.

"Think broader."

Joe sighed. "So it's not one or the other. It's not only all connected, NINA's after all of them. Why?"

"I don't know." Nick let his worry show in his expression and darken his tone. "But I fear it's after all of them and about even more."

"Don't go back out to the Lodge." Olivia issued Johnson the warning then slid out of the car in the motel parking lot. "They'll be expecting you next time. You won't get a friendly reception."

Paul Johnson nodded. He didn't like Phoenix. He did respect her enough to never let her know he didn't like her. She was a powerful woman in the organization and he'd worked too hard for too long to get where he was to cross her. She didn't give second chances and she never permitted any obstacle in her path to stay in her path. She'd either get rid of him or send him to some obscure assignment on the other side of the planet. Neither option suited him. Working for Jackal did.

When Jackal had bought Paul's way out of prison, Paul had thought Jackal worked for Phoenix. He'd also thought Phoenix was a man: a deception she deliberately perpetuated to protect herself and to diminish anyone prone to challenging her authority.

That fear of challenges had to be a carryover from early on in her managerial career, though. Only a fool dared to challenge her now. About her, Paul had been wrong on both counts.

Fortunately, he hadn't revealed his thoughts to anyone. They, and his erroneous assumptions, remained hidden. Even more fortunately, Jackal, who worked directly under Phoenix, remained extremely ambitious.

After being released from prison, Jackal remained Paul's handler, yet they both remained acutely aware that NINA owned Paul. He had no choice but to do as he was told, when he was told, the way he was told.

So long as he followed orders issued by Phoenix, her boss Hawk, and his boss, Sage, and Paul covered Jackal's back by briefing him on all his orders, Jackal would bring Paul up the ranks with him and provide him cover along the way. For a man in Paul's position, having an extremely ambitious handler was his best possible outcome.

"Are you listening to me, Johnson?" Phoenix asked, looking in through the open car door.

"Yes, ma'am."

"Pick me up in three hours at the pier. Better make it four. Traffic is wicked between here and Panama City Beach during tourist season."

Panama City Beach was a solid hour and a half drive east of Seagrove Village during tourist season. What was Phoenix up to there? He didn't dare to ask, just checked his watch. "Yes, ma'am."

"See if we've had any luck tracking down Jaycee Cole. I want to question her as soon as possible."

Jaycee Cole. Sue Ellen Montgomery. Lizzie's mother. "Yes, ma'am."

Phoenix frowned, shut the door, and then stepped over to her sleek silver Jaguar.

Paul waited until she pulled onto the street and, at the corner red light, turned right. Then he pulled into the parking slot she'd vacated and retrieved his phone.

He left the engine running, cranked up the air-conditioner, and hit number one on speed dial. A cup of coffee from Ruby's Diner would be fantastic, but he'd be recognized and that would spell catastrophe. The kid might have identified him to the Shadow Watchers already. Going out to their Lodge had been a mistake. He'd tried to tell Phoenix that, but she wouldn't listen. She never listened.

"Yeah."

Jackal. "Phoenix delivered the ring to the girl." That innocent bump to dislodge his glasses had been anything but innocent. He'd seen her pass the ring to the kid. "You might want to take extra precautions to protect yourself, sir."

"You're sure."

"Positive." A maid pushing a cart down an upstairs walkway paused outside a second-floor room, gathered supplies, and then knocked on the door. "I'd be remiss if I didn't recommend Hawk replace her on this mission." Paul had already pushed as far as he dared to push, warning Jackal that his not objecting to NINA honchos activating Phoenix on this mission was a mistake. Her daughter was one step from center with the Shadow Watcher team involved.

"I understand your concern, Paul, and I appreciate it. So do the powers that be. But they've determined that if we want the parent, the most direct route is through the child."

So Hawk or Sage planned things to unfold this way? For Phoenix to return the ring? But NINA had wanted it. Now it didn't? Strange. No, it wanted that ring. But it wanted more. Did NINA want it and Elle Bostwick? Or the woman now going by Sue Ellen Montgomery?

Paul had no way of knowing. Staying true to NINA policy, an operative was given only the information required to successfully accomplish his specific assignment. Normally, Paul saw the wisdom in the policy. Any upset or complications, and an operative could reveal only what they know. The less they know, the greater the odds for mission success. Yet in this case? Here? With these people? What an operative didn't know could get him killed. Or worse. Captured.

Paul shivered. "May I ask a question, sir?"

"Go ahead."

"Why don't I just tag Elle? She and her father… shouldn't that be enough."

"Elle is under the protection of an entire team of Shadow Watchers. We've challenged them before. You know this, Paul. You were there. I shouldn't have to remind you what those altercations cost us. Considerable revenue lost, operations disrupted and, some permanently destroyed. We lost valuable operatives and even more connections."

"I'm aware of that, sir." He'd lived it. Gone to prison for it.

"Then tell me how you plan to beat them? Because you know Hawk and Sage are going to want to know. You can't buy them off and they're like dogs with bones. No matter what you throw at them, they just keep coming. No. No, we can't afford another botched run-in with those people. We need to let this play out as planned."

But Phoenix—"

"I said I understand the situation with Phoenix, Paul. Hawk and Sage understand it, too." Jackal firmed his voice. "Let me worry about her—and remember, things are not always as they appear."

"Yes, sir. Of course, sir." Irritated, Paul shifted in his seat. Easy for Jackal to say to let him worry. He was parked in a sweet chalet in Switzerland. Safe and sound and a long, long way from Seagrove Village and the Shadow Watchers. When Phoenix crashed and burned on this—and she would—Jackal, or Hawk or Sage, wouldn't be a convenient target, available to take the fall for her. Paul would…unless…

The idea in his mind solidified. A little self-protection insurance was definitely warranted.

CHAPTER TEN

Sunday, June 7ᵗʰ, 3:00 p.m.
The Lodge Lake

ELLE CAST INTO THE LAKE. THE POPPING CORK BOBBED ON THE water's surface. The sun felt warm, the breeze light and cool, and calm wanted to soothe her, but with no word on her dad or Jaycee, even fishing without feeling antsy just wasn't going to happen.

A short span down the grassy bank, Sam and Lizzie prepared to drop their lines into the water.

"I ain't baiting your hook, half-pint." Sam held out a little metal bucket. "Grab a worm and get it done."

Lizzie pulled a frown. "I don't want to touch worms, Sam. They're slimy."

"If you're gonna fish, you got to bait your own hooks."

"Why?"

"So you know how to do it." He sighed. "What if I ain't here to do it for you? What then? You can't fish. If you can't fish, you don't eat. You need to be able to fend for yourself, Lizzie. That's just sensible."

She squinted up at him against the sun. "A body sure has to be sensible a lot around you. Do you know how many times you've said that to me?"

"Apparently, not as many as I needed to." He wiggled the bucket. "Your hook's still shy of bait."

"Oh, all right." She dipped her fingers into the bucket and pulled out a worm. "Now what?"

"Run it length-wise on the hook." He reached over. "Like this."

"It ain't gonna bleed, is it?"

"Just bait the hook, half-pint."

"But if it bleeds, then I'm hurting it."

"Fish have to eat, too."

"But—"

Sam's jaw tightened. "Bait the dang hook."

Lizzie made quick work of it. "There. It's done. Satisfied?"

"Now cast, like you did into the cup in the basement."

"Joe didn't talk mean to me, showing me that."

"Last I checked, cups don't bleed." Sam sniffed.

"Do it again, and I'm telling Nora you cussed."

"Dang ain't cussing."

"To Nora, it is."

"You really gonna tell her?"

Lizzie stared at him and the fire drained out of her expression. "Not this time, but stop doing it or I will. Cussing is the sign of—"

"A weak mind," he interrupted. "Nora told me."

"Then how come you still do it?" Lizzie frowned. "You ain't weak-minded, are you, Sam?"

"Naw. I just forget."

"Well, don't forget no more." She grimaced. "That jalapeño pepper juice burns out your gut, and what happens to the rest of you? And if you ain't around, who's gonna look after me?"

"I'll do my best to remember, okay?" He grunted. "Now hush or you'll scare off the fish."

Elle smiled. She couldn't help it.

"Those two spat more than any two people I've ever seen." Nick dropped down beside Elle on the grass.

"She's squeamish," Elle explained. "He's teaching her to fend for herself." She held her smile and looked at Nick. "I can't believe you're wearing a tie fishing. Do you ever dress casually? I don't think I've ever seen you when you weren't wearing a suit."

"Suits are comfortable. They remind me to stay alert and on my game."

"Like you'd ever not be on your game," she countered. "At least take off your jacket."

"It's not a jacket, it's a coat." She was as bad as Joe.

"Your coat, then."

"Why?"

"We're fishing on a grassy bank at the lake." She reached for his tie and unknotted it, her fingers warm on his throat. "There's nothing comfortable or relaxing about wearing a tie to fish, Nick Sloan." She pulled it off and stuffed it in his pocket.

"Why does what I have on affect you relaxing?"

"Because I can't relax if you're all tied up in knots." She stilled and sat up straight. While she'd deliberately forced herself to be patient—he'd tell her if he knew anything—the words tumbled out of her mouth anyway. "Has there been any word on my dad?"

An apology filtered through his eyes. "Not yet. I'm sorry it's taking so long, Elle."

She cupped his face with her hand. "Not your fault. I know if you could, you'd have this all worked out already."

"I would." He eased off his coat, folded it neatly then set it down in the grass.

"My cork's under water! Sam, look!" Lizzie shouted. "What do I do?"

Sam moved behind her and held up the tip of the rod. "Easy, half-pint. Now reel it in, slow and easy."

Elle laughed. "Oh, I'm so excited. She's getting a fish, Nick. Isn't that fantastic?"

He watched, a nice twinkle in his eye.

"Oh, he's a fighter, Lizzie. Must be a big one." Sam tipped the rod, lifting its tip higher. "Keep the pressure on so it doesn't slip off the hook."

"I'm trying. He's strong!" Her face flushed from excitement, her eyes sparkled and she fairly danced on the bank.

Finally, the fish broke the surface of the water. "Wow, half-pint. He's a nice one."

Lizzie squealed. "Nick. Elle. Look! I got me a fish."

Elle laughed and Nick smiled.

Overwhelmed, Elle shouted at Lizzie. "You clean it and I'll cook it for you."

Lizzie went stock still. Her laughter faded. "Clean it?"

Sam's expression turned deadpan flat. "You don't expect it to clean itself, do you?"

"No. But…"

"Don't fret." Sam winked at her. "I'll show you how to do it."

"It's gonna bleed." She squeezed her eyes shut. "I know it's gonna bleed."

"Ten says she might watch him clean it, but she won't be able to swallow it," Nick whispered to Elle.

"I'll take that bet." She smiled over at him. "By the time he's done, Lizzie will have the food chain all worked out. She knows she needs food to live, and Sam will talk with her about that," Elle predicted. "But, I'll bet another ten Lizzie prays for the fish tonight before going to bed."

"Gratitude for food?"

Elle nodded.

"I kind of like that." Nick's phone rang.

He stepped away and answered it, obviously recognizing the ring tone. "Yeah, Tim."

A moment later, Nick hung up and returned to Elle. "Joe found something in the setting of your ring."

"He did?" No way was she touching that. Not happening.

"Yeah. He says it's encrypted and breaking the code will take some time."

"Okay."

"Does your dad do that?"

"Do what?"

"Use encryptions to conceal things in objects?"

133

"I honestly don't know, Nick." She tilted her head. "I haven't been in the lab since Jaycee had to go into hiding, and he didn't say anything about any encryption when he gave me the ring."

"You haven't been in the lab at all?"

"No." She shrugged. "I didn't intend to stay away. Well, not at first. But after they bombed Jaycee's car… I knew I'd never go back. I just couldn't make myself do it."

Nick looked down at the grass. "You know, I get it that you feel guilty for what happened to Jaycee and Lizzie. I do. But I've seen the other side of it, too."

"The other side of what?"

"Your systems. The lives saved because we had your systems. I never hear you acknowledge that."

She let him see the truth in her eyes. "I never saw anyone saved. I did see Jaycee's life destroyed."

"You have no idea, do you?" Nick clasped her hand. "I've seen many saves, Elle. Thousands."

"Seriously?"

He nodded. "I can't estimate accurately beyond that, but I'll tell you. The team has been in situations so sticky the bean counters gave us one percent odds. Your systems got us out alive, and anyone on the team can vouch for that."

A tear slipped from her eye. "I, um… thank you for telling me, Nick."

He brushed at the fallen tear on her cheek with the pad of his thumb. "If you're going to feel guilty about the one bad outcome, then you need to feel wonderful about the thousands of saves. Fair is fair, Elle."

A knot swelled in her throat. She tried to talk around it. "It's hard to be fair to myself when Jaycee and Lizzie pay the price, but I do understand what you're saying, and I am grateful for you telling me about the other side. It helps."

He let his fingertip slide across her lips, along her jaw. "Just stating the facts."

His phone rang again. Different ring tone.

He hauled himself to his feet and again moved down the bank. This time, well out of hearing distance.

Elle watched him, fascinated and totally breathless. He'd touched her. Her hand, her face, her lips. Intentionally and deliberately.

Sweet progress!

Her heart soared.

What had he been thinking? Why had he touched her like that?

Worse, his fingers tingled, eager to do it again.

Angry with himself, Nick jerked out his ringing phone and answered it. "What?"

"This is not me."

Omega One. "Okay. Secure?"

"Yes."

Nick double-checked the app, saw that they were secure, then asked, "Developments?"

"Information you need, but since I can't give it to you, I'm not talking to you. I'm just out for a walk, talking to myself."

Nick said nothing.

"You're going to find a connection between Elle and Jaycee Cole because there is a connection. Elle designed a system someone wants. Jaycee was the contract negotiator on it. As soon as we discovered that, the honchos upstairs yanked the mission and cut us out of the loop. Ever since, Hip Pocket and Hamster have had my entire team under intense scrutiny. I'm not sure why—none of us are—but I am sure, if my people seek Jaycee and find her, she's as good as dead, and I'm not sure it'll be our mutual enemy doing the killing."

Again, Nick held his silence. Omega One obviously thought NINA had infiltrated his task force. Or the honchos worried someone had. Either way, this wasn't good news for Jaycee or Elle.

"When you crack the code," One went on, "you might have better insight. All I can tell you about that is it's stiffer than military-grade encryption. Our guys haven't seen anything like it before, so I have nothing to offer on that front. Whatever it is, NINA wants it and the CIA doesn't want them to get it. Otherwise, they wouldn't have returned the ring to Elle." He paused a long second, then added, "There's always a reason for that level of encryption. And it always extends beyond the usual rationale. In this case, that'd be beyond using Elle as ransom bait to get the encryption code from her parents."

Did that mean NINA had her father? Nick didn't dare to ask.

One clearly anticipated the rise of the question. He said, "I don't know where her father is or who's holding him. I do know he's alive—he has to be kept alive to decode the information in the ring in case Elle doesn't know the code."

She would have told him if she did know it. Would revealing that she didn't make her situation better or worse? How would that impact her dad?

"Olivia made a drop in Panama City earlier today. She reported that she returned the ring and NINA knows it. They have scanned copies of the encryption and are working as hard as we are on breaking the code. She says you're safe at the Lodge but not away from it. To stay put. NINA operatives have been ordered not to go anywhere near you guys. But she also said to get Lizzie out of there. One of our associates gave Jaycee a heads up that trouble was brewing. Their intention was to give her and Lizzie new identities and move them again. Jaycee agreed but then before the arrangements were complete, she took off. She called the associate the day after she left and said she'd tried handling this his way and it had failed. Now she's handling it her way. She must, for her daughter."

A lump lodged in Nick's throat. *What had Jaycee meant by that?*

"NINA will be looking for a way to use the girl to flush out her mother. If you want us to intervene and retrieve her, report your concern for her in your next official update. If not, report alternative plans have been made for her and refuse to disclose them."

He shouldn't ask, but Lizzie... The abandoned kid in Nick had to know. "Jaycee coming back?"

"Doubtful. She says so long as she stays away, Lizzie will be safe with Ben and Kelly Brandt, the owners of Crossroads Crisis Center."

Ben and Kelly would keep Lizzie safe, and they had the resources to do it. Jaycee must have talked to one or both of them about Lizzie already. Nick's money was on Kelly. Which meant, One was right. To protect her daughter, Jaycee wouldn't be coming back. Not now. Not ever.

Lizzie would be devastated.

The lump in Nick's throat swelled, doubled. Jaycee had sacrificed her life with Lizzie to spare her. But that isn't how Lizzie would see it. And it's not how she'd feel.

Left behind. Abandoned. Discarded and forgotten. Thrown away.

Just like Nick…

Elle took one look at Nick's face and asked, "What's wrong?"

"I, um, need to go to Crossroads Crisis Center and talk to the Brandts."

"Who are they?"

"Ben and Kelly. They own the crisis center."

"We met briefly at Lisa and Mark's wedding." Elle stood up, slid into her sandals. "Has something bad happened?"

He didn't answer.

"You're not driving. Not like this," Elle said.

"I'm fine."

"You are not." She turned and raised her voice. "Sam, you and Lizzie fish and get enough for dinner. Nick and I are going to Crossroads to see the Brandts."

That alerted Sam but one look at Nick had Sam on his feet, walking over. "You okay, bud?"

"I'm fine."

Sam grimaced. "I heard the ringtone. What's up?"

Nick dropped his voice. "Jaycee isn't coming back."

Sam closed his eyes and his huge shoulders slumped. "What

about half-pint?"

"Jaycee wants her with Ben and Kelly. That's why I'm on the way over there now. We have to move her."

"Because…?"

"CIA says it's imperative."

"That's it, then." He glanced back at Lizzie. "I ain't telling her. Not until you get back."

"I'll tell her," Elle said, understanding Sam didn't want to taint the bond of trust he'd built with Lizzie.

"No, I'll tell her myself." Nick insisted. "Tell Joe to hit that code hard. Half the world is trying to break it."

Elle gathered her gear and she and Nick headed toward the house.

Half an hour later, they were seated in Ben and Kelly Brandt's kitchen.

Ben was about Nick's age, dark hair, intelligent eyes. Kelly was a petite blond with a strong personality and a will of steel. Elle liked them both very much.

"I don't have another number for her, Nick. Nora and I tried to call her to let her know Lizzie was with you guys at the Lodge. The number had been disconnected."

Nick frowned. "It seems strange she'd take off and not leave a number where she could be reached by somebody here." Time for Kelly to fess up that she knew all this and more. "What if Lizzie needed medical treatment or something? Seems pretty irresponsible, and that's not like her."

"All right, Nick. Point made." Kelly refilled their coffee cups and returned the pot to its warmer on the kitchen counter. "Lizzie is covered."

Elle, Nick, and Ben turned to look at her. "What?" Ben asked.

Kelly shrugged. "Anything that could come up with her is taken care of. I—actually, we and the center, as our successors—have full authority to do whatever Lizzie needs done. We, um, have guardian-ship papers, too, and if when Lizzie is sixteen, she wants us to adopt her, we have those documents as well."

Ben just stared at his wife. "Kelly, explain."

"I'm sorry for not telling you, honey," she said. "Jaycee swore me to secrecy. I couldn't tell anyone unless it became absolutely necessary." She shrugged. "Now, it's necessary."

Nick frowned. "Did she tell you why?"

"I didn't ask and she didn't offer." Kelly sat back down in her seat. "Look, I've worked with Jaycee for months. She's a wonderful mother. She said it was a matter of life and death and that she had to know Lizzie would be safe." Kelly shrugged. "That was more than enough for me."

"Sorry, Nick. The signs were there, but I didn't put them together." Ben sipped from his cup. "I should have known."

Kelly raised her eyebrows.

"You just redid the bedroom next to the baby's. I should have realized it wasn't random timing, you had a purpose."

"I did." Kelly looked at Nick. "If Lizzie had to come to us, I wanted her to feel like this was home. Not like she's a guest. You know what I mean. She needed her own room with her own things —her space so she belongs."

Nick's voice went gruff. "That's very thoughtful of you, Kelly."

Her gaze turned liquid. "I remember how I felt. I didn't have any of that for a long time, and it hurt."

Nick hadn't had any of that since he was six until he provided a home for himself. It had hurt. But he couldn't talk about it like Kelly did. Sometimes, though, he wished he could. "Lizzie could be in danger," he warned them. "You need to know that, especially with the baby and all…"

"I promised Jaycee, Nick." Kelly lifted her chin. "We've got protection. Mark's seen to it and I'm having faith that we're in capable hands."

"You can rest easy on that front." Ben reassured Nick. "Lizzie will be safe here. We'll do whatever we have to do to protect her."

Elle spoke up. "She's lucky to have you."

"We all need someone we can count on." Kelly swallowed her coffee. "Lizzie can count on us."

Nick cleared his throat. "Well, I guess we'd better go tell her. We'll bring her back in a couple hours, if that's okay."

"We'll be ready and waiting." Ben stood up and shook Nick's hand. "I don't envy you, having to tell her. But, Nick, don't worry. We'll make a home for her here."

"That's…good." It was all he could manage. From the compassionate look in Ben's eyes, it was more than enough.

CHAPTER ELEVEN

Sunday, June 7th, 5:00 p.m.
The Lodge

WHEN NICK AND ELLE WALKED INTO THE LODGE, SAM WAS AT the stove frying fish and Lizzie stood on a stool beside him, taste-testing a filet.

Sam took one look at Nick's face and dread filled his eyes.

"What do you think, Lizzie?" Elle asked.

She cocked her head, studied Elle and then Nick. "You've got bad news or else you guys have been fighting again."

"We don't fight," he said. "We discuss."

"Nick's right." Elle slid onto a stool at the breakfast bar. "But I was talking about the fish. What do you think of it?"

"It's good. I didn't let Sam burn it." She shoved the plate toward Elle. "Have some." She looked at Nick. "You, too."

"Thanks, Lizzie." He sat down beside Elle. Grabbed a piece and took a bite. "Mmm, it's good."

Lizzie drank down a gulp of water. "So is my mom...hurt, or what?"

Leave it to Lizzie to be blunt. Nick admired straight-talk, but he hated that any kid had to go through this, worrying about a parent. He knew how that could rip you apart inside. "We don't think so. We just don't know yet."

She chewed slowly, then screwed up her courage to ask the question she most wanted answered. "So what's the bad news?"

"Your mom wants you to go to stay with Ben and Kelly." Nick answered quickly. Prolonging her agony wasn't just cruel, it was a sure-fire path to hyper-anxiety. Between the wreck, the unexpected guests here at the Lodge where she was supposed to feel safe, the stint in the vault and everything else, the last thing Lizzie—or any of them, for that matter—needed was more anxiety.

Elle licked at her lips. "Kelly's fixed you a room at their house, Lizzie. She showed it to me, and it's beautiful."

Lizzie bit into a piece of fish, and chewed it at a snail's pace, glancing at Sam and then at Nick, gauging their reactions. "My mom isn't coming back, is she?"

Nick could lie. His heart squeezed so hard he wanted to lie. But he couldn't make himself do it. He'd known lies when he'd heard them and Lizzie would, too. "Right now, it doesn't look like it, no."

She sucked in a sharp breath. Stilled.

Sam put down the pinchers and held open his arms.

Lizzie leapt into them and Sam scooped her up. "I'm so sorry, half-pint."

She cried, soft sobs that shook her shoulders and ripped Nick's heart to shreds.

Elle discreetly grabbed his hand and squeezed, her cheeks wet.

When Lizzie's sobs softened to sniffles, Sam dabbed at her cheeks with the edges of a wadded paper towel. "We'll be here for you, Lizzie. No matter what. You know that, right?"

She nodded. "But how am I gonna know if she's okay or not? What if she needs me? I won't even know it, Sam."

"You're going to have to have faith. Sometimes things happen we can't control. We have to trust that nothing is going to happen to your mom that she and God can't handle. He'll be with her, Lizzie. She's never gonna be alone, and that's the way it works."

"Trust God?" she said. "After our house blew up?"

"Hey, you weren't in it."

"Well, that's true."

"You got out of there and you've been safe here."

"Yeah." She sighed. "For a while, anyway."

"Your mom's really smart, Lizzie," Sam said. "She'll be thinking of a way to get back to you every single day."

"I don't know about that. She's smart, but I think she'll stay away." Lizzie looked at Nick then Elle. "She told me this could happen one day."

"That she'd leave you?" Nick asked.

Lizzie nodded.

"Because she didn't want you to think she just left you," Nick said. "She wanted you to know that she had no choice—to keep you safe."

She looked him in the eye, challenging him. "It still hurts."

He looked right back. "Yeah, I know it does. Part of you will always hurt."

"That's true," Elle added.

"How do you know?" Lizzie asked Elle.

Elle worried her lower lip with her teeth, not eager to disclose. "My parents pretty much kept me a secret," she admitted. "They gave me a different name, and even when I worked with my dad, everyone thought I was his cousin. No one knew I was his daughter —at least, not until he told Nick."

"That's just crazy." Lizzie sniffed and asked, "Why'd they do that?"

"They were scared." Elle shrugged. "They thought it was the best way to keep me safe."

"From what?" She sniffled. "Are bad men after you, too?"

"They have been for my whole life. But not the same kind of bad men after you and your mom. At least, I don't think they are." Elle paused, thought, frowned. "Well, maybe now they are the same." Elle stiffened. "I'm just not sure yet."

"It's hard not to be confused, huh?"

"It is." Elle nodded at Lizzie. "Angry, too."

Lizzie's brow furrowed. "You're angry at the bad men?"

"I really am. And I'm angry at my parents, too," Elle admitted. "Actually, I've spent more time being angry with them than with the bad people. In my head, I know they were just trying to keep me safe. But in my heart, all this time I've been worried that I'd done something wrong to make them do what they did."

Lizzie's jaw dropped. "Me, too."

"Well, you just get that thought right out of your head. You didn't do anything wrong, Lizzie. You either, Elle," Nick said. "Not a thing."

"How do you know?"

"Yeah?" Elle asked. "How do you know?"

Nick bristled, looked at Sam in a silent plea for an escape or diversion. None came. "Because I do."

Elle stilled, blinked twice, then gave him a reprieve. "Nick's right," Elle told Lizzie. "For a long time I was sure something was wrong with me and that's why they didn't want anyone to know I was their daughter. I thought they were ashamed of me because I was kind of weird. You know, with building things and loving my dad's work. Most little kids don't care about those kinds of things." Elle sighed. "But they weren't ashamed. It just wasn't true. They were scared and trying to do the best they knew to do to keep me safe—even if it didn't feel that way." Elle stiffened. "That's what they were doing."

"But you were still mad at them."

"Well, yeah. Sure, I was. Sometimes, I still am." Elle sighed. "Sometimes even when someone does something really hard for them to do because they believe they must, it still hurts. It's okay to be mad about it. It took me a while to figure that out." Elle reached for a second filet of fish. "Now, when I get mad at them about it, I think about how hard it must have been for them to act like they didn't have a daughter. Especially my dad. He was actually pretty proud of me and what I was doing, working with him. But he didn't say much because he worried someone might figure out the truth. "

"It was hard for them and you," Lizzie said.

Elle nodded. "Very."

"Does that make you feel better?"

Pausing a long second, Elle admitted the truth. "You know, it does."

Lizzie went silent for a long beat. Then another, clearly mulling things over in her mind. "I think I'm not mad at my mom. I'm not going to get mad at her, either."

"Why not?" Nick asked, fascinated. How had Lizzie processed this so quickly?

She looked across the bar at Nick. "My mom doesn't cry much. But when she told me this could happen one day, she cried." Lizzie pulled in a shuddery breath. "She didn't want to leave me. But she didn't want our new house to blow up with me in it, either."

"You're lucky to know she didn't want to go," Nick said.

"You weren't lucky?"

Nick nodded that he wasn't. "Mine wanted to go and she did."

"No. Why?"

"I don't know." He started to ignore her, but she needed the reassurance she'd found in her mom. He couldn't give her peace but he could give her honesty. "I was six. I got up and ate cereal for breakfast, dressed, and went to school. She wasn't up yet, so we never even said good-bye." He remembered coming home, facing his father's fury, being blamed for her going. "She left and she never came back."

Lizzie walked around the edge of the bar, put her hand in Nick's and held them clasped. "Why would she do that to you?"

"I'm not sure," he said, staring at her tiny hand offering him— him—reassurance. A lump formed in his throat. "She wasn't happy. I am sure about that. My dad was gone a lot on business and she hated that. They . . . discussed it all the time," he said, deliberately toning down the screaming matches he'd covered his head with his pillow to snuff out.

"But he said it was your fault she left."

"He did." Over and over. "Maybe it was. I was smart and she didn't like it."

"Why didn't she like it?" Lizzie asked. "Parents usually like having smart kids, don't they, Sam?"

"Yeah, they do. Bragging rights."

Nick looked up at Lizzie. "I think she kept a lot of things to herself and she didn't want me to know them."

"Secrets?"

He nodded.

"What kind of secrets?"

"I don't know." How many times had he asked himself that question? Strained to remember every word overheard? Wondered what could be so awful she'd desert him?

"Maybe she didn't want to leave you," Lizzie said. "Maybe she had to leave to protect you."

"I thought that for about a minute, but she really was not happy." She'd locked herself in the bath but he'd heard her muffled sobs through the door too many times to think anything else. "She left because she didn't want to be there."

"So how come she didn't take you with her?"

"I don't know that, either." He let out a sigh of sheer frustration. "It's not like my father would have missed me. He sent me away right after she left."

"Sent you away where?"

"Boarding school." Nick grimaced. "He got married again and his new wife didn't want me around, so he sent me away."

"He left you with nobody?" Lizzie's indignation was swift and strong. "What did you do?"

"I learned to never need or trust anyone."

"Well, did he ever come get you?"

"No, he never did." She innately squeezed his fingers. Feeling the sting, Nick let his gaze fall again to their clasped hands. "I lived at the school until I grew up, and then I started my own life."

Lizzie's jaw clenched. "You didn't see your dad anymore, either?"

"No, I didn't."

She stilled, went silent for a long minute, then said, "You learned not to trust anybody but I know you trust Sam and Joe and Tim and Mark and Elle."

"I have to work at it. Honestly, it's hard." He didn't dare look at

Sam. "But, yes, you're right. I do trust them. It just took me a long time."

"Cuz you're still mad at your dad for sending you away."

"Yeah, I am." He'd gone this far. Might as well confess the rest. "At my mom for leaving me. At my dad for throwing me away and forgetting I existed, and mostly I'm mad at Jacinda."

"Who's she?"

"My dad's wife," he said. "She hates me. She always has, but I don't know why."

Lizzie stepped closer, craned back her neck and looked up at Nick. "Ain't nobody ever loved you, Nick?"

"My grandma did, but she died when I was little—before my mom left." He hiked his eyebrows. "For some of us, life's that way, Lizzie. Everyone dies or leaves us. Sometimes because they want to go, and sometimes because they can't help it. Either way, they're gone, and we're on our own."

Unshed tears had her eyes shiny, overly bright. "That's sad."

"That's life." He studied her a long second. "Until right now, I've only ever told one person about all this—even Sam didn't know it."

Surprised, she glanced at Sam.

"I didn't."

She pivoted her gaze back to Nick. "Why'd you tell me?"

"Because I want you to know, whether they go because they want to or because they have to, it's hard not to be mad. But either way you have to accept it, Lizzie, and you have to go on and do the best you can do to make yourself a great life. You're one of the lucky ones. You have Ben and Kelly, and they'll be a family to you."

"And I have you and Sam."

"Dang right."

Nick didn't think to complain about Sam's language. Hearing this from Nick for the first time, Sam was pretty emotional, too. "All the team—Joe, Tim and Mark, and me."

"Me, too, Lizzie." Elle's voice sounded rough, thick.

She hugged Elle then turned and hugged Nick, catching him by surprise.

VICKI HINZE

He hesitated, hands mid-air, then gently let them close around Lizzie's slim shoulders. "You're definitely a lucky one, and we're lucky to have you in our lives, too."

Lizzie glanced up at him, her expression frank, her eyes earnest. "I ain't abandoning you, Nick. Not ever. And I ain't dying or leaving you, either. Never. Ever. And that's a promise." She held up her little finger. "I pinky swear."

Moved, he linked their little fingers, then lifted his free hand and touched her face. "Thank you, Lizzie."

"Can I ask you something?" she asked.

He nodded, too tight-throated to speak.

"How long did you miss her? Your mom, I mean."

"I'll have to let you know."

Lizzie's face riddled with confusion. "What's that mean?"

Elle clasped Nick's hand. "It means a part of him still misses her."

"Sensible," Sam said. "She is still his mom. Of course, he still misses her."

"Yeah." Nick agreed, then cleared his throat. "Now, I'm not going to blow smoke at you about Ben and Kelly, Lizzie. But I promise you they're good people and they will take great care of you."

"I know."

"You do?"

"Sure." She went back to her stool and snagged the last filet of fish. "I know them all really well. They've got a baby, Susan. She's new."

Elle smiled. "You can be like a big sister to her, then."

"Yeah, but I sure am gonna miss my mom. She could do anything."

Sam stroked Lizzie's hair. "She had to go, half-pint, but when she can—when it's safe—she'll come back."

"No, she won't." Lizzie's voice was deadpan flat. "She'll want to every day but she won't do it. She'll be too scared to ever come see me again."

The certainty in Lizzie's voice cracked Nick's heart. "You can

148

hope she will."

"No, I can't."

"Why not?" Elle asked.

"Because it ain't gonna happen. When you know something ain't gonna happen, you don't hope for it. You just hope for things you can believe."

"Well, I'm going to believe things work out and she can come back someday." Elle told Lizzie.

Sam stroked his beard. "The thing is, we never know exactly what's going to happen. If we don't know, we don't know. What do we have to lose by hoping?"

"It hurts when it doesn't happen."

"But we don't know it ain't gonna happen, half-pint. It might."

"I suppose."

Nick cleared his throat. Forced strength into his voice and courage from inside that he feared he didn't have but sorely needed. "Lizzie?"

She paused and looked at him.

"I didn't hope. I hurt instead. I still do. That's not good." He blinked hard. "I wish I had hoped, even if it never happened."

"That's what broke you inside? Not hoping?"

Nora's words. He nodded. "We need hope." He didn't dare look at Elle. "It's too late for me, but it isn't for you. Hope, Lizzie. Enough for both of us."

She thought a long moment. "No. But I'll hope if you will. I figure if you can do it, I surely can."

"I told you, it's too late for me."

"I'm saying, it ain't." Lizzie jutted out her jaw. "You're still breathing."

"You sound just like Nora." Nick said.

"That's the truth," Sam said, a smile in his voice.

Elle smiled.

"Well?"

"Okay, Lizzie. I'll try." Nick said. "But only for you."

"Well, all right, then."

Amazingly like Nora. Nick couldn't help himself; he smiled.

CHAPTER TWELVE

Sunday, June 7th, 6:00 p.m.
Three Gables

NICK AND ELLE GOT LIZZIE SETTLED IN WITH BEN AND KELLY, then Lizzie walked them to the door. Nick struggled to find something to say to her worth hearing, but the girl had opened old wounds in him, and he felt raw. Still, Elle had trusted him and so had Lizzie. He had to have their courage and dare to trust them a little, too.

"If you need or want anything, you know how to reach us, Lizzie." Elle stepped back.

Nick stepped closer, squatted so that he and Lizzie saw eye to eye. "I'm going to hope with my whole heart your mom comes back, Lizzie."

"You are?"

He'd surprised her. Surprised himself, too. He nodded. "Right now, you're hurt and sad and confused. I was, too. But whenever you feel that way, I want you to remember something."

"What?"

"How brave you were to tell us about you and your mom. That took a lot of courage."

"You're the official secret keepers."

"Yes, we are. But trusting even us was still really hard for you to do." He sucked in a breath, praying the right words would come with it. "One day, you're going to be brave like that again, Lizzie. Lots of days, really. Until then, just relax and live your life, okay? I'm going to hope about your mom enough for us both."

"Seriously?"

He nodded. "Hey, a pinky swear is nothing to mess around with. I meant it."

She gave him a shaky smile. "Thanks, Nick."

He winked at her, then turned solemn. "No matter what, you can always call me for anything. Day or night—it doesn't matter. About anything. You said you wouldn't abandon me or leave me. Well, I'm not abandoning or leaving you, either."

She lunged at him, hugged him hard.

Stiff and unaccustomed to hugging, he forced himself to relax and hug her back.

Elle watched Nick, a man she knew had put his life on the line countless times, a man who ran into danger when others fled from it, and tears blurred her eyes then slipped down her cheeks. She knew what this whole conversation and commitment to Lizzie had cost him.

"You'd better get going, half-pint." He let her go and rose to his feet. "Kelly's waiting for you to help give Susan a bath."

She nodded. "Don't worry about me." She looked into his eyes, studied them. "I'm good here."

She'd better be great here. If he weren't convinced Ben and Kelly would move mountains to keep her safe, there's no way he could let her stay.

Lizzie walked inside and shut the door.

An empty feeling seized his stomach. Nick blew out a sharp breath, then turned to Elle. Silently, they walked toward the car.

Three steps from it on the driveway, Elle paused and kissed Nick, letting him see without words all the emotions she was feeling. When she could, she lifted her head and gazed into his eyes. "Sometimes you awe me, Nick Sloan."

"Awe?" He wouldn't have said it, but it fit what she did to him. "That's a little over the top, don't you think?"

"It's honest." She opened the car door. "You awed me the first time I saw you and every time after that—until you left without saying good-bye. But you awed me again, being like you were with Lizzie. I know that was difficult for you, opening up to her like that, but you did it."

"Why does that awe you?" He didn't understand. "Knowing what it's like to be an outsider and alone, how could I not try to settle her fears?"

"Because you don't trust. Period." Elle paused at the car door. "Yet you saw her pain and you trusted Lizzie. It's incredibly hard for you to let anyone get close to you, Nick. Actually, I doubt anyone really has gotten close to you until today. You did it—for her. And there isn't a doubt in my mind that you'll be there for Lizzie until you die of old age."

He motioned for Elle to get into the car. "Unless I'm wrong, she won't need me."

Elle waited until he walked around the front-end of the car and got inside. When he settled on the seat and clicked his seat belt, she asked, "What do you mean by that?"

"Nothing."

Clammed up. Again. "Tell me." She hiked a shoulder. "I trust you. Do you think maybe one day you'll trust me just a little?"

He looked over at her. "Why is my trust important to you?"

Good question. Elle had an excellent answer to it, of course, not that he was ready to hear it. He wasn't. But, honestly, for a brilliant man, he could be slower than sludge where feelings and emotions were concerned. "You're important to me," she said. "Therefore, your trust is important to me. That's how it works."

"Don't." He cranked the engine. "Let someone better... someone not damaged be important to you. I'm no good for you, Elle."

"I disagree." She frowned and held it so he wouldn't miss it. "You don't get to dictate what matters most to me, by the way. Just pointing that out because you don't seem to know it."

He frowned back, also holding it so she wouldn't miss it. "Listen to what I'm telling you. I can't ever love anyone or anything. I won't."

Laughter bubbled in her throat. "Didn't you hear Lizzie, Nick? If you're still breathing, you can love."

"Maybe you can, but I can't. I won't—"

"Won't what?"

He hesitated, then clearly changed what he was about to say. "What's it going to take to make you understand?"

"I do understand. You're—"

"It's not fear," he told her, then stared out through the windshield for a long moment, as if gathering his thoughts. "It's me," he said. "Elle, you look at the world and everything in it and see goodness and beauty. I see the dark side because that's all I know. It's all I've ever known." He paused, then added, "Your parents denied you their name, but privately, they were there for you. It's different. In my whole life, nobody stayed. They never stay."

"I will."

"No you won't." He lifted a hand. "You're a big star. You've got a career, money, everything anyone could want. You don't need me. If I'd paid attention to you like you wanted from the start, we wouldn't even be having this conversation."

"If you'd give me a chance—"

"For .what?" he asked with more heat than he'd intended. "You'll go just like everyone else."

"Look at me, Nick." He stopped the car at the end of the driveway and stared at her, waiting. "You think you've got me all figured out, but you don't. You might have been right about other people in your life. Likely you've been right a lot to feel so certain of this. But you're wrong about me." She took a moment, searched his eyes, and let him see the honesty in her own. "If you asked me, I'd stay with you forever."

She didn't waver. She had to seem sincere, to convince him she believed what she was saying. It should be easy; she was sincere and did believe every word. But his expression tightening proved he thought he knew better. That she'd say it, break her word, and leave him heartbroken and alone all over again.

"I think you mean that."

"I do."

"Then it's just a temporary thing." He stopped and shook his head. "Look, I can't do this, Elle. I won't ask you to stay. Not today or tomorrow or six months from now. It's just not going to happen."

"You're telling me what I think again." She sighed. "You really need to work on that, Nick."

His snapped his jaw shut. "I don't want to talk about this any more. That's it. Discussion, over. I've said all I have to say about this." He turned onto the street and took off.

She stared out the window, tempted to let it go, but something inside her pushed. Hard. She swerved her gaze over to him, kept her voice firm. "I know you're a brave man, but about this, you're a coward."

His temper flared. "Excuse me?"

"This is all fear talking, not you. You have feelings for me, Nick. I see it in your eyes when you don't know I'm watching. I know you do—so don't even bother trying to lie to me about it."

"I don't lie."

"Good."

"Now, that's it," he warned her, a hard bite in his tone. "No more on this. The end."

"The end." Elle had to work at it hard to not dispute him. He'd come a long way today. No sense in getting his back up even more and making her work harder. He could say what he wanted. This wasn't the end. He hadn't disputed her about having feelings for her. If he had none, he would have fired back a hasty and firm denial. One sputtered so quickly her head would be swimming. But he hadn't even hinted at a denial. Not even hinted. Her lips curved into a smile.

A smile that infuriated Nick. "I tell you there is no us and never will be and you smile?" He grunted. "I was right. You're moving on already."

"Don't be melodramatic." She broadened her smile. "I'm just happy."

"Happy?" He looked totally baffled. "That's an unusual reaction, considering the circumstances."

"Not at all." She lifted her chin. "Even under the best circumstances, relationships have no guarantees. You can vow, promise, or even swear, but things can happen that you can't control and *poof!*"

"That kind of nightmare makes you happy?" He looked at her as if she'd lost her mind.

"Of course not. It's not a nightmare, it's just reality, and sometimes it bites."

"I don't get it."

He genuinely didn't get it. Tender, she softened her tone. "You're with me now, Nick. I'm happy because you're with me now."

That confused him even more. He was mystified, puzzled, and totally lost—it riddled his face, clouded his eyes, and, not knowing what to do with it, he did what Nick always did. He shut down and changed the subject. "You want to be happy? Be happy when Joe cracks that code."

Elle felt more satisfaction than she had since writing *New Dawn*. But now wasn't the time to savor it. Later, alone and away from Nick's watchful gaze. Then, she'd celebrate this small victory.

He hadn't denied he had feelings for her or that he was with her now.

Elle looked away. It was progress. Small. Maybe tiny progress, but progress. She'd take it. At this rate, another twenty years or so and she just might crack *his* code.

Dabbing at his sweaty brow with a precisely folded handkerchief, Paul Johnson pulled into the roadside park and left the engine running. He hated Florida. He hated the heat and he really hated the humidity. But in all of Florida, the place he most hated was this forsaken village. He'd been humiliated here; tried, convicted, and sent to prison for a murder he committed but he should have walked away from—and would have walked away from had he committed it anywhere else. Anywhere the Shadow Watchers were not. They had been responsible for his disgrace, and for the position he found himself in now.

Nothing enslaved a man like owing one for your freedom.

Moonlight slanted across the hood of his car. He pulled out his phone to report developments.

"Jackal."

"Yes, sir, it's Johnson." He scanned the parking lot to be sure no one was anywhere near his vehicle.

"What is it, Paul?"

"Lizzie is out of the nest. She's moved in with Ben and Kelly Brandt."

"At Three Gables?"

"Yes, sir." Jackal wouldn't like that. Benjamin Brandt took security seriously. Nothing moved anywhere near Three Gables without his security team being fully aware of it. That was another lesson Paul had learned the hard way.

"Perfect."

Surprise skittered up Paul's back, settled in his neck. "You're not upset?"

"Of course not. Things are proceeding nicely."

The truth smacked Johnson between the eyes. "Phoenix is sealing her fate."

"Indeed, she is."

Jackal's ambitious streak ran even deeper than Johnson realized. He'd held his tongue when Sage or Hawk appointed her to head the mission, and then Jackal had allowed Phoenix to jeopardize it unheeded, to set herself up to fail. The honchos would eliminate her...and Jackal would move up the ranks and into her slot. *Beyond extremely ambitious.*

"Anything else to brief?"

Should he tell Jackal that Phoenix headed to Panama City? Anticipating his *what for* and not having an in-depth and accurate answer to give the man just yet, Johnson opted not to mention it. "No, sir. Not at this time."

"Keep me posted."

"Yes, sir." Johnson ended the call and dropped his phone onto the center console, again weighing the risks of grabbing a coffee at Ruby's, and warning himself to never again underestimate the devious nature of Jackal.

CHAPTER THIRTEEN

Sunday, June 7ᵗʰ, 7:30 p.m.
The Lodge

Nick walked into the Lodge with Elle on his heels.

He couldn't get that smile of hers out of his head. Her joy at him telling her he could never love her, and that's exactly what it had been—*joy*. The only way that smile made sense was if she hadn't believed him, but that wasn't possible. She knew him, knew he talked straight, and Elle was far too sagacious for that kind of delusion. *What then?*

He thought and thought and came up with only one thing. Maybe she believed that he believed what he was saying, but she didn't believe what he was saying was really true. That would be logical, he supposed. Reasonable, too. Wrong, of course, but logical and reasonable.

Joe stood in the kitchen, putting ice into a glass. Sam and Tim were seated at the bar.

"You're frowning, buddy," Sam said. "Lizzie have a rough time settling in at Ben's?"

"No, she didn't. She's a brave kid." Nick gave her what for him was high praise. She'd earned it…and more.

"When you left, did she cry?"

Sam sure worried about Lizzie and tears. Why was that? Girls cried a lot, didn't they? "No, she didn't," Nick admitted. He omitted he'd had to fight himself to leave her. How she'd wormed her way into his heart like this, he had no idea. Yeah, they had a lot in common, but he'd had a lot in common with others before and he hadn't gotten emotionally wired into their situations. Lizzie, though, was different. Wise as an old woman in her own way. "We discussed all this before we went, Sam. If you'd dropped her off, she'd likely have bawled herself to sleep for a week. She's invested in you. But me leaving her was fine. Not a problem."

Elle frowned at him. "That's not exactly the whole story," she told the other men. "Lizzie was worried, but Nick reassured her."

"Yeah?" Sam sounded as skeptical as Joe and Tim looked.

Elle answered. "He told her he'd be there for her forever, and she could call any of you day or night for anything. She was okay after that."

Joe filled his glass with tea. "Sounds like you did good, bro."

Nick shrugged in Joe's general direction. "I didn't want her to feel like we'd jumped at the first chance to dump her. That's all."

A look passed between Joe and Sam that told Nick all he needed to know. Sam had briefed Joe and Tim about Nick's family situation. What it had been like when they'd dumped him. Wisely, none of them said a word about it.

"One called." Joe drained his glass. The ice clinked against the glass. "He wants you to call him back as soon as you can."

Nick nodded. "Any luck on the encryption?"

"Not yet." Joe swung his gaze to Elle. "Your dad's very good at coding. I hit a trap every move. How about some lemonade?"

"I'd prefer iced-tea with a little lemonade in it." She slid onto a stool. "Don't push the traps. He gets testy when that happens."

"Testy how?" Joe asked, filling her glass with ice, splashing lemonade in and then filling it with tea.

"Think self-destruct." She took the glass he offered. "Totally and completely irretrievable."

"Handy information to know." Joe cut a sharp glance at Sam. "The kind we should have had earlier."

"I just thought of it." She shrugged. "Remember, I've been away from all this for a good while."

Joe didn't push her on it. Neither did anyone else. Nick wasn't buying it. She had a reason for not telling them. What it was, only she knew, but he didn't like it—and he would insist she explain herself…just not right now. When the time was right, then he'd push and push hard.

Tense, he stepped out onto the porch and then down to the lawn and phoned Omega One. "It's me," Nick said, hearing the muffle of voices from inside. "This a good time?"

"Perfect," he said. "In the middle of a five-mile run."

"Secure line?"

"Absolutely."

"We haven't yet cracked the code on Elle's ring."

"We haven't either, but I have reason to believe Elle's father encoded the ring with plans to a new non-invasive system designed to neutralize troops on the battlefield, on airplanes, ships—places bullets can't fire without causing a lot of damage."

Who'd reported that? Nick didn't bother to ask. "Have you verified he's working on such a system?"

"Actually, Elle was working on it, before she left the company. He took over the project when she got the European tour. Guess he figured she'd be back to finish it herself until then."

Her getting that tour likely had convinced him she was gone from the lab for good. Nick borrowed a phrase from her. "Reality bites."

"Yeah. Guess he didn't want to accept it." He grunted. "I had no idea she was behind the system. I mean, the woman's a star. But the honchos are glad he's picked it up. If the development is successful, the system will be an amazing asset for us in the field. It doesn't shoot, makes no noise, and it doesn't kill."

It didn't do a lot, which left Nick wondering. "What does it do?"

"Totally neutralizes human targets for up to twelve hours."

Did it knock them out or what? "How?"

"I have no idea, but they're conscious and communicative, I'm told." One sighed. "I also have no idea how Phoenix got the ring from our agents to return it to Elle. That's caused quite a stir here with Hip Pocket."

He was raging, to be sure. Nick knows how that happened, but Hip Pocket leaving him and One flying in the dark... he and his insiders could figure it out for themselves. It wasn't complicated. Phoenix is CIA *and* undercover. She infiltrated NINA years ago, and has been an essential asset at checking NINA's missions. It's never been beneficial to remove her. Omega One clearly wasn't in that need to know loop, which seemed rather odd to Nick, but since he wasn't, Nick couldn't bring One into it. "How did Phoenix know where to find us?" The Lodge was supposed to be off radar.

"We suspect she followed you with a simple tracking device. On the car or attached to something she gave to one of you—"

"The flower. She gave Elle a begonia." He'd known it was a warning and hadn't bothered to check it for a device. *Stupid mistake. Totally his fault.*

"That's it, then." One sounded happy to have at least that mystery solved. He didn't like unanswered questions any more than Nick. "To tell you the truth, I've been wondering whose side Phoenix was on."

"Been there, done that."

"Any conclusions?"

"Yes." He didn't dare to say anymore.

"Okay, then," One said. Clearly, he'd spun it out and decided if Nick didn't trust her, he'd be reporting it. Which meant Nick did trust her. "That opens a whole new can of worms, then."

"What kind of worms?"

"From what I've gathered—strictly under the table and outside official channels—NINA really wants that system. If their honchos know she had it and gave it back to Elle..."

"Bad news, definitely." NINA would kill Phoenix for that action... normally. But this situation wasn't normal. "I think they got boxed into a corner, and they do know what she did." *Traps. Self-destruct.* "I think they tried and failed to crack the code and feared destroying it by trying further."

"Destroying it?" One sounded worried. "What do you mean?"

Nick hadn't been through all of Howell's work, but he had been over his company with a fine-toothed comb. The man had kept some things deliberately out of Nick's reach—like the fact that Elle was an engineer and held multiple patents of her own on a variety of systems she'd developed. But he'd seen enough to draw some conclusions, and with her disclosures, to do so with confidence. "Howell—Elle's father—permits dabbling with his encryptions, but only to a point. Hit it and cross the line, and you're trapped. The encoded message self-destructs."

"You're kidding me. He can do that?"

"He has done it on many of his systems."

"So you think NINA hit the wall and knew it couldn't go any further," One said, then paused. "That would make them snatching Howell logical. They need him to open the encrypted vault."

NINA had snatched Howell? Nick's stomach caved. Elle knew the man she'd spoken to hadn't been her father. Did he dare tell Elle this? Could he not tell her? Maybe she already knew it—like she knew about the encrypted traps. "Possible," he told One. "NINA knows Elle's stashed here, and it was initially her system." He followed what could be their line of thinking. "So they return the ring, hoping Elle can break the code?"

"Maybe. Her design, after all. She might have coded it."

"I don't think so." Nick felt sure of it. She felt responsible for Jaycee and Lizzie. If the mother and daughter were in jeopardy, and the mother was, and Elle knew something that could help her, she'd do it. "But if she didn't code it, then Howell did. Makes sense if NINA knows Elle is Glen Howell's daughter and Howell knows they tried to kidnap Elle to coerce him into giving them the plans for the system in exchange for NINA leaving Elle alone."

"Not NINA," One said. "But Howell and his wife are sequestered. That's confirmed."

Their side, not NINA, had sequestered Howell. Surprise streaked up Nick's back. "Where?"

"That I don't know. I'm not in the loop, remember?" His bitterness about that came through in his voice. "My source says the CIA snagged and stashed them at the Pentagon's request before NINA could. NINA was reportedly on the verge of getting them so we interdicted. That was passed on to me inadvertently by a trusted source at the Pentagon who had no idea Hip Pocket had removed me from the need-to-know loop."

"Just like with Elle."

"Yes," One admitted. "Source says we can't risk Howell giving NINA the plans. He'll do anything for Elle. Anything. And NINA knows it."

So they'd nixed Howell from having the opportunity and from being forced to make the decision. Where the CIA would hold the Howells baffled Nick. They normally functioned only outside the US.

Which meant, for them to drop into this at all, the implications of that system had to be broad, deep, and potential consequences, beyond staggering.

What NINA could and would do with the technology sent chills through Nick. And what they'd do to the Howells to make them give them technology did worse. Frightened him in ways he didn't think he could be frightened. For them, and for Elle.

"Gotta go. Keep me posted."

Nick heard the line go dead. Elle's parents sequestered. Elle being set up as a pawn...

Even in his darkest thoughts, he'd hated few things in life. But he hated NINA as much as he... no. No, he didn't love. Not now, not ever.

His chest hollowed. He sat down on the steps. What was he going to do about Elle? Was she being straight with them? She hadn't been totally open, but not knowing who to trust could explain that. Except she'd said she did trust him.

He rubbed at his eyes, weary of the emotional turmoil she

aroused in him. He didn't live his life on emotion. Turmoil, yes. It was a constant companion. But emotions? No way.

At least, not until now.

The door opened and Joe walked out onto the Lodge's front porch.

Nick sat on the steps, waited for Joe to settle on the step beside him. "Was the call with One that bad?"

"I'm not hiding out. I'm thinking."

"Ah, figured that."

"Elle knew and held out on us."

"Yeah, she did." Joe snapped up a little twig and studied it in the light from the porch. "Question is, why didn't she tell us?"

Nick glanced over. "No idea...yet."

"Mmm." Joe worried his lip with his teeth. "Well, don't convict her just yet. I think if she figured it made any difference, she'd have spilled it out right up front. She's just that kind of woman."

She was. Nick agreed with that. "She irritates the fire out of me, Joe." Nick sank into a dark place.

"Because...?"

Nick growled his frustration, stared off into the distant trees. "She's smart and sunny. How can someone in danger be like that?"

"She wasn't so sunny coming out of that box. Sam's jaw is still sore from where she laid one on him."

Frowning over at Joe, Nick said, "You know what I'm saying. She knows she's in trouble. She knows the man on the phone posing as her father wasn't actually him. She's worried sick about where her dad really is, but she still comes across calm and controlled and..."

"Sunny?" Joe suggested.

"Yeah."

Joe stretched out his leg, crooked his knee and leaned his arm on it. "She seems pretty normal to me. Strong, but then she'd have to be, growing up like she did. Maybe she seems so sunny because you're so... not sunny?"

It was a kind shot at diplomacy. "I know I'm grouchy and cynical, okay? I see the worst in everyone and in everything. That's a perk in my job—and it's worked for me in my life, too."

"Worked how?"

Seeing no judgment only curiosity, Nick answered. "I'm not disappointed all the time."

"So you see the worst in people to avoid being disappointed by them?"

"Yeah." Didn't everyone, to some extent? From Joe's expression, apparently not. "When you expect nothing and get it, you're not surprised."

"I hear a but in there."

There was one. "But Elle... I hear her laugh and it lifts my spirits. She makes me want to see...something else."

"Something not the worst?"

"Yeah. Exactly." Nick stroked his thigh, thinking. "It's crazy, I know. Sets me up for a fall I know will come."

"How can you know that?"

Nick pivoted and looked Joe right in the eye. "Because a fall always comes."

Joe held his silence. Laughter from inside filtered through the wall to the porch. Elle, Sam and Tim joking about something, and guitar music.

Nick slid a questioning look at Joe.

"Sam brought it. He thought Elle might like to play some."

Nick nodded.

"You know, bro, I think she's getting to you."

He'd rather cut out his tongue than admit it—even to himself, but truth was truth. "She is—and I hate it."

"You shouldn't." Joe waited until Nick looked at him to go on. "Her getting to you isn't a bad thing. She's a good woman."

"She lied."

"Maybe, or maybe she was just waiting to figure out the lay of the land to decide the time was right to tell. She deserves the benefit of doubt on that. The woman was snatched off the street in another country, you know?"

"I know." He'd had nightmares about it even when awake. NINA could have gotten her. That didn't bear thinking about. "But she'll leave me, Joe. Everyone always leaves."

"We didn't."

"That's different."

"Maybe she's different, too." Joe stood up. "Look, she could leave or not. But if she did, at least you'd have time with her now. You could enjoy that, Nick. And we'd all love to see you enjoy something other than solving risky missions. You're overdue for some happiness, man."

They knew, and they cared. He would love a little happiness. The kind he saw in Mark and Lisa and Tim and Mandy. The kind Elle just seemed to have inside with no one around. Problem was, Nick didn't trust happiness. And if he did let himself feel it, how would he go back to life without it? He'd made peace with his lot in life a long time ago. The day his father moved and hid to avoid seeing him.

Joe clasped his shoulder. "Give her a shot, Nick. It's fair. You do fair."

"I don't think I'm that brave," Nick looked up at him from the step.

"Nobody's that brave. Relationships don't come with guarantees. They come with leaps of faith. Sometimes you splat, sometimes you soar—and there's no telling which it's going to be." Joe smiled, slow and steady. "But here's the thing, bro. Either way, what a ride!"

The door opened and Elle walked out, Sam's guitar in her hand. "You finished with your business?"

"We are," Nick said, confused and a mass of nerves inside.

"Great." She came out and sat down in the porch swing. "It's wonderful out here. Love this swing." She settled in. "If it won't bother you, I'd like to play a little. I've missed it."

"Awesome. I need to grab my tea." Joe stepped inside and nearly collided with Sam and Tim. "Stay," he told them.

Elle chuckled. "It's okay. Everyone can come out."

"Shortly. You go ahead," Joe said. "I need to brief them."

Setting him up. That's what Joe was doing. *Brief them?* Yeah, right. Nick frowned.

Elle strummed the guitar and began singing a tender ballad. *I Still Miss You.*

It'd been a big hit for her. Double platinum. Beautiful song, even if the longing in her voice did rip at his heart. Envy flooded him. Envy and the same resentment he felt every time he'd heard the song.

But up close and personal, it sounded… different. Even more beautiful. And that catch in her tone… unique and haunting. She was getting to him all right. More like, she'd gotten to him. What did he do with all these feelings?

He had no idea.

When she finished, she stilled. "Did you like it, Nick?"

"Yes. Since the first time I heard it," he said, avoiding her eyes. "But I do have a question." He paused, waiting for her permission to ask. When she gave it, he dared. "What man put that kind of longing in your voice?" He shouldn't have asked. Would having someone specific to be angry at do any good? It never had.

She didn't seem to take offense. Actually, she seemed pleased by the question. That mystified him.

Her skirt hem rustled. She left the swing and joined him on the step. "You did."

His heartbeat doubled. "Excuse me?"

"I wrote that song for you, Nick. Right after you left without saying goodbye."

He'd never even considered it could be about him. The possibility hadn't once crossed his mind. "Me leaving… that really hurt you, didn't it?" He understood that now in a way he hadn't before. The song in context had made it clear.

"It did hurt—for a long time." She smiled. "I know you thought I was a kid with a crush, but I wasn't. I've never really been a kid." She set the guitar aside, propped it against a porch post. "We're not so different, you and me."

"Your parents loved you."

"Yes, but they denied me, too. I thought they were ashamed."

She smiled. "Like you, I'm an outsider. Always have been and always will be."

"Still, it's different. You know they're there."

"My father is there—when he can be. My mother, not so much. But I don't want to talk about them." She reached for his hand, clasped their fingers. "I cared about you then and I care about you now. For me, nothing's changed except our geography. We're sharing a location right now. But I could be on the moon and it wouldn't change the way I feel about you at all. If after this moment, I never saw you again in my life, that wouldn't change anything either." She smoothed her skirt. "I know that doesn't sit well with you, but it's the truth, so you're going to have to just get used to it. It is what it is, as you so often say."

He squeezed her hand. "I want to believe you, Elle." Man, was that the understatement of the year. He craved believing her. "But I have so little to lose. I—I don't dare."

"It's okay." She stroked his jaw, then borrowed a phrase he'd spoken to Lizzie. "I'll believe enough for both of us until you do dare. No pressure, no rush."

What did he say to that?

Before he could decide, Elle leaned over and kissed his lips.

Phoenix left the pawn shop, a front for one of NINA's other projects, and heard her phone. She retrieved it from her handbag and paused near a tiny park sandwiched in between two buildings. Light from the busy street streamed in, reflected off the stone pathway and blended with the twinkling lights hung in the trees. *Jackal.* She depressed the icon and answered. "Yes?"

"How are you, my dear?"

"I'm fine. You?"

"Busy," he said, his voice warm and tender.

"Enjoying the chalet?" Switzerland was wonderful any time of year, but that home was particularly lovely in summer. "Caring for my flowers?"

"Of course. I enjoy being here more when you're here."

"Thank you for that." She smiled. This man had always had the ability to turn her mind to mush. And he'd been doing so for thirty years. "Everything going well?"

"Johnson phoned again. I'm afraid he's becoming a problem."

"What's he reporting?"

"He isn't reporting that you're in Panama City for an unknown reason."

"He doesn't know why I'm here. Is there more?" She didn't understand the reason for Jackal's concern or the purpose of the call, not that there had to be one. He phoned at least once a day. Often more.

"The problem is he's elevated the nature of his concern. From mild mentions to straight-up warnings."

That wasn't good news. "Warnings about what?"

"Your allegiance."

"I see." Anger churned in her stomach and blended with a healthy amount of fear. Since their daughter Mandy had married Tim, a former Shadow Watcher, NINA's scrutiny on Phoenix had doubled. If it knew Jackal was Mandy's father, neither of them would be alive. But more attention—warnings or mentions outside the chain of command—was the last thing she needed. Hawk likely would shut her down, and that created a host of challenges for her and Jackal within NINA and the CIA. "Thanks for alerting me, darling. I'll rein Johnson in."

"Do it quickly," Jackal suggested. "He's close to becoming a major liability we don't want or need."

"I agree, he's walking a thin line."

"Thinner than you think," Jackal warned. "He recommended I issue an advisory on you to Hawk or Sage."

Alarmed, she slumped back against the building. "You're kidding me."

"I never kid when it comes to your safety or that of our daughter."

"Where is Johnson now?"

"Reconnaissance."

Her stomach sank. "I know he didn't go back to the Lodge after I expressly ordered him not to do it."

"No, the fool spotted Jaycee and intercepted her at Three Gables. Stunning that Mark Taylor allowed it."

"He didn't. He's away on his honeymoon." Phoenix rushed to her car, certain Ben Brandt was having fits at Three Gables. "Is Jaycee alive?"

"Last Johnson reported, yes. Now? Who knows?"

"Where's he taking her? Did he say?"

"To join the Howells," Jackal told her. "I don't know where they are. I wish I did."

Thankfully, Phoenix knew exactly where the Howells had been stashed. The question was, how did Johnson know their location? He had to have followed her. How else could he possibly know? "I'm on my way."

"Drive safely, but do hurry," Jackal said, his concern escalating to worry he didn't bother to hide. "All the reasons we wanted Johnson working for us also make him formidably dangerous—especially right now."

Easy to control. Too afraid of elimination to cross them. But if he'd gone rogue and bypassed her to warn Hawk about her...? *Very dangerous.* "Knowing Johnson," she told Jackal, "he could convince himself that killing Jaycee Cole is helping you, and going over my head and straight to Hawk is saving you."

"That's my worst fear. I tried to convince him both Hawk and Sage would be pleased. That things were developing exactly as planned, but I'm not sure he bought it."

Her worst fear, too. "I know you did your best to be convincing." The CIA wouldn't be able to protect them. No one would. Hawk would act against them both without lifting a brow. He'd put out kill orders, assign them priority one with his authorization code, and there's no way in the world either Jackal or she could survive.

Reaching her car, Phoenix ended the call and quickly sped toward the village. She and Jackal had one chance: to stop Johnson before he destroyed them and those they were trying to protect.

CHAPTER FOURTEEN

Sunday, June 7th, 11:00 p.m.
The Lodge

THE PHONE RANG.

Nick rolled over in bed and glanced at the clock. Eleven? Couldn't be good news. He lifted the receiver. "Yeah."

"Nick, it's me, Lizzie." Her voice cracked.

"Lizzie?" He sat straight up. "What's the matter, half-pint?" She sounded terrified.

"The bad man was here. He—he took my mom." A sob escaped her throat. "He left a flower. A poppy."

Her *mom*? Surprised streaked through him. "Where are you?"

"Three Gables."

"And your mom was there?"

"Yes. Nick, you have to come. He took her, and I don't know where."

"On my way, Lizzie. Are you safe?"

"Yes. He locked me in the bedroom."

"He who?" Nick stood on his feet and grabbed his pants, started stuffing his feet into them.

"The man from the wreck."

Johnson. Wow, this was bad news. Johnson had snagged Jaycee for NINA—from Three Gables? Nick blamed himself. He should have eliminated Johnson when he'd had the chance. "But you're safe now?"

"Yes, we were in Ben's cottage. I crawled out the window and came back in through the door to get to the phone."

"Do Ben and Kelly know what happened?"

"I—I called you."

Trusted him. "I'm on my way, half-pint."

"Bring Sam."

"I will."

"And Elle."

"All right." He jerked on a shirt. "Lizzie, you call Ben and tell him what happened. He'll stay with you until we get there."

She screamed.

Nick's heart stopped, then thudded. "Lizzie! Lizzie!"

"I—it's okay. It's Ben. He scared me, but it's okay. He's here."

"Put him on the phone, honey." Nick slid into his shoes and opened his bedroom door, nearly colliding with Sam, Joe, and Elle.

"What's wrong, bud?" Sam asked, his hair poking out in every direction.

"It's Lizzie." Nick held up a finger. "Ben?"

"Yeah, Nick," Ben said. "Jaycee's been snatched. She's been hiding out in my cottage. Don't come unglued at me. That was another little detail my wife failed to mention until now."

That explained why they hadn't been able to pick up a trail on her. "Is Lizzie hurt?"

"No, she's physically fine. But she's freaking out at her mom being taken."

"We both know she has just cause. You keep her safe, Ben. We're on our way." Nick hung up, then looked at the others.

"Someone hurt Lizzie?" Sam's voice thundered.

"No, she's fine. Apparently, Jaycee's been hiding out in one of Ben's cottages."

"He held out on us?" Joe asked.

"Kelly failed to tell him," Nick said. "Lizzie's safe. Unhurt. She says the man who took her mom was the man from the wreck."

"Johnson." Sam shook. "I should've—"

"I know, but we didn't," Nick cut in. "He left a poppy."

Elle frowned. "What does it mean, Nick?"

Oh, how he hated to answer her. "Death."

Elle dragged in a sharp breath. "Let's go."

"Lizzie wants us all there."

"She needs us all there," Joe said. "To feel safe."

"Maybe," Elle said. "But she wants us all there to find her mother."

"Elle's right." Nick started moving toward the door. "Let's go."

"You and Elle head out," Sam motioned. "I'm going to gather some tools. Meet you there shortly."

"I'll ride with Sam," Joe said. "Go, go. Lizzie's got to be frantic."

Nick and Elle ran to Nick's car and took off. As soon as he turned onto the main road, he dialed Omega One. "I have an emergency. You take it to Hip Pocket. He gives you any flak, you go straight to the White House. Where is Glen and Daris Howell? I need to know, and I need to know now."

"What's going on, Nick?"

"NINA just snatched Jaycee Cole." He went on to share details with One, then added, "Either the Howells aren't where they were sequestered anymore, or Jaycee and NINA are now with them."

"I don't follow."

"Elle was a decoy. NINA's using Jaycee. Her car was bombed, she lost her job, her identity, everything. Howell will do anything for her—so will Elle. You can bet NINA's playing that angle."

"I don't know where they were sequestered. All I know is it was a remote location."

"Find out—fast. Otherwise, Jaycee and the Howells are as good as dead."

Nick hung up.

"I need that." Elle grabbed his phone. "How do I get Sam?"

"Sam? What for?"

"Just give me the number, Nick."

"Speed dial two."

She pressed the buttons. "Sam," she said. "You still at the Lodge?"

His voice carried to Nick. "Just leaving."

"Go back. I want you to get to the lab and try this code."

"Now?"

"Right now," Elle said. "I'm not sure it'll work. I could be wrong. But if I'm right, it'll give us a location."

"Location of what, Elle?"

"My parents and Jaycee."

"Walking in now," Sam said, sounding a little winded from the stairs. "Go."

"Seven, one, fourteen, twenty-nine, thirty-two."

"That it?" He harrumphed. "It can't be that simple, Elle."

"Read it back to me." Elle snatched a tissue from the box on the console, then swiped at her nose.

He did, then she added, "Immediately after entering the numbers, key in Purple People-Eater. Cap just the first letters, and add the hyphen between People and Eater."

"You're joking, right?"

"I'd never joke about this."

"That's the code word—between you and your dad?"

"Yes."

"Try it, Sam. And when you get what you get, start on the third line of code. Read it backwards and skip every third letter in every third word. Then drop the first, third, and last. My guess is what's left is going to be coordinates that will take us to him."

"Not the system?"

"Not on a piece of jewelry. Everything but the third line exactly as I just described to you is just stuff and traps." Elle risked a glance at Nick. "He always told me if no one else could find him, he'd find a way to let me know where he was. I think this is it."

"Will do. I'll call you back."

Elle hung up the phone and passed it back to Nick.

"You knew this and didn't tell me?"

"I had no idea it was related."

"After your father went missing, you knew something was up. You should have told me then, Elle."

"If I'd realized he was involved in all this, I would have. I didn't —and I needed time."

"Time? For what?" He pulled up to the gate at Three Gables. It swung open and he drove thru.

"Us. I wanted a chance for us, Nick."

"Unbelievable." He stopped at the head of the driveway and shut off the engine. Ben and Lizzie walked toward him. He slung open the car door and got out.

Lizzie ran and launched herself into his arms.

"Hey. Hey, it's okay, half-pint." He gently patted her shoulder. "We've already got people looking for your mom."

"Sam?"

"Yes," Nick said. "And Joe and Tim." No doubt they'd already called him in.

Ben nodded at Elle and motioned for her to take Lizzie aside.

"Lizzie." Elle held out her arms.

Lizzie told Nick to put her down. "Elle needs a hug."

"She does." Elle smiled and hugged Lizzie, and led her a few feet away.

Ben sighed. "Sorry about this. Kelly told me after you and Elle left. I thought she'd be safe here."

"What happened?"

"Not sure. Security's still working it out."

"Security better thank their stars Mark's not here. He'd have them for a snack."

"He would," Ben agreed. "Still might. Should I give Jeff Meyer a call?"

Local police. "No, we have other resources on this."

"Anything I can do?"

"Keep Lizzie safe."

Ben nodded. "We didn't realize. Now, we do. It won't happen again."

Nick nodded. "Elle?"

She walked back over with Lizzie. Nick squatted, so they were eye to eye. "We're going to go help Sam and Joe and Tim. You stay with Ben and Kelly."

"Are you going to find my mom, Nick?" Her eyes were earnest and deeply worried.

He wished he could offer her certainty, but he couldn't. "We're going to do everything we can. I promise. Everything."

She nodded. "Be careful."

"We will. You try not to worry."

"I'm going to be brave."

"Again," Elle said. "You crawled out of that window to get to a phone. That was brave."

"It was," Nick agreed.

"I was scared."

"Of course, you were scared," Nick told her. "It's sensible to be scared when you're in danger. And you're a very sensible girl, Lizzie. Sam says so all the time."

"He does?"

Nick nodded. "We're going now. But we'll be in touch."

"Anything you find out—"

"We'll call you."

She nodded and watched them get back in the car and head down the driveway.

They hadn't gone twenty yards down the street when Sam phoned.

"Yeah?" Nick answered.

"Elle was right. It's a location. A little airport in the north end of the county."

"The one the former mayor's wife owned?" Nick asked, stunned.

"Yeah," Sam said. "She apparently sold it to Glen and Daris Howell about two years ago."

"About the time Jaycee and Lizzie moved to the village."

"Yeah. We figure that's why he bought it—for her. A safe shelter, should she need one."

Nick had driven by that little grass-strip airport many times, taking Nora to visit her friend's grave. "There's nothing on that land, Sam."

"It's not on it, it's under it."

"A bunker?"

"Yes," Sam said, verifying it. "Omega One just sent art and there's a green sedan on the far end of the property right now.

"Drone or satellite?"

"Drone."

Quicker, more efficient, and something he could do without Hip Pocket coming unglued.

"Tim's on his way. Joe and I are out the door in five. Need heavier tools. Ten minutes behind you."

Nick hung up and briefed Elle, finishing with, "I'm going to drop you off at Crossroads Crisis Center. You can stay there with Peggy and the staff until we resolve this."

"You will not." Elle added a shake of her head and grabbed another tissue. "These are my parents, Nick. After what I've already cost Jaycee, I will not be tucked safely aside while she and they are in jeopardy. I'm going with you."

"Can you even shoot a gun?"

"You tell me. You trained me, remember?"

He had. And she'd done well. "All right, but you will hang back —and I mean it, Elle."

"Fine."

"And for the record, the only reason I'm agreeing to this is because it's faster than arguing with you. We don't have the time to lose—not if NINA is already there with Jaycee."

"What are you saying?"

"Johnson is sadistic and he enjoys being cruel. He'll do whatever to get what he wants from your father. If not to your mother, definitely to Jaycee."

"You mean torture?"

"I mean torture—anything he must to get what NINA wants."

"Hurry, Nick." Elle squeezed her eyes shut.

"Pray hard enough for me, too," he said, pressing down hard on the gas pedal. "And when we get there, you do exactly what I tell you to do."

"I will."

She wouldn't. But right now, he had enough on his plate to worry about. He needed the lie.

Phoenix spotted Johnson's green sedan and parked beyond it, snapped her fanny-pack into place, grabbed her binoculars, and then disabled the interior lights in her car. There wasn't anything in the area but trees, weeds, and wildlife. Mosquitoes buzzed, thick as thieves in the air.

She made her way through the brush, sliding her feet, hoping to avoid snakes. Rattlers and cotton-mouths were common in this area. So were coyotes, black bears, and panthers. She popped her spare magazine into the double pouch at her waist, then checked her Glock. Locked and loaded, she grabbed her phone from her light-weight red jacket's pocket and dialed Jackal.

"Is he there?" he said, on answering the phone.

"Yes, he is." She let Jackal hear her irritation. "I spotted his car. Prepared to approach the bunker now."

"He called here about ten minutes ago."

Why hadn't Jackal reported that to her?

"I knew you'd be phoning, so I waited."

Reasonable, but still irritating. "What did he want?"

"To report you. He's beyond concerned and is now suspicious. He said you met a contact in Panama City—"

Surprise rippled through her. "He knows the pawn shop is a drop site?"

"He suspects it's something. He doesn't know what, but he wanted me to report it to Hawk right away. He figures Hawk knows the place."

"Why would he figure that?" Had Johnson erroneously tagged Hawk as CIA and not her? Maybe he'd pegged Jackal as a double agent? Her worry meter shot up.

"Because I told him nothing moves within a hundred miles of the village without Hawk knowing about it. I thought that'd be enough to convince Johnson a report wasn't necessary."

"Logical. Did he accept it?"

"I think so."

"I'd feel better about this if you were more confident. Johnson's gone rogue, snatching Jaycee, Jackal. Are you sure he isn't taking orders from Hawk and us?"

"He's been taking orders from Hawk, Sage and us. But snatching Jaycee… he did that on his own. I'm sure of it."

"How? I mean, how do you know?"

"Mostly because you and I are still breathing."

"Valid point." If Hawk or Sage suspected either of them, they'd be in a warehouse somewhere being tortured or else shot dead. She gave Jackal that one. "We can't let him go straight to Hawk."

"There's no sign that he has—"

"Yet."

"Yet, and I can't really explain his death, so we're between a rock and the hard place with him."

"For the moment, anyway."

"For the moment, but you're right. We can't let him go around us. Any evidence he is or might, and he has to go. We have no choice."

All these years and the upper crust of NINA hadn't come close to questioning her loyalty or Jackal's. Then the CIA honchos intervene and force Johnson in, then he puts them both in jeopardy. "The CIA won't like it."

"I agree," Jackal said. "But better them than our daughter. She would not be happy to bury either of us, much less both of us."

An image of Mandy standing alone at her grave flashed through Phoenix's mind. Her throat went tight. "We've been through that once with her already, if you recall. She was devastated."

"I remember." His voice shuddered. "When this is over, I want you to think about something."

"What?" Phoenix unzipped her fanny-pack and fingered the loose flower petals filling it. The light scent stirred, filling her nose.

"We need to retire."

"What?" People like them didn't get to retire. The only way out of NINA was to die.

"I said, we need to retire."

"Your timing isn't great for talking crazy." He knew better. She sprinkled flower petals along her path.

"We've managed to stay alive this long. If we can do that, we can figure out a way to retire."

She stared through the woods to the clearing ahead. "I don't know how to live like that, Jackal." This double life was all she'd known for decades. She barely remembered a time when duplicity didn't rule her life.

"Me, either," he admitted. "But what an adventure it will be to find out."

Twigs snapped. She strained to see through the tree branches. Moonlight slivered and fanned the clearing. Something rustled straight ahead, at the entrance to the bunker. Phoenix stilled, lifted her binoculars to her eyes and spotted Johnson, walking behind Jaycee, obviously with his gun pointed at her back. "I have to go," Phoenix whispered.

"Be careful."

"Always."

CHAPTER FIFTEEN

Monday, June 8ᵗʰ, 1:10 a.m.
The Bunker

NICK AND ELLE WAITED IN THE WOODS. "HOW ARE THE GUYS going to find us?" Elle kept her voice soft and low, worked to keep her fear buried deep inside.

"Sam's more bloodhound than man. He'll lead them to us."

Elle swatted at a mosquito, determined not to complain once about anything. Nick didn't want her out here; no sense in reminding him. He'd insist she return to the car.

Not knowing what was happening would drive her over the edge. Not that she would go, but taking precautions avoided an argument neither of them had the time to engage in right now. She wanted Nick focused on her parents and Jaycee. She wanted to focus on her parents and Jaycee.

All the way up here, she'd prayed harder than for anything in her life, trying to keep her imagination in check and horrific images out of her head. She asked repeatedly for intervention and that they all emerge from this collision with NINA alive.

Considering the organization's reputation and what she knew

from experience they'd done in the past, the odds were admittedly against it, but she had to hope, and she dared to believe.

Something moved close behind them. Elle whipped around and saw Sam, Joe and Tim. Relief washed through her, yet the tension remained. Their faces were smeared with greasepaint, their clothes dark, and every one of them stood armed to the teeth.

"You're here. Good." Nick quickly briefed them on the lay of the land. "Clearing is twenty yards due north."

"Bunker is on the far side, eleven o'clock when standing squared to the road," Sam said. "Consider this a refresher, Nick. I briefed them on the way in."

"Great." Nick looked pleased. "I'm taking point. Tim you run command and control from here. Sam head east and cover the back side of the bunker entrance."

"I'll take west," Joe said. "You planning to flush them?"

"Yeah."

"Any sign they're still alive?" Tim asked, shooting Elle an uneasy look.

"None." Nick avoided glancing her way. Swatted at a mosquito.

"Uh-oh." Necks snapped toward Sam. He hiked his chin toward the clearing. It was filling with smoke. "Either we're too late or someone's beat us to it, trying to get them out of there."

"Let's move." Nick shot Elle a hard look. "Do exactly what Tim tells you to do. No matter what you see, you stay with Tim. Got it?"

"Be careful, Nick." Their gazes clashed. She wanted to say more, to offer him something to let him know how much he meant to her. But she didn't dare. Nothing would send him running as quickly as knowing she cared, and nothing would mess with his mind as much as knowing she cared. Now just wasn't the time. She wanted him to live.

Holding his gaze, she added nothing. Her heart thudded against her ribs, her pulse pounded in her temples, and her throat constricted. Silently, she watched Nick and Sam and Joe disappear into the woods and split off from each other.

A warning fired through her and a little mewl escaped.

"They'll be careful," Tim assured her, clearly sensing her fear. "They've done this kind of thing a million times."

Cold and bitter, her anger at knowing that clawed through her. "Yes, but not against these people."

He didn't dispute her, and the warning inside her deepened to a droned beat. This effort would be extremely difficult and it would not go as planned. How she knew it, she had no idea, but she was certain of it. Certain they could all become NINA victims.

Fear crackled through her like an errant live-wire whipped by storm-driven wind. "Tell me they'll be okay, Tim." Elle hated the pleading she heard in her voice but she seemed helpless to infuse it with any strength.

Sympathy flickered through his eyes. "Don't ask me to lie. I won't do it. But I do hope they will be okay. They've faced daunting odds many times." He hiked a shoulder. "That's the best I can give you."

There was an odd tremor in his voice. Had he sensed a warning, too? It wouldn't surprise her. People accustomed to intense, dangerous situations had honed instincts.

An explosion split the air.

It shook the ground under her feet, rocked the east half of the clearing. Leaves blasted from the trees, swirled to the ground, twigs snapping, branches crackling. The dry brush burst into flames and quickly spread, fanning out over the land.

Tim instinctively grabbed her arm. "You need to get back to the car. Can you find it?"

"I'm not leaving the rest of you here." Some movement—a person running through the flames—caught her eye. "Look! Over there. Two o'clock."

"I see him." Tim flipped down his lip mic. "Nick? Joe? Sam? Report in."

Elle stared at the zigzagging figure hustling through the woods at the edge of the clearing. Pivoting and ducking to avoid the spreading fire. "Who is that?"

Tim frowned. "Not sure."

"One of ours?"

"Not wearing a red jacket."

Elle gauged the person by size and the way he or she moved. The facts became obvious. "It's a woman. I can't see her face, but I'm sure she's a woman."

"No need to see her face," Tim muttered, then spoke into his lip mic. "Phoenix is departing the fix."

Phoenix. He recognized her? And the others knew her also? If she wasn't one of theirs, then she had to be with NINA. Elle strained to keep an eye on her through the trees. She slipped from the firelight into deep shadows and then disappeared in the darkness. *Lost her.*

Tim listened for a moment, then spoke again. "No, no confirmation on whether or not she was solo. Doubtful, though. She's consistently been teamed with Johnson. He's likely in the bunker or the immediate area, so stay alert."

"I'm going in." Nick's voice sounded enough that Elle heard it.

"Negative." Tim mumbled a curse. "Without a breathing apparatus, you won't make it. The smoke's too thick."

"They're in there. I have to try."

"I said no, Nick. Stand down."

"I'm going. My responsibility."

That declaration spurred a flurry of exchanges between the other men and Nick. Them opposing Nick going in, him letting them know he was doing it anyway.

Terror sank in and Elle's whole body clenched as if caught in a seizure. Nick was risking his life to save her parents and Jaycee. Doing it, knowing odds were against him making it out. She stepped closer to Tim, took control of his mic. "Don't do it, Nick." No one would expect him to sacrifice himself. No one. She couldn't lose him and all of them. "Listen to your team."

"Get her off this frequency."

Tim frowned at her, reclaimed his mic. "Control resumed."

She looked up into Tim's eyes, let him see her emotional turmoil. "He's going to do it."

"Yes."

Tim couldn't stop Nick and neither could she, which left her one choice. "I'm going to help him." She took a step.

Tim snagged her arm, jerked her back. He gently squeezed her arm. "Stay put, Elle. I don't have time to fight them and Nick and you." Tim shot her a warning look. "I'd rather not restrain you, but if I have to, I will. Your call."

Only a fool wouldn't believe him. "But I might be able to do... something."

"Getting yourself killed won't save them or Nick."

She looked at Tim, struggling to check her emotions. "Okay. Okay." Tim meant every word he'd said, and his words left her feeling drenched in water cold as ice. She nodded her acceptance, and fisted her hands at her sides, willing herself to stand in place and not to run to the bunker.

On a secure phone, Tim relayed developments to Omega One. "Nick's moving into the bunker to attempt a rescue. The smoke's way too thick for it, One."

Tense minutes crept by. Minutes in which Elle silently screamed, begged and bargained and frantically searched the patches between the flames stretching into the trees, licking at the branches and beyond into night sky.

"We need to pull back," Tim said. "Fire's getting too close."

"Wait. Look. I see something..." Shadows appeared in the smoke. "Look!" Her parents stumbled toward them, disheveled and grimy, hands bound behind him, breathing hard and faces contorted in fear and angst. "Hurry!" her father urged her mother, his voice husky and scratchy. "This way!"

Elle rushed forward through a break in the thorny brush and intercepted them, hugging her father and then her mother. *Oh, thank you. Thank you for letting them live!* "Are you okay?"

"Elle? What are you—"

"Later, Dad." She tugged at his sleeve. "Come on." She led them back to Tim, eager to get them away from the heat of the fire and its encroaching flames.

"You shouldn't be here," he said, tromping behind her. "I can't believe Nick brought you—"

"He had no choice." Elle cut him off. "Your shirt looks scorched. Are you sure you're all right?" Her mother hadn't said a word, but she didn't look much worse for the trauma. A little stressed, her forehead puckered and her jaw tight. "Mom?"

"We will be fine, Elle."

"As soon as we get these restraints off." Her dad half turned so Elle could reach his hands, bound at the small of his back. "You?"

"I'm fine. Worried to death about the guys, but fine." She looked to Tim. "I need something to cut them loose." Their hands were wrapped with silver duct-tape. "Where's Jaycee?"

"I don't know." Her father looked at Tim, nodded his thanks for the rescue then briefed him on specifics. "The same man who snatched us brought her into the bunker before the fire broke out. I figure she must have started it. That's the last we saw of her."

Tim retrieved a knife from a pocket at his knee. "How long ago?" Tim sliced through the duct tape.

"Twenty minutes before the fire," her mother said, nodding her thanks to Tim for cutting her hands loose. "No more than that."

Tim focused on the two of them. "About five ten, black hair, thick glasses."

Her mom nodded, and her dad said, "Sounds like him."

Tim adjusted his lip mic. "Confirmed that Johnson is on site. He interdicted the Howells and Jaycee." Tim then repeated that transmission into his secure phone, informing Omega One.

"Did you see Nick?" Elle asked her parents, her gaze darting between the two of them. She'd tried and failed to sound calm.

"Our feet were bound and our eyes taped closed. We didn't see much," her mom said.

"Daris, be honest about him. You owe the man your life."

"I just didn't want her mistaking gratitude—"

"What you want is insignificant. It's what *she* wants that matters." Her dad frowned at her mother, then told Elle, "One minute there was nothing. The next, someone snatched the tape off our eyes and the gags out of our mouths. It was Nick, Elle. He saved us. He cut our feet loose and pointed us to you."

Relief washed through Elle. Unfortunately, more fear chased it.

The fire was ballooning, but moving away from them. In the distance, a huge tree fell, landing on the ground with a loud clap rivaling thunder. "Why didn't he come out with you?"

Her dad sucked in a sharp breath, coughed and sputtered. "He went back for Jaycee."

Nick was alive and moving. She had to hold onto that. Determined to think no deeper, to not imagine him struggling for air in the smoke-filled bunker, Elle asked her dad, "Who was holding you?"

"The man I described to him," he said, referencing Tim. "I don't know him, but I suspect—"

"NINA," Elle finished for him, sensing his reluctance to mention the organization. It had to be Phoenix's partner, Johnson. Had to be. "It's okay to speak freely, Dad. These guys have clearance. They know more than we do."

Her mother grunted. "The man's a sadistic troll. He knocked out my masseuse and manhandled me. At the bunker, he battered your poor father, but he told him nothing."

"The system?" she asked her dad.

He nodded.

Johnson was still after the system specs. Elle grimaced. Tim asked her dad a series of questions. Rapid-fire, they exchanged information. Tim relayed it to the guys and then reported it to Omega One.

Elle heard the discussion, every concise word, but it all faded into the background, growing weaker and weaker as if from far, far away. The fire captured her, thoughts of Nick and what he could be going through. She squinted to see through the flames, scanning and searching for some sign of him—any sign of him. But she spotted nothing.

Panic rolled through her, swelled and expanded. The smoke grew thicker, the flames inching higher up the trees, growling and hissing and setting more and more branches aglow. "Anything?" she asked Tim.

"Sam and Joe are in constant contact," he said.

"Nick?"

"Not yet." He nodded to her parents. "I need you to get them to the car. They need water, Elle. There's a cooler full of it in the trunk."

She didn't move. If she left, Nick might not make it back. She couldn't leave.

"They're dehydrated." Tim studied her, saw or sensed the stark fear and raw emotion eating her alive. His voice gentled. "Elle, look at me. Into my eyes." When she did, he went on. "You've got to take care of them. Get them to the car and stay put. As soon as Nick comes back, we'll meet you there." She hesitated. Tim cocked his head, then told her, "Sam says for you to be sensible and do what needs doing."

"Sensible." The phrase he often used with Lizzie. "He's threatening to tell—"

"Half-pint, yes." Tim grunted. "Go on now, Elle."

Elle reacted outwardly, doing what he asked of her. She ushered her parents away from the fire and clearing, the bunker, when everything in her wanted to turn and flee to it, to Nick. "The road is this way," she told her parents. "I know you're weary, but we need to move quickly. I have to get back for Jaycee and Nick."

"Elle, no. He said for you to stay with us. The fire—"

"No, dad. I don't take the safe way and leave them in harm's way. I did that once." She had, with Jaycee. "I can't do that again and live with myself. I won't."

He stilled, stared at her, and seeing her resolve, finally relented. "Where is the car?" he asked.

She pointed. "About four minutes, straight ahead."

"You go back, then. I'll get us to the car."

"Get the water out of the trunk, but wait for us away from the car. Stay within spotting distance." Elle brushed his sleeve. "There's a woman out here in a red jacket. I believe she's with NINA. Avoid her."

He nodded. "You stay away from that bunker. If there's a way out, Nick will find it. He'll take care of Jaycee. I need you safe."

"I will." Elle gave him the words because he needed them, then turned and ran back toward where she'd left Tim. Safe? How could she think about safe? Was Nick safe? Jaycee? Elle didn't want to look at Lizzie and tell her she'd been safe while Lizzie's mother and Nick were... Oh, she couldn't think this way. She couldn't!

Counting oaks, she made her way back to Tim.

He was stunned to see her. "I told you to stay with your parents."

Elle ignored him. "The fire seems to have exploded."

"It has. We're pulling back." Tim guided her back toward the road. "Sam's worried. So is Joe."

These men didn't worry needlessly or easily. They'd endured too much. "No word from Nick?"

"Not since he went in." Tim's concern was evident. "But it might be inconvenient to talk at the moment. That happens. Depends on where Johnson is now. We have to trust Nick."

"Time's up, bro." Joe's voice came through the receiver dangling from Tim's collar. "Sam's with me. We're going in after him."

"No," Tim said, putting weight and authority in his tone. "If he fell to the smoke, you and Sam will, too."

"You're cracking up, buddy." Sam's voice, now. "Can't hear you."

"Sam! Joe!" Tim elevated his voice. "Do not enter that bunker. That's a direct... order."

Elle squeezed Tim's shirt sleeve. When he looked at her, she added, "They're not in the military anymore. I think they're beyond direct orders."

"Yeah. Dumb jerks."

Tim's voice wasn't steady. He hadn't meant that, of course. Everyone on the PSC team was brilliant in his own way, but when worried, we all grab on to anything we can to cope.

"We got him!" Joe's voice broke the tense silence.

"Both of 'em!" Sam added. "We're coming out."

The anxious dam in Elle burst and tears flowed down her face.

Tim's expression said it all. Relief, sweet and sure. He blew out a sharp breath. "What about Johnson?"

"No sign of him."

"We're going to have to hike around," Joe said. "Nick's maxed on smoke. Need to get him to fresh air."

Elle's nerves sizzled, like they were riding too close to her skin. "But he's okay, right?"

She motioned for Tim to ask, and he complied. "Elle wants to know if he's okay."

A long hesitation set in, then finally Joe answered. "He's a little singed—hair and, I think, hands. But otherwise, he looks okay. Well, as okay as he ever looks."

That bit of sarcasm told Elle exactly what she needed to know. If Nick were in jeopardy now, Joe would be all business. Not a speck of sarcasm in him. She smiled at Tim, let out a nervous laugh. "He's okay." She silently repeated that to herself three more times, hoping it would sink in and her heart rate would slow down and the bottomless pit of fear in her stomach would settle.

"Yeah." Tim smiled back at her. "Yeah. Let's move out."

They made their way back to the car. About twenty feet to the left of it, her parents squatted low to the ground in a clump of palmettos. Three empty water bottles lay on the ground beside them.

"Seen anyone?" Tim asked them.

"Not a soul." Her dad shot them a negative nod. "Glad to see you, though. The fire looks like it's bursting at the seams."

"It is," Tim said. "I take it this is your land."

Elle's dad nodded. "Jaycee needed a safe place in case of an emergency." He grunted. "Turns out it wasn't so safe after all."

"We're nearly there, Tim."

On hearing Sam's voice, Elle scanned the woods for signs of them. She saw Joe first. He was out front, carrying a limp Jaycee. "Is she…"

"Drugged," Tim told her.

"Where's Nick?" She tiptoed, craned her neck looking for him.

"Behind Sam. Ten yards back."

Elle saw the wisdom in them making their way back separately but she'd expressed all the restraint she had left. She glanced at Tim. "I'm going to Nick."

He nodded. "Go."

"She lasted a lot longer than I expected," her dad told Tim.

"It took effort," Tim admitted. "She's got discipline."

"She's terrified she'll get someone else killed."

"That, too," Tim said. "If I live to be a hundred, I'll never forget the fear for Nick etched in her face."

"She still loves him." Elle's dad looked at her mom. "You will not interfere with them again."

"But, Glen, I—"

"I said, not again, Daris. Never again."

Elle rushed into a thicket and spotted Sam and Nick making their way toward her. "Nick!" He was covered in ash. His hair standing straight up and bits of brush clinging to every surface on him. His hands were wrapped in wet towels. Another was slung around his neck. Where had they gotten wet towels? What kind of facility was this bunker? She stopped on a narrow path before him. "You okay?"

"Yeah." He looked down at her, his expression grim. "I could use some water, but otherwise, I'm okay."

"How bad are your hands?"

"Not burned. The towels were preventative. I breathed through them."

"Sensible. Course, not lingering would have been more sensible."

A twinkle lit in his eyes. "Course."

"Spar later." Sam kept walking. "Johnson and Phoenix are out here somewhere."

Unable to restrain herself another second, Elle rushed Nick and hugged him hard. "You scared me to death. I wish you wouldn't do that, Nick."

He lifted an arm and circled her back. "It wasn't intentional." He trembled.

She shook. "I know." She pressed a kiss to his neck and then another, and then looked up into his face. "Thank you for getting my parents and Jaycee out of there."

The look in his eyes remained distant. "You're welcome."

"And thank you for not dying." Her voice dropped, her tone deadpan flat. "I would have been so ticked off at you if you'd gotten yourself killed, Nick."

That distant look faded and softened and a lovely twinkle lit in the depths of his eyes. "You know, I knew that. I thought, if you mess up and die, she's never going to forgive you. She'll spend her eternity nagging you about it."

Elle sent him a flat look. "You're right. I would."

He released her and started walking back toward the others.

She couldn't yet not touch him. She clasped his arm. "So why did you linger so long?"

"I couldn't see. Too much smoke."

"How did you find Jaycee and get out then?"

"It was the oddest thing," he said, his puzzlement tinting his tone. "There were flower petals the whole way. It was like following a gingerbread trail. Well, not whole flowers. Peony petals. I just followed them."

Phoenix? Had to be her. She might work for NINA but she'd interceded for them—again. First the warning at the wedding, then bringing back the ring, and now this. "What do peonies mean?" Every flower meant something, and it didn't occur to Elle that Nick wouldn't know.

"Protection."

"We saw Phoenix leave," Elle admitted. "She protected you."

"Yeah, she did."

"Why would she do that?" Elle called the question, not at all sure if Nick would answer.

"I can't read her mind, but she surely has her reasons."

Cagy and vague and either he didn't want to disclose the answer to Elle's question or he couldn't disclose it. Either way was fine by her. He was safe. She linked their arms. "Don't scare me like that again, Nick. My heart can't take it."

He frowned, and held his silence.

Elle tried not to let that reaction drag her down. He was alive and well. She was grateful—and dead certain he was nowhere near ready to take down the walls he'd built around his heart to protect himself from being hurt.

They walked on and joined the others.

Already he was pushing her away, keeping himself and his emotions apart and separate, and there seemed nothing Elle could do to stop it. The man was so terrified of being abandoned that he left first.

What he needed was to face his fear… and maybe he would. She let that notion ramble through her mind, studied it, tested it. Maybe that would crumble the walls…

She thought about it from different angles and concluded the outcome could go either way. *Something* would surely crumble. But would it be his walls or her heart?

The first time he'd left, she'd been a wreck for months, nursing a broken heart with no hope of it ever mending. It'd been so hard to pull herself together. To go through that again…?

Things were different. Now, she wasn't a young woman in love for the first time in her life. She was a grown woman still in love with her first love. That made the potential for getting hurt even greater.

Big risks.

Huge risks. Question was, did she dare take them?

CHAPTER SIXTEEN

Monday, June 8th, 5:30 a.m.
The Lodge

IN THE KITCHEN OF THE LODGE, EVERYONE WAS TALKING AT once. The Howells, Jaycee, Tim, Joe, Sam, and Elle was making breakfast. Wounds had been tended, showers taken and fresh clothes put on. Elle had inspected Nick's hands herself, touched his hair at least a dozen times, and issued orders to Joe and Sam like a seasoned drill instructor. Everyone ate and ate and still she kept cooking. Even Sam had refused to eat more.

"What's up with that?" Joe asked Nick, keeping his voice low so no one else heard.

"The cooking?" When Joe nodded, Nick shrugged. "Adrenalin. Some people drink to get it down. Elle walks or cooks."

"She's not getting far enough away from you to walk unless you go with her. So I guess she'll be at the stove a while, then."

"Not too long." Nick's emotions were all over the place on this. "Her dad's got a chopper coming to pick them up."

"She's leaving?" Surprise rippled through Joe's voice. It was mirrored on his face.

Nick's heart hollowed. "Yeah." He shrugged. "It's over. Of course, she's leaving."

Joe took a bite of blueberry muffin and slowly chewed. "And you're all right with that?"

He was but he wasn't. Torn, Nick paused. He loved being around her. Seeing the world through her eyes. She always found something good to see and say, and she worried about him. He'd never had anyone worry about him before. He watched her at the stove. The way she coerced Sam into eating one more pancake. The tilt of her head, the way she danced foot to foot, the flipper in her hand slicing through the air, and the truth hit him like a sledge. He loved her.

Impossible.

No. No way.

He shunned the truth, closed his heart. No way was he going to allow himself to love her or anyone. Not now. Not ever. She'd break his heart. He'd had enough of that. His whole life, everyone he'd ever loved, ever even cared about had left him. And he'd had to deal with the fallout, the isolation and devastation, alone.

"I asked if you're all right with that, bro." Joe searched Nick's eyes.

"Yeah, sure. I've had a lifetime of training at this." Nick shrugged again. "That's what people do. They leave."

The door from the porch swung open and Lizzie ran into the kitchen. "Mama! Mama!"

Seated at the bar, Jaycee stood up and rushed to embrace her daughter. "Lizzie…"

A lump settled in Nick's throat.

"And sometimes, bro, they come back." Joe whispered low and deep.

"They do," Nick conceded. "Just not in my world."

Watching the reunion, Sam sniffed. "That's what I'm talking about."

Elle brushed at an errant tear. "Sometimes life's just good, Sam."

Nick frowned. And sometimes it was anything but… like two hours from now when Elle would walk out of his life for good.

By eleven o'clock, Jaycee and Lizzie had returned with Ben and Kelly and their baby, Susan, to the cottage at Three Gables, Tim had phoned his wife, Mandy, and filed his reports with Omega One. Joe and Sam were working contacts, including Jeff Meyer, trying to pick up a trail on Johnson. According to the fire department, he wasn't in the bunker and the fire on the property was contained.

Elle had tried several times to talk with Nick, but he'd kept his distance. No matter what was said, she would leave with her parents, and he'd prefer she not leave knowing he'd done the dumbest thing he'd ever done in his life. It was cold comfort but, hey, he'd take whatever comfort he could get.

Just after noon, the chopper arrived and landed on the helipad between the Lodge and lake. Nick joined the other guys and walked the Howells and Elle to it.

"Thanks, Nick." Glen Howell extended his hand.

Nick shook it, then nodded at Elle's mother. She remained distant and removed, but he didn't take it personally. For her, that was normal. He supposed, being a mother, she held him responsible for breaking her daughter's heart four years ago. She'd warned Elle he wouldn't fit in with them or their life. If she knew he'd fallen for Elle and now he'd be nursing a broken heart, would she laugh now and feel vindicated?

A moot point since she'd never know.

Elle stood before him, her jaw trembling. "Thank you, Nick. For everything." She tiptoed and kissed him good-bye, then backed away. "Just so you know, I'll always care enough for both of us. I did four years ago, and I do now. I always will." She licked at her lips, as if her mouth had suddenly gone dry. "If you ever want me, you know where to find me."

Don't believe it. Don't. Her mother is right. You have nothing to offer her. "Good-bye, Elle."

Pain flashed through her eyes; his words stung her. She stared at him a long second, then got onto the chopper and sat down.

Minutes later, Nick watched the bird go airborne, Elle's face at the window, her fingers touching the glass.

Joe stepped up to him. "Why didn't you ask her to stay? She would have stayed, Nick."

"Dang right." Sam grunted.

"I agree," Tim added. "That woman loves you."

"It would just have delayed the inevitable." Nick sighed, watched the chopper soar over the trees and out of sight. "Sooner or later, she would have left."

"Fool." Sam dragged a hand through his hair.

Tim looked away. "I hate to say it, but Sam's right, Nick."

"Sam is not right."

"He is," Tim insisted. "I saw her face. When you were in the bunker, I saw the fear in her. It was the kind that only runs shotgun when someone you love is in danger. She was terrified for you. And when she heard you were okay... man, I've never seen anyone so relieved."

"She got to you." Nick glared at Tim.

"I saw what I saw—and I never want to see that kind of fear in her again."

"Yeah, buddy." Sam nodded. "Like it or not, we all saw what we saw."

"Too late, Tim." Joe cocked his head. "I already did see it again."

The others turned to look at Joe, including Nick. "When?"

"When she turned her back on you to get in the chopper." Joe paused, then added, "That woman loves you and she was terrified she was never going to see you again." Joe lifted his hands. "You should have risked it, bro."

Anger churned in Nick. "You don't understand. None of you understand."

"We all understand, Nick, Tim argued. "You've been walked out on all your life. You don't want to love her and for her to walk out on you, too."

"Exactly." Certainty he'd done the right thing pounded through Nick. "You tell me to risk it, but you wouldn't want it, either. None of you would."

Sam nodded. "I get it."

Finally, one of them using their brain. "Yeah?"

"Sure, buddy." Sam looked Nick right in the eye. "You risk your life all the time. No big deal. But your heart? You ain't risking your heart."

"It's not that I won't," Nick shot back. "I can't." He paused, collected himself. "I know how this ends, okay? I've been there. It's always the same."

"Interesting." Tim crossed his arms.

"What?" Nick glared at Tim.

"You've got only a little to risk. I get that, too." Tim hiked a shoulder. "But what if this time, it isn't the same?"

Joe shrugged. "That's a fair question, bro."

Sam mimicked Tim. "Yeah, what if this time it ain't? It's possible."

Nick grimaced. "Anything different is *not* possible. I told you, it always ends the same way."

"It is possible. Ain't nothing ever exactly the same," Sam insisted. "It could happen."

An emotional volcano, Nick erupted. "You're all nuts. Get out of my face." Nick stormed off, down toward the water. "You're dead from the neck up—the whole crazy bunch of you."

Sam started after him.

Tim blocked him, pulled Sam back. "Let him go."

"So he can sulk?"

"No, Sam," Joe answered, a twinkle in his tone. "So he can think."

Nick heard every word…and played stone deaf. The last thing he wanted to do was think. Especially about Elle.

She was gone.

Forever, this time.

His heart squeezed tight in his chest. What kind of life would he have without her?

The kind he'd always had.
Alone.
Empty.
Abandoned…

CHAPTER SEVENTEEN

Wednesday, June 10th, 8:30 p.m.
The Lodge

DARKNESS SETTLED IN OVER THE LAKE.

Nick hauled himself to his feet, sighed, then left the grassy bank and walked back to the Lodge. Unfortunately, the persistent thoughts of Elle he'd hoped to leave at the lake followed him.

Resigned to living with them for a long time, he opened the door, and stilled in surprise. The guys were still there. Even Tim.

"Good, you're back," Sam said from the stove. "Dinner's almost ready."

Smelled like chicken. Joe sprawled on one end of the long, curved sofa, watching a baseball game on the TV. "Why are you all still here?" Nick wasn't opposed, he just didn't expect them to hang around. The reports had been filed. The case, for them, was closed.

"I was hungry," Sam said. "You've got better food than I do at the apartment, so I figured I'd cook here."

Nick looked at Joe. "Beth's in Atlanta," he said. "No reason to go."

True, but not the truth. "And you?" Nick asked Tim.

"Mandy's cooking. I figured I'd better get something solid in my stomach before eating it. You know, to coat my stomach for protection."

"Probably a good idea," Nick said. He sat down on the opposite end of the sofa. They were there for him. For moral support. He wasn't sure how to react to it; he'd never really had personal moral support before because he'd never before revealed anything personal. He liked his skeletons in the closet where they belonged. And yet there was something… comforting… about the guys hanging around for him. Something… reassuring… He didn't have to face this alone…

That stirred emotions in him he didn't want stirred. Already he couldn't see his way forward. He'd cobbled together a life that worked for him, but Elle blasted that to kingdom come. What did he have now? Shattered pieces. What did a man do with shattered pieces?

Elle was gone. For good. He couldn't go back to the darkness and undo knowing what light was like. Somehow he had to find his way back to existing. But how? In uncharted territory, he had no idea.

After living with her around, he didn't know how to forget what it had been like. What she had been like. How could a man who had never mattered to anyone ever forget mattering most to a woman like Elle? How could he forget finally, for the first time in his adult life, feeling loved?

"Let's eat," Sam said.

The guys grabbed plates and filled them buffet-style at the breakfast bar. Avoiding the table, they all went to the sofa and parked before the ballgame.

Nick went through the motions of eating, hoping he could swallow.

"Wow, Sam," Tim said. "This is actually good."

He nodded. "Elle—" he stopped himself, then finished "—told me how to make it."

Silence fell.

She'd touched them all, in one way or another. Nick lifted his chin toward the TV and asked about the game. "Who are we for?"

Joe responded. "Cards."

"They winning?" Nick asked.

"Um, yeah," Joe finally said, proving he'd been distracted, too.

They watched the game with only the sounds of forks scraping plates competing with the announcer's calls.

The game ended.

Joe and Sam gathered plates and hit the kitchen to load the dishwasher. When Joe had put the leftovers in the fridge, he and Sam returned to the sofa. No one was talking.

Before long, Sam signaled Joe, who signaled Tim. He frowned his irritation that the task had fallen to him, but took it on. "So, Nick, you wallowed in it long enough yet to come to your senses?"

Whatever Nick had been expecting, that wasn't it. "Excuse me?"

"Come on, Nick," Sam cut in. "You know what he's asking."

"I don't." He really didn't. "Wallowed in what?"

Joe chimed in, lifting an impatient hand. "The elephant in the room nobody's talking about, bro."

Sam grunted. "Not that Elle looks or acts like an elephant."

"He knows what I mean, Sam."

"I know, Joe. I'm just saying."

Nick started to shut down. To back away and shut down. But the guys weren't expressing idle curiosity, they were concerned. It showed in their body language. If Sam's cap got pulled any lower, its brim would rest on his nose. "I can't get her off my mind," Nick admitted.

"Well, all right." Sam slapped his thigh.

Joe glared Sam silent, then prodded Nick. "Because...?"

Nick shrugged, shook himself, then dragged an annoyed hand through his hair. "I don't know." He hesitated, let it grow to a pause, hoping someone would fill the silence. No one did. He took in a deep breath and admitted aloud something he'd sworn all his life never to feel. "Because I love her." He spat, glared at Joe. "Satisfied? You got what you wanted. I love her."

Joe gentled his voice. "Admitting it is a start."

"Slow start," Sam amended. "But I get why, okay? In your case, slow is good. Probably just a shade shy of a miracle."

Miracle? More like, crazy. But knowing his history gave Sam, all of them, perspective and, because of it, they were giving him a pass. He didn't need a pass from them, but he kind of liked having one. Nick nodded. "It doesn't change anything. It's just, now I know."

"Know you love her?"

Nick looked at Joe. "Know what I am missing."

"I get what you're saying, but I don't get what you mean." Joe turned halfway toward Nick. "If you love her and she loves you, why don't you just go get her, bro?"

"Now, we're talking." Sam shoved his ball cap back on his head, spun it around until the brim rested on his neck.

"It's not that easy. Oh, we could grab her. That'd be easy enough. But then what?" Nick laced his hands, his elbows parked on his knees. "Love. What is it, anyway? Maybe she doesn't love me, she just thinks she does. Put it to the test, and…"

"She'll leave like everyone else?"

Nick's gaze locked with Joe's. He nodded. "I don't know if I can take her leaving me twice. To tell you the truth, I'm not sure I'll recover from this time."

"She would have stayed," Joe said. "I saw, okay?"

"Joe's right. You didn't ask her to stay." Sam reminded him. "I got ten says she'd have parked it right here."

"And I'd have made her miserable." Nick worried his lower lip. "You guys know me. I'm too broken. It'd fall apart and—"

"You're not," Tim said. "Look at Mandy and me. You can't get any more broken than we were, but we glued ourselves together, and it all worked out."

"The women in your life don't leave and not come back."

"You don't know that Elle wouldn't come back. It's worth the risk, Nick. For this woman, for you, it's worth the risk." Tim leaned forward. "I've seen a lot of women in love in my life, and—"

"Not as many as Joe."

"True, Sam. But I have seen enough of them to know what I'm

looking at." Tim swung his gaze back to Nick. "Elle Bostwick loves you, Nick. It's that simple."

"I need to think." Nick stood up, headed for the door, and grabbed the knob.

"Nick?"

He paused, looked back over his shoulder at Joe, and lifted his chin. "Yeah?"

"Courage isn't out there. It's inside you. That's all this is about, bro—in case you aren't knowing."

He was right. Nick risked his life routinely. He knew how to do that. How to handle the ups and downs and the emotions. He knew how to be intense and to decompress. But this—he had no idea how to deal with this. "I don't know if I have that kind of courage." He opened the door then stepped outside.

On the edge of the porch, he nearly tripped over a bunch of flowers. Bending down, he lifted it. Sage.

Opening the door, he called out to the guys. "Phoenix has been here."

They joined him on the porch. Sam asked, "Why are you sure Phoenix and not Johnson left the sage?"

Nick glanced Sam's way. "Who else has been sending us messages using flowers? Technically, it's an herb and not a flower, but…"

"Good point." Tim added, "But Johnson left a poppy with Lizzie."

"Framing Phoenix for snatching Jaycee." Nick lifted a hand. "Warning us… that's Phoenix."

"So what does sage mean?" Joe asked. "Someone wise?"

"Doubtful."

"I think she's worried," Nick said. To come back to the Lodge, she had to be deeply worried. "She helped us with Jaycee and the Howells. That could put her in jeopardy."

"Yeah, NINA won't be happy with her."

"If they know it, they'll kill her," Tim said. "Unless they sanctioned it."

That obviously worried him, but it should. His mother-in-law being eliminated. Mandy would be devastated at losing her mother. "Phoenix could bury it, if Johnson doesn't out her." Nick frowned. "What's his status?"

"Gone aground," Sam said. "One's got alerts out worldwide. Nothing yet."

"It's getting old, him giving us the slip—or being cut loose by our side. I wish we could get and keep him out of commission." Joe voiced what Nick had been thinking.

"Be glad he didn't take out Olivia and the Howells and Jaycee." Nick reminded them. "The man's a psychopath."

"I'm grateful," Tim said. "He'll bury himself underground for at least a year. He always does."

"So you think Olivia's safe?" Nick asked.

"I think Jackal will do all he can to help her be safe, and that means the two of them will handle Hawk."

Her NINA boss could be problematic. "We better let Omega One know about this visit."

"I agree, Nick," Tim said.

"Why would Jackal cover for Olivia with Hawk?" Sam frowned. "I know he's Mandy's father, but—"

"Why wouldn't he?" Tim cut in. "He and Phoenix have been together over thirty years."

"Jackal and Liv are married?" Sam asked. "How did I not know this?"

"We didn't exactly announce it," Nick reminded Tim.

"Does anyone else know it? Our side or NINA's?" Sam asked.

"It's not been disclosed to me through official channels." Nick shrugged.

"Well, that explains that," Sam said. "So if Hawk's her boss, then who is Sage?"

"Has to be Hawk's boss," Tim said. "Aren't you paying attention, Sam?"

"I am, it's just—" Sam suddenly stilled. His expression hardened and he looked at Nick. "Incoming."

Seconds later, Nick made out the faint familiar sounds of

chopper props slicing through the night sky. "Friend or foe?" he asked no one in particular.

The men drew their weapons. Unsure, they collectively prepared for either.

The chopper landed on the helipad. The door parted and someone's silhouette appeared in the opening.

"Stand down," Sam said. "It's Elle."

Elle. Nick's heart skipped a full beat, then thud against his chest wall. Nick couldn't believe his eyes. It was Elle.

She spotted Nick, and seemingly oblivious to the weapons drawn and aimed at her, she ran across the wide expanse of lawn to him, hurling herself into his arms.

They closed around her, and he breathed his first easy breath since she'd left. "Elle, what are you doing here?"

She reared back and smiled up at him, her fingers clutching him at his waist. "I found the daisies." She smiled. "You put them in the bag with my things. I didn't know what they meant, so I did what I thought you—never mind. I know what they mean now."

The woman was happy. A half-glance at Joe told Nick not to ask the question burning his tongue. *What daisies?* Instead, he asked another. "What do they mean?"

"Keeping secrets."

She looked awfully pleased by that. He hesitated, then told her the truth. "I didn't put the daisies in your—"

Joe elbowed him in the ribs. "Not now, bro. Think tactical."

"I found three of them." She looked deliberately to Joe, then Sam, and finally to Tim. "Three."

"Obviously you interpreted them to mean…" Nick let his voice fade, then quickly added, "Never mind." The chopper hadn't yet departed. One wrong word and she could get right back on it and fly out of his life again as fast as she'd flown into it.

He had been miserable.

She returns, and he's got a life as bright as the sun.

Take a chance, Nick. Just once, take a chance.

His mouth went dry. "So you found the daisies and looked them up and found out someone is keeping secrets. That doesn't explain why you're here."

She faltered, but held on to him. "I decided to care enough for both of us up close." She borrowed the words he'd told Lizzie. "Not from thousands of miles away." She glanced at the guys, clearly guessing that they and not Nick had stashed the daisies in her bags.

Sam went poker-faced.

Tim looked away.

Joe winked.

"Just tell him, Elle," Sam suggested, tapping his temple. "He ain't as swift on the uptake as usual today."

Tim nodded. "Go for it."

"Go for what?" Nick asked.

"She knows," Joe said softly.

Elle swallowed hard, looked up into Nick's downturned face. "The thing is, I love you, Nick. I thought I could leave you because that's what you wanted, but in my heart, I don't believe that is what you really want. Even if it is, I can't do it because it doesn't matter where I am or where you are, I'm still going to love you. My pride was hurt that you wouldn't ask me to stay, so I left."

"But you came back."

"Yeah, I did." She worried her lower lip with her teeth. "I had to because my heart said even if I went to Mars, it would still be here with you. Then I found the daisies, and I figure if these three— she motioned to the guys—are warning me you're keeping secrets, then I need to know them or they wouldn't bother telling me you had them. So I want the truth, Nick. I want to know..." her voice cracked. She shook herself and pushed on. "I want to know the truth. Do you love me?"

Tension crackled between them, rippled through the group. No one moved. Spoke. Breathed.

Nick stared at the helicopter, squeezed his eyes shut. *Please, don't let this be a mistake. Please, not a mistake.* He lifted his arm, signaled the chopper pilot to depart, then looked at Elle. "I want you to stay."

She searched his face. "Why?"

She wanted and needed the words. "Because I love you, Elle."

"I left because I love you," she said, her expression solemn. "You feared me leaving, and I didn't want you fearing it every day for the rest of our lives. So I left. It's done and behind us." She let that sink in, then went on. "But I came back. Remember that, Nick. I came back because I love you." She tilted her head. "I'll always love you, and I'm never leaving you again."

Her words were a warning.

And a promise.

He pulled her closer, tightened his hold, and kissed her.

He had rescued her from NINA's clutches. But she had rescued him from far more. Why his parents had done all they'd done no longer mattered. It wasn't due to something in him that made him impossible to love. Elle had left him, and she'd returned to rescue him again.

To love him.

To forever be the marked star of his life and his heart.

ABOUT THE AUTHOR

Vicki Hinze is a *USA Today* bestselling author who has written nearly forty books, fiction and nonfiction, and hundreds of articles, published in as many as 63 countries. She's won a wide array of awards, including novels of the year in multiple genres. All of her novels include suspense, mystery and romance. The focus determines genre. Her works have been classified in nearly every genre except horror, with the majority being suspense, thriller, mystery and romance.

A Vice President for International Thriller Writers, Vicki also served as a consultant to the Board of Directors for Romance Writers of America and multiple other notable organizations. She is the former radio talk show host of *Everyday Woman*, and a columnist for Social In Global Network. Vicki was the first RWA PRO Mentor of the Year, and the recipient of RWA's National Service Award. She's recognized as an author and an educator by *Who's Who in the World*.

For early access to new releases and more, subscribe to the monthly newsletter at http://mad.ly/signups/82943/join

    f facebook.com/vicki.hinze.author

    🐦 twitter.com/vickihinze

    ⓟ pinterest.com/vickihinze

    BB bookbub.com/authors/vicki-hinze

    g goodreads.com/vickihinze

ALSO BY VICKI HINZE

Clean Read or Inspirational:

S.A.S.S. Unit Series

Black Market Body Double | The Sparks Broker | The Mind Thief |
Operation Stealing Christmas | S.A.S.S. Confidential

Breakdown Series

so many secrets | her deepest fear (Short Read)

Down and Dead, Inc. Series

Down and Dead in Dixie | Down and Dead in Even |

Down and Dead in Dallas

Shadow Watchers

(Crossroads Crisis Center related)

The Marked Star | The Marked Bride | Wed to Death: A Shadow
Watchers Short

Crossroads Crisis Center Series

Forget Me Not | Deadly Ties | Not This Time

Inspirational

The Reunion Collection

Her Perfect Life | Mind Reader | Duplicity |

Lost, Inc.

Survive the Night | Christmas Countdown |

Torn Loyalties

Inspirational

General Audience:

War Games Series

Body Double | Double Vision | Double Dare | Smokescreen: Total Recall

| Kill Zone

(out of print)

The Lady Duo

Lady Liberty | Lady Justice

Military

Shades of Gray | Acts of Honor | All Due Respect

Paranormal Romantic Suspense

Legend of the Mist | Maybe This Time

Seascape Novels

Beyond the Misty Shore | Upon a Mystic Tide |

Beside a Dreamswept Sea

Other

Girl Talk: Letters Between Friends | My Imperfect Valentine | Invitation to a Murder | Bulletproof | The Madonna Key (series co-creator) | Before the White Rose | Invidia

Multiple-Author Collections

Dangerous Desires | My Evil Valentine | Risky Brides | Smart Women and Dangerous Men | Christmas Heroes | Love is Murder | Cast of Characters | A Message from Cupid Seeing Fireworks

Nonfiction Books

In Case of Emergency: What You Need to Know When I Can't Tell You | One Way to Write a Novel | Writing in the Fast Lane | All About Writing to Sell |

Mistakes Writers Make and How-To Avoid Them

For a complete listing visit http://vickihinze.com/books

www.ingramcontent.com/pod-product-compliance
Lightning Source LLC
Chambersburg PA
CBHW022057170626
46808CB00002B/490